SILHOUETTES IN THE MOON

A Novel

Kathryn Horsley

Vendera Publishing

Chapter 1

Humans say to truly find love, you must first find yourself, but humans are often wrong. I have centuries of coming to terms with my best qualities and my innermost demons. Love is an unobtainable gift for most vampires. Impulsive, greedy, and naturally cold, vampires are not particularly soulmate material. It cannot possibly be fair to ask anything other than another vampire to share in this curse. Only our own kind truly understands what drives us and knows to expect disappointment from having a vampire as a mate.

I had loved as a human. I loved my Ann wholly before she was ripped away from me. I tried with Claire; and I tried with Kate. Neither ended well. No, the only thing I have learned from finding myself is that the greatest plight of being a vampire is that we rarely love anyone more than ourselves.

Doomed to be alone even in a crowd, we fill our time with lustful flings and gluttonous bingeing. While fun, it is meaningless. Perhaps that is all we can ask for. We have incredible strength and skills along with a sort of immorality, it would not be fair for us to be truly loved by another too. We simply cannot have everything. That would not be just.

Coming home had brought me no closer to the man I once was though, honestly, I'm not sure I want to be him again anyway. London forgot me- my friends, my family, and even my Ann. London looked nothing like the place I left so long ago. Only the people seemed the same; warm smiling faces in a cold, gray land. Being home, I realized, I needed to forget London as it had forgotten me.

The first month there was the hardest. I would walk past my childhood home where a church now stands without even the slightest hint of the people I once knew. I spent hours at the marina watching the ships and yachts. I knew the world had changed, I watched it; but I suppose a part of me still expected London to be the same as when I left it. Despite moving back to the United States a year ago, I remember leaving London like it was yesterday...

*   *   *

I had stayed in London for nearly two decades hiding from my former family. Things seemed to be going well for once. A warm arm draped over my ribs, reminding me of our recent feedings, and I could not help but rub my fingers over hers.

She moaned as she awoke and pressed her lips to the back of my shoulder, "Good morning," Yen whispered in my ear, sending chills along my skin.

Her hand pressed into my chest, pulling herself onto my back as Big Ben chimed in the distance. I rolled over to face her. Staring at her it was hard to believe that I would ever meet someone more beautiful, at least, physically. However, as far as personalities go, there are more than enough women who could easily make me happier; but, somehow, I always end up in her arms.

I trailed my fingers over her cheek and pulled her chin toward me, caressing her lips with mine. Her long hair rested against my chest and I brushed it behind her ear gently as her hand glided over my muscles. She slid her body on top of mine, her bare skin warming mine and making me remember why I called her. It was not the sex; although, with her, that is always great. No, it was because we were both the same inside. We were both alone.

She kissed along my jawline and down my neck. Then resting her head on her hands which were folded over my chest, she sighed lightly.

My fingers flowed along her arm, feeling the softness of her skin.

"Why don't you make me breakfast in bed?" she asked innocently.

Laughing to myself quietly, I reminded her, "Julia's not for you."

Rolling her eyes, she smiled, "What good are sheep if you can't share them?"

It is not that I do not share. It is that I do not share with Yen. Julia has been my feeder human for close to eighteen years. Ever since I had come to London, I had managed to keep the same sheep. I had no plans to create a new drone, so I had no choice but to keep Yen from sinking her teeth into her even once.

"You don't need to share sheep if you're too busy sharing a bed. Besides, the good thing about vampires,"-I pulled her along my body quickly so that her face was close to mine and she inhaled sharply with surprise- "is we don't need to stop for food."

She kissed me with a blind hunger behind her lips that is not for any sheep. My hands tangled in her hair as I rolled her over onto her back and positioned myself on top of her flawless body.

I did not plan on stopping, after all, this was what she came for. A few weeks in my bed and we would both forget the hollowness inside. However, when I heard my front door slam shut, I froze where I was, listening intently.

Despite the familiar mumbling, it was the heavy footsteps heading toward my bedroom that I recognized first. Quickly, I jumped out of bed and slid on my pants as I heard Julia in the hallway insisting, "You can't go in there!" and Tara burst in.

Yen huffed irritably, under her breath, "Mutt."

"Skank," Tara acknowledged Yen.

But I ignored them both and focused on the distraught look covering Tara's face, "Tara, what's wrong?"

Hurrying to me, Tara wrapped her arms around my neck, "It's terrible, Nick. What am I supposed to do?" She stepped back and paced the floor, "What if the humans attack? I don't want to have to kill any humans."

Grabbing her shoulders, I stopped her in front of me, "Slow down. What happened?"

"You've not heard?" Tara asks woefully. Her face grew blank but I could still see the worry in her eyes, "Werewolves have been exposed. Humans know we're real."

At the time, I did not understand why that is such a big deal. Humans had been told before, seen videos, even heard the howls in the distance. They always discredit the things they do not want to be real.

"Give it a week. It will pass. Humans never believe."

"Well, they do now. It's all over the news. It's not going away this time. Everyone is in a panic. Humans. Werewolves. Everyone."

My heart sank for Tara. Humans were never supposed to know about the supernatural. They were not ready for it. We are vicious beasts; however, we are all aware that humans can be just as fearful, quick to judge and murder, especially with things and people they do not understand.

Yen laughed to herself, "You know, Nicolas, if she dies, you could always buy a Great Dane. It's basically the same thing."

With her emotions spiraling, Tara's words rushed out as quickly as they came to her, "Oh, please. Don't pretend to be anything other than whore of the month, Yen."

Yen's eyes glazed over into black quickly as she hissed at Tara but I stepped between them, "That's enough. Both of you."

I took Tara's hand and pulled her close, holding her against me, trying to ease her angst, "Don't worry. I won't let anyone hurt you."

"Ugh," Yen groaned, "I think I just threw up in my mouth."

Disregarding Yen, Tara said quietly, "I'm not worried about me. It's Roddy. What if there is a war, Nick? What if something happens? I can't feel his pack bond anymore. I'd never know if...," she trailed off.

She rested her cheek on my chest as guilt crept in. I should have told her about Roddy when I found him so long ago. I thought I was protecting her. Her pack was not ready to know everything about him. But now, after eighteen years, I was stuck keeping her son a secret.

"Well, then you better go fetch him," Yen said, making my breath catch. "He's in Santa Fe, right Nick?"

Slowly, Tara looked up at me hesitantly with a mix of emotions scrolled on her face, "What's she talking about?"

Before I could come up with an answer that would keep her from hating me, Yen spoke again, "Oh, that's right. You're not supposed to know."

Yen's mouth twisted into a satisfied smirk as Tara stepped back, her breathing quickened with anger. Her eyes darted over the floor as her thoughts sped through her mind.

"Tell me she's lying, Nick," Tara said. "Tell me you don't know where he is."

That would have been easy. Just cover up a lie with another lie and I could have because I am good at it. I probably should have lied. But it was Tara and I was tired of lying to her so I told her the truth. And that was a mistake.

"I wanted to tell you," I tried, as I reached for her hand, "Tara-"

She backed away slightly, "How long? How long have you known where my son is?"

I am not usually a nervous person but something about the intensity in her glare made me swallow hard.

"Relatively, not that long," I told her which was somewhat true. I had been a vampire for five hundred eighty-seven years so comparatively eighteen years was not so long.

She stepped close to me with her face near mine, "Relatively...," she said with a cold, harsh tone and somehow I believe she knew exactly how long I had known.

"You know where he is now. Isn't that what's important?" I tried.

She shoved me back harder than I expected her to, "Tell me the truth!" she shouted.

"Why does it matter?"

Pushing me, she screamed, "You're so selfish and arrogant, Nick! I don't know why I thought you could care about someone other than yourself for even five minutes. I guess I shouldn't be too surprised that you are such a dick! But somehow. Somehow, Nicolas Rider, I am surprised. Every time! And pissed! So very pissed!"

Her words stirred more anger in me than they should have. Looking back, I could say that it was just my defenses coming out but right then, it just felt like fury.

Yen leaned toward the edge of the bed, smiling widely like a kid with ice cream.

Tara stepped toward me and my back hit the wall. She poked her finger in my chest repeated, "I want to know, and I want to know now! How long have you been lying to me?"

"Since Alaska!" I snapped at her. Like a horror film, I knew what was about to happen, what I would say, but I could not change it. It spilled out of me like red wine on a white sofa, staining and tainting everything it touched. Even if she did forgive me, the marks of my words would always be visible. "I've always known! Look, I'm sorry that I had to hide Roddy from you. Trust me when I say your pack would turn on him like dogs."

What was I saying? I do not use the word, *dogs*, not to her. But I could not stop myself. "And let's face it, that's what they are, a bunch of wild mongrels pretending to be domesticated."

There was a sharp smack and the sting of her hand on my face before my words were even out.

Frigidly, she told me, "I'm lifting the order not to have you hunted down. You come close to me again and just see what happens."

Hearing the honesty in her voice, my face dropped as she turned and stomped out.

I chased after her, "Tara, wait!" But she did not slow her pace as she walked down the hallway. "Tara, let me explain!" I tried.

Grabbing her arm, I turned her toward me but was not ready for her black wolf to explode out of her clothes, knocking me to the floor. Keeping my head to the side, I tried not to make eye contact, knowing that would only anger her more, as her teeth hovered only inches from my cheek.

With her paws pressing into my chest, her lip curled over her teeth with her deep growls and I felt the warmth of her drool roll down my cheek. Yen watched with enough intensity that I could feel the air grow tense. I still do not know exactly what she was waiting for. Did Yen want to see Tara sink her teeth in me just so she could justify killing my friend? Or did she believe that Tara would not actually hurt me? To be honest, in that moment I was not so sure that Tara would not rip my head off. I am still not sure I would not have deserved it.

There were so many things I could have said. I could have told her how many days I stayed awake, crippled with guilt, or how many times the words nearly slipped from my lips, but everything seemed like too little, too late.

I only managed a few desperate words in a quiet whisper, "Forgive me, Tara."

She leapt off of me and rushed down the hallway. Sitting up, I watched as my best friend ran out of my life. It is not over. It could not be. I have a lot of years left to live and that leaves a lot of time for my repentance.

She rounded the corner and burst through the door, letting the sunlight shine in. In the shadow of the wall, I shielded my eyes from the sudden brightness but it was not the pain from the light that wet my eyes. My eyebrows came together as I wrapped my arms around my legs and leaned back against the wall.

Yen stepped into the hallway but I did not look over at her, staring, instead, at nothing in particular as sorrow filled my heart.

"It's better this way," Yen says gently, "Your friendship with her was doomed from the beginning. An abomination like that is a tragedy."

There was nothing wrong with my friendship with Tara. It was perfect; well, as perfect as could be expected. It was not my fault that her pack constantly got in the way.

My British accent laced over my pain as I whispered only loud enough so that Yen can barely hear me, "There is beauty in tragedy."

Then standing up, I refocused and called, "Julia!"

Walking past Yen, I opened my closet and looked through my clothes. I tossed my favorites on the bed as Julia walked in with a curious look on her pale face.

Along her hazel eyes were the beginnings of wrinkles but they did not take away from her kind appearance. Her light brown hair hung straight down almost hiding her face.

As Julia shoved her glasses further up, I took her shoulders gently, "I need you to pack your things."

Her heavy English accent highlighted her every word, "Are we going on holiday?"

Smiling, I told her, "Something like that."

She smiled back and started to leave when I added, "And get Roddy on the phone. I need to warn him."

*   *   *

And just like that, the world had discovered the reality of werewolves and Tara had discovered the reality of me. Lying and selfish, I am no friend worth keeping. But true to my selfish nature, this will not stop me from eventually making Tara my friend again. I have not yet, but I will.

Humans did not attack the werewolves as much as I anticipated but they still managed to overreact. After Clinton passed a massive two-thousand-page bill dictating where the wolves could live, attend school, work, and basically everything but breathe, several gated communities, or *sanctuaries*, as they are often called, sprung up for the wolves. Separate but equal was unconstitutional but somehow this is not. It generally takes humans several decades, sometimes longer, to see their errors. Maybe that is because the ones that see them are not the ones who made them in the first place.

After their 'voluntary' registration, werewolves have been excluded and treated like outcasts which even vampires realize is ridiculous. I mean, really, nothing happened. Werewolves did not start killing hordes of humans. They did not just appear one day. They have always been the humans' friends and neighbors. The only difference is now the humans knew.

But despite the obvious discrimination, werewolves took the new laws in stride. Not even one human was harmed. The same would not be true if it had been the vampires who were exposed and governed so harshly. But luckily for everyone, vampires are still the best-kept secret, even from some of the werewolf packs, such as the one that lives near our house in Montana which is where I am headed now.

It has been a year since I left London and losing Tara has not gotten easier. I still try to call her to ask how her day was. Each time, I pick up the phone only to be reminded that my call will go unanswered. It was a year of being completely without friends or family before I become lonely enough to cave. I called Marcella.

She tried to apologize for how our last conversation had gone. It was not sincere but I do not really care. I must admit, I have missed Marcella, and maybe even Luther, a little. At this point in my loneliness, I am willing to give my dysfunctional family another try.

So as I pull into the gas station, I contemplate whether or not our reunion is to be just another colossal blunder I have caused myself. Listening to the gasoline funnel into my bike, I hear a more merry sound. A group of twenty-somethings standing near the ice bins laughs at some hushed joke that escaped my attention. The wind carries their scent to me. Two are human; their blood is rich and heavy, untainted. However, most of the small group are werewolves. Their odoriferous stench coats their blood with an earthy, robustness that would deter even the hungriest vampire.

I watch them as my gas pump clicks to a stop. Their joy seems light and untethered by past wrongs. That is the difference between vampires and werewolves. Werewolves do not carry guilt. They have protected humans for so long that they justify any crimes they commit against us and therefore, simply have no guilt. Whereas, vampires have learned to embrace the guilt that often accompanies killing for pleasure. We use it to control our lust and retain some sense of humanity. Without our guilt, vampires would deplete this world with carnal cravings seemingly overnight.

As I place the nozzle back in the pump, someone catches my eye. Inside the gas station, buying some insignificant item, is a woman unlike any other. The thick glass separates her from me but it cannot hide her rarity. Her brown hair is pulled back into a loose ponytail, exposing her fine skin along her neckline. Her long ponytail brushes over her shoulder as her locks bounce into large curls at the ends. Her beauty is not like a model in a magazine; no, she is much more approachable.

I watch as her supple lips part as she speaks to the cashier. The thick glass protects her voice from finding me but it would not matter, I cannot focus on words. I cannot hear anything above my own heart beating in my chest.

The delicate coral color accentuates the flawless way the brim of her lips holds its bow shape, curving gently upwards in the corners. Full and inviting, her lips rival any trap Cupid could have designed himself.

Standing straight, yet relaxed, she projects confidence without arrogance as she smiles at the cashier. Her beauty has not made her vain.

It is as though she does not realize that her soft, delicate skin radiates even from across the parking lot.

The light catches her deep-set, almond-shaped eyes as she makes her way toward the door. Bright and lively, her eyes hold a joy and innocence in them. Her smiles pushes her cheeks upward, narrowing her eyes without hiding the way they sparkle. The vivacity to her eyes is as though she has never felt true pain or loss. Pure and untainted, there is a virtue in her that has yet to be spoiled.

She has not tried to be so striking. Her makeup is extremely minimal, just a small bit of eyeshadow that is hours old. Probably not touched up since it was applied this morning. She does not have to try. She simply *is* stunning.

If her personality is even a quarter as remarkable as her appearance, she is an oddity among women. A rare gem that, once acquired, should be cherished and kept forever. Definitely not a woman to be wasted on a vampire.

She pushes the door open and I realize, I have been holding my breath. I inhale deeply, hoping the wind will bring her scent to me, that I might have that small piece of her to keep. But, alas, the wind does not cooperate and I find myself watching her walk across that lot thinking, '*please, out of all the cars she could go to, do not let it be with those dogs.*'

I sigh to myself as she joins the group of wolves. Of course, that is where she was going. Realistically, I know I should let her be. There is no place for me in the life of such an untarnished human but deep down, I was enjoying lying to myself about the potential of it. Now that hope is gone. Squashed by a horde of werewolves and I hate them for it. Why should they get to keep such a perfect human?

Contemplating the injustice of it all, I watch as they all pile into a few cars and drive off, taking with them the most remarkable human I have seen in over a hundred years. I grab my helmet and start inside to pay for my gas. There was something about her. It wasn't just her outward beauty that was remarkable. She emitted something more. There were confidence and kindness in her but it was something else about her that I cannot shake from my mind. Some kind of magnetism that compels me to pursue her, to fall into her heart and become unequivocally lost in her arms, and every other part of her for that matter. What I wouldn't do to feel her wrapped around me. The heat of her skin warming mine. Her soft hair brushing over my chest...

As I push the door open, I hear the click of a gun being cocked and an angry male voice shouting, "Get on the floor!"

My eyes meet the young cashier's as she shakes behind the register for a moment. The man presses the tip of the gun against my head, "I said on the floor."

Against my natural instincts, I slowly lie down on my stomach as I am sure any human would. The robber walks over to the register and screams at the cashier to hurry as she empties the drawer.

Vampires are not supposed to get involved in human affairs. I should just let the robber go. Let him get away. Let the police handle this. But I do not like being told to get on the floor like a weak human and I do not enjoy pretending to be timid. Besides, I am already annoyed that werewolves drove off with the beauty I want for myself. I am in no mood for this robber.

Slow enough to appear human but still fast enough to have the element of surprise, I stand up and slam my helmet into the robber's head. His head flings forward, smacking onto the counter hard enough for me to hear his skull crack. The cashier screams but not because she is afraid of me, simply the situation.

I can smell the blood from the robber's head smeared on my helmet. Perhaps I hit him too hard. It will be difficult to explain his death to the police with a witness.

I lay a twenty-dollar bill on the counter for my gas and nod to the wide-eyed cashier, "Keep the change."

However, before I can make my escape, a police cruiser pulls in. Its lights are not flashing as it pulls up to the gas pump. A human would say it is a lucky coincidence but for me it only makes it harder to sneak away unnoticed.

The cashier rushes past me, running to the police. I watch her as she tries to explain everything frantically. For a moment, I consider sneaking out the back door but the security camera behind the counter would only lead to more questions.

I try to put my story together quickly, something the police will believe without question. Maybe a surge of adrenaline caused me to hit the robber harder than necessary. No matter what story I give, I cannot let myself be arrested, show up for court, or even have my name in the paper. I will most likely have to enthrall this police officer to get my way.

My thoughts stop short when I hear a familiar southern voice, "Nicolas Rider! Well, butter my butt and call me a biscuit. Didn't expect to see you tonight."

Snapping my head up, I am thankful to see one of my oldest friends. The blonde vampire stands in the doorway donning a police uniform, "Levi! What are you doing here?"

He rushes over to me and hugs me tightly, "And what are you wearing?" I laugh.

"Hell, the ladies like the uniform," Levi tells me with his thick Alabama accent. "They think it makes me hotter'n a billy goat's butt in a pepper patch. Not that I need help with that," he winks.

I chuckle to myself but it is not just his lighthearted joking that makes me smile. Unlike most men, I actually do like Levi.

He nods toward the body on the floor, "So what happened? He didn't get in the way of a meal, did he? You know this is a no-kill zone, right?"

No-kill zone. His phrasing for a safe haven for humans makes me smile. The only real purpose of a no-kill zone is to keep suspicions away from any vampires who have set up a permanent residence which from the looks of it, he has. Nodding, I tell him, "I'm not here to kill humans."

"Well, you cain't be killin' the wolves here either. There's a couple us on the force that want to keep those pups about one fry short of a Happy Meal, if you know what I mean."

I smile to myself. Levi always has a way with words. Of course vampires would want to keep such a large pack in the dark about us. The less they believe in us, the more of us that get to live.

"I understand, Levi."

"Be sure that you do," He smiles as he continues, "Listen, I've got to clean up this mess you made but me and you need to run up to Missoula and catch a drink sometime, what do ya say to that?"

Nodding, I tell him, "I'd like that."

"I'll be callin' ya then," He nods toward the door, "Go on, get outta' here before the rest of the cops show up. This gets harder and harder to explain the longer you're here."

As I open the door, he adds, "Hey, Nick,"-I turn toward him-"it dills my pickle to see your face again."

Laughing to myself, I respond, "If I knew what you just said, I'd probably agree. I'll see you later, Levi."

I hurry across the parking lot to take off on my bike, smiling at seeing Levi again. We have not seen each other for some time now but we did get to share a few years in Alabama just before Marcella decided to go to Alaska in 1977. Every time I see Levi, it is as though no time has passed for him at all, always the same jovial Levi.

His deep Southern accent always makes me smile despite not truly understanding most of the phrases he uses. There is no pressure to be better than him or more dominant, not because he is insignificant in any way. Quite the contrary, he makes you feel better about yourself just from his acceptance of you. It is a powerful personality trait that I am sure keeps the humans right where he wants them. However, behind his lovable, carefree persona is the heart of a killer that nobody wants to believe exists.

It is odd that he said there are others on the force that want to keep vampires a secret, as though there are many other vampires parading as police. How could so many vampires infiltrate the police force and manipulate the public in such a small town without being noticed? It is a risk, for sure.

I walk across the now mostly vacant parking lot determined to take my leave before there are any more surprises. I sit on my bike and start sliding my blood-smeared helmet over my hair when my eyes fall on the cashier. Sitting on the sidewalk, her eyes are fixed straight ahead of her but she is not focused on anything in particular. Her trembling hand lifts a cigarette to her lips but she does not take a good inhale. Her actions are automatic, like reflexes, and she is lost in her head. No doubt replaying the past few moments.

Despite my better judgment and my imperative need to leave, I walk over to her and kneel down in front of her. Her eyes still do not meet mine until I place my hand on hers. Like a scared cat, her head snaps to face me, panic-driven and intense.

"Oh... um ... thank you for... um...," she stumbles out.

With my hand still on hers, I wait for her eyes to meet mine so I can enthrall her. I do not have sinister plans. I merely need some information and she is in no state to give any without my help calming her nerves.

Her eyes stop darting long enough for her to become enthralled and her body begins to relax. I tell her calmly, "You're alright. I know it was scary but that is over now. You are alive and you *are* safe." Looking down at the cigarette in her fingers, I add, "And you are going to quit smoking because it is disgusting. Smoking is harmful and you refuse to let it steal any more of your life."

I take my hand away slowly. "Are you okay?" I ask her quietly.

No longer enthralled, her mind is quieter with my calming persuasions polluting her thoughts. Thinking, she sighs and lightly smiles, "Yeah. I think I am."

Good. Now, for my real question. "Do you remember just before the robber, there was a woman? She was the very last customer before the gunman came in. She was a brunette, beautiful-" I stop my sentence when the cashier nods.

"Yeah, she bought gum, I think."

"Do you know her name?" I ask although, I am not sure why I am asking. This human is not for me. The less I know about her, the easier it would be for me to ignore her. Perhaps the cashier will say that she does not know her name. Perhaps the cashier will protect her without even realizing it.

However, the cashier responds, "Krista Hartley. She lives on Honeywood, over in the Lock."

My stomach twists at the knowledge. Part of me is elated to know. Part of me wishes I had not asked. I should have left when it was smart to. I should not know her name. And I definitely should not know her address. I want to know. But I should not.

The more I know, the more difficult this gnawing in my stomach is going to be to overlook. I know myself. I am weak in this regard. Denying myself is not one of my stronger traits. It is not a matter of inner strength at all. It is my selfishness that will get in the way.

"What's the Lock?"

The cashier looks at me as though I should already know the answer, "Lockwood Estates. It's a werewolf community just outside of town."

Of course it is.

Grabbing the cashier's hand once more, I tell her, "Thank you," then locking her eyes, I enthrall her one last time to add, "It is a shame that you cannot remember my face."

I quickly go back to my bike, having already wasted more time than I should have. As I slide my helmet on, I hear the cashier say, "You should stay away from Krista. She's trouble. They all are."

Looking up, I watch the cashier toss her cigarette to the ground and walk inside the gas station. Perhaps, Krista Hartley is not as innocent as she appeared. If she is trouble than she would not by too perfect to be tainted by me. I could justify manipulating her, relish in the privilege of being the one to tarnish her. Make her mine for just one night.

No, I stop myself from thinking further.

I will stay away from Krista. True, her purity does beckon to be corrupted; it also commands to be protected. She is not one to be exploited. Not even by the unscrupulous. And especially not be me.

So despite the opinion of some pimple-faced cashier, I will not pursue Krista Hartley. She is not for me. It is that simple.

Chapter 2

The smell of cinnamon fills my kitchen. As the rotating fan placed in the corner of room whirls and wafts the pleasant scent with each pass, I recall a time long past. A time when my life was much simpler, despite not realizing that then. A time when I lived by the sun, not the moon. A time when food was sustenance, not fun. My human life, though brief, had perks I can still recall.

The neighbor's wife would occasionally bring me a sweet bread. Not like the cinnamon roll I spent the past thirty minutes making from scratch, not near as sweet. Hers did not smell quite so appetizing or sugar-laced but, just the same, I would inhale her sweet bread both literally and figuratively. One big breath in was all I could do before I would shove my mouth full of the dry, crumbling bread.

She was a lovely lady, much older than my father, or at least she appeared to be. My father did not dislike her but he did avoid her. Looking back, I know his distance was merely because she would bring up my mother's name quite often. She told me more about my mother than my father ever did.

She loved my mother as a sister and she had been there helping bring me into this world. Within a few short moments, she witnessed my first breath and my mother's last. It changed her. Aged her eyes in a way only loss can.

Despite being neighbors, I really did not see her often. Her health was not the best and she passed away when I was ten. No more stories of my mother. No more of my father dodging her presence. And no more sweet bread for me.

Most of the time, I quite enjoy being a vampire- the strength, the youth, the vigor. These are things that humans cannot capture long; and things I take for granted. There are things that I miss, however. Times when I long to stop killing and return to a simpler life. Days when I wish to cook *and* eat what I prepare.

More recently I discovered that I can keep food in my stomach longer than I used to. It does taste pleasing and it helps me appear human. However, this does not change the fact that I still cannot digest it and forcefully purging my stomach contents is something that should simply be avoided when possible.

Human-like qualities such as being able to walk in the sun and enjoy a dinner would make luring a human into my bed much easier. Not that I have any particular human in mind. I mean, I already promised myself that I would not entertain even the idea of being with Miss Krista Hartley of Honeywood Drive. And I do not break promises I make with myself... Well, sometimes, I keep them.

The bell of the oven timer chimes and I set the cinnamon roll on the table. It looks like an article in a food magazine. The cinnamon roll browned to perfection, sitting on a delicately painted floral plate. A bead of condensation rolls down the orange juice placed near a single flower. I smile to myself as I am sure Julia will be pleased. Julia would be satisfied with anything I offer her but her complacency does not deter me from attempting to earn her smile with small efforts.

As I start into the study, the phone rings. I pick it up, sighing. I already know who is on the line.

"Hello, Luther." I grit through my teeth.

"I see you made it to Missoula," he states.

"Clearly," I say dryly.

"Marcella says hi."

"I bet she does." Luther is not my favorite vampire. Actually, he is one of the most pathetic vampires I know and definitely not someone I would want to speak to regularly, or at all, so I get to the point, "What do you want?"

His voice is lighter than mine, almost as though he does not hate this conversation as much as I do, "I just wanted to make sure we're still a go for joining you?"

He states it like a question and he should. I may have told him a few weeks ago that I would try to be a family again but I am not exactly thrilled about the idea. The last time I saw any of them ended in tears and pain, but mostly, it ended in betrayal. It is a betrayal I have not forgotten.

"That's the plan," I sigh.

"Great." There is a long pause but the silence is not awkward. Neither of us feels the need for pleasantries that we do not mean.

"Well if that's all you needed, I'd like to get back to life," I state plainly.

I do not like Luther. That has never been misunderstood. But if I am honest with myself, it is not Luther that has my irritation on edge. It is Marcella. However, knowing this does not change the exhausted disdain in my voice.

"Okay. I'll see you in a couple of days," he says.

"Yeah," I hang up the phone feeling more depleted than I should, "in a couple days."

Part of me has missed having a family. The other part cannot change the pain they caused, cannot forget the life they robbed from me, and cannot forgive, no matter how much I try. I have tried for years to forgive, to see it from their perspective. Every time ends in failure. That is why I agreed to allow them in my life again. Perhaps forgiveness is something that has to be obtained face to face.

Having lived with Marcella for centuries, I should have been immune to her selfishness and stony nature. I should have known she was capable of violating my trust for her own purposes. However, either I did not see it or I did not want to. The past happened and no number of apologies can reverse the wrongs.

Marcella always treated me differently than the others. Being her favorite, I believed she cared for me. I trusted that she cared enough to understand how much I had grown to love a child. Her name was Penny; however, I never called her that. She had renamed herself Punzi after her favorite princess Rapunzel. At the time, I believed Marcella understood why I cared. I was wrong.

Punzi was six when we met. She was gentle and sweet. She did not see the darkness in me. She was alone in this world but she did not need to be. I wanted to raise her as a human. Never turn her into this nightmare. Or, at least, ensure that she found a human family to love her. She deserved that much. But all she got was a raw deal from a cruel woman.

A little girl I almost called my own, but, like most humans that are close to vampires, she died. Marcella promised to help find her a family but all she helped Punzi find was a quick death. Marcella did not do it herself but it was her influence that directed Kate's fangs. Like a puppet on a string.

I am sure Marcella does not feel guilty for Punzi's death. She is merely distressed by the distance it put between us. It is a distance that I fear may be too great to ever really bridge.

I sink into the couch, letting my head fall onto the back. Closing my eyes, I let out a long breath. Even the idea of seeing my family is mentally draining. How will I ever survive learning to live with them again?

Before I have time to consider my inner dilemma, there is a knock at the door. My eyes spring open and I listen intently as Julia opens the door. There is a muffled conversation about cleaning. It is most likely the housekeeper. Nothing Julia cannot handle. So I allow myself to relax into the cushions once more.

Once I knew I was moving back here, I had hired Simone to clean weekly and check on the house over the past few months. I had explained to her that I would not need her services while I was living in the home. From the sound of their brief conversation in the doorway, she has left something here and simply wants to retrieve it.

"Let her in," I call from the couch. "It's fine."

Without my approval, Julia would never invite someone into our home. She knows better than to let some unsuspecting human stumble into a vampire's house. Nothing forces us to have to relocate like killing or even maiming some poor door-to-door salesman.

I hear Simone walk through the house to the kitchen but I do not leave the couch until her scent trickles its way down the hall to me. As she rummages through the cabinets, I smell *it*. Like a wall slamming into me, that is no human that wandered into my house. That is a werewolf. The smell of her perfume may mask her husky wolf smell to humans but not to me. My inner monster perks up at the idea of an intruder and my eyes glaze into black. I do not make a habit of hiring wolves but I also do not make it a habit of killing them in my home when it can be avoided. I refocus and let my eyes change back to my very human-looking green. No sense in being obvious about my being a vampire. After all, not all werewolves believe in vampires.

I walk quietly to the kitchen to assess the beast properly. Her long dark hair is pulled back into a loose ponytail. The fallen strands rock back and forth as she bobs her head around quickly, scanning the counters for her lost item.

I recognize her identifying wristband. One of the newly adopted werewolf laws is that all werewolf must be immediately recognizable as a werewolf. Some packs tried tattoos, others tried uniforms, but the wristbands with a symbol to indicate which pack they belong to were quickly accepted as the easiest means to abide by this law. Her wristband confirms what my nose already established; this woman is definitely a werewolf.

I entered the kitchen unsure of what I was walking in to, determined to find out how much this werewolf knew about the occupants of the house she has been cleaning. I was planning on lying to end our contract so that she would never need to step foot in my home again. As I watch her though, I realize she is no threat.

Her relaxed posture indicates that she knows nothing of vampires. Nothing about my scent that lingers on every surface of the house raises an iota of suspicion in her. She is as clueless as any human. Perhaps she does not know how to recognize a vampire or she simply does not believe we exist. Either way, she definitely has not met one and I can end our cleaning contract without any messy details.

Distracted by her searching, she does not notice me. I stay very still in attempt to not make a sound that would make her stop because, for some unknown reason, I am compelled to keep watching her. There is something in the way she moves that draws me in. My eyes roll over her every curve. Even though as a wolf she is off-limits, it does not hurt anything to look. I cannot help but smile at her scattered rifling.

Snagging something from the bread box, she spins around to face me. Startled, she hops back slightly. In her hand is an old Walkman but that is not what takes my breath.

"Oh." She smiles with a heavy exhale, "You scared me." But she has no idea of how scared she really should be.

Unable to move, I can only stare at her. This is not Simone. Standing before me is Krista Hartley. In my home. Krista Hartley of Honeywood Drive is in *my* home. And she's a... werewolf.

She reaches her hand out toward me and my breath catches, "You must be Nicolas."

I had not expected her to be so alluring. I did not expect the copper flecks in her brown eyes to shift and dance along the iris. I was not prepared for her silky skin to call to me, tempting me to feel its softness. I did not choose to get lost in her voice but here I am, taken aback by the most attractive werewolf I have ever seen.

The pause is too long and she mistakes my hesitation. Darting her eyes, she starts to drop her hand, "Actually, you know what, I should go. I'm late for a thing...," her words fade off.

She starts toward the door when I call out, "Wait." She looks over her shoulder at me and her hair brushes across her back. "Sorry, I um... I forgot my manners."

Stepping toward her with my hand outreached, I add, "You're right. I am Nicolas."

She smiles warmly and slides her hand in mine making my stomach twist.

"I'm Krista. I help Simone with her cleaning jobs sometimes. You have a beautiful home," she says gesturing around.

"Thanks." Letting go of her hand, I look into her eyes before continuing, "You'll have to excuse my awkwardness. I am usually very good with words but at this particular moment I seem to be fall-failing," I correct myself quickly, "I seem to be failing."

Her cheeks flush bashfully. She opens her mouth as though she is about to say something but nothing comes out and she bites her lip instead.

Watching her, my heart races. It is not until she glances to the side, her cheeks still burning with fresh blood, that I realize I have stared too long to be comfortable.

Eager to rectify the situation, I blurt out, "Um, do you want something to drink? Water or something?" Gesturing toward the refrigerator, I spin around, knocking over the orange juice and flowers that had been sitting on the table with my hand.

I groan under my breath as I stand the bottle of juice back up. Utterly mortified to be making such a fumbling, bumbling fool of myself. *Come on, Nicolas, pull yourself together.*

Smiling kindly, Krista goes to the cabinet near the sink. She sets down her Walkman and graciously grabs a towel to help me with the mess I have created, both on the table and with this conversation.

"Let me," she offers. Standing close to me, she dabs the juice with the towel as I pick up what I can. Her perfume wafts into me, beating my will like waves battering a ship in the most vigorous storm.

Smiling, she looks over at me warmly. Her face is closer than I expect and her eyes meet mine. There is no sense of authority exuding from her. Like all single female werewolves, she is low on the totem pole of influence. Despite her position, her eyes burn with an intensity that rivals even the most powerful beings. My breath quickens as I find myself held captivate in her eyes. With her face close to mine, she pushes her hair behind her ear.

It is that moment, that simple act, that my resolve is broken. Deep down, I know that I will not stop until she is mine. I do not just want her. I need her.

I know enough about werewolves to know that to date outside of your own pack, even to date a human, you have to get permission from the alpha. I ask quietly, "Krista, I know this might sound a little brash, since you don't know me, but I'd like to take you to dinner."

Her smile dims regretfully, "Nicolas, you don't know what I am."

Yes, I do. She is perfect. But in lieu of not frightening her with my forwardness, I say, "Yes, I do. You are a werewolf. And a beautiful one at that."

"How did you...?" As her voice wanders off, I reach out and touch her wristband. My fingers slide over the black and white elastic band.

Taking her hand in mine, I turn her wrist to expose the black wristband on her, "I know *what* you are. What I want to know is *who* you are."

She looks down at her wristband, staring at the full moon with the silhouette of a human hand print in the center. Levi had told me of a large werewolf pack nearby. The symbol must be for that pack. To a human, the wristband indicates that she belongs to a pack that would die to protect her. To me, it only means that she belongs to a pack that would kill to protect her. But, mostly, it means she does not belong to me.

Letting go of my hand, she asks quietly, "Does that bother you?"

Her unease is understandable. The wolves have had mixed reception into the human world. Even after a year, most humans still hate them. Some love that having a "werewolf best friend" makes themselves feel as though they are more acceptable, trendy, and prevalent. Others still treat them like circus freaks. Only a handful of humans are indifferent to their existence altogether.

She rubs her arm nervously waiting to find out which group I might fall into. Standing there unsure of herself, she seems very human and it makes me smile.

"No. It doesn't." It should though.

Her eyes meet mine once more. This time, however, they are soft, exposing a vulnerability that was not there before. "My alpha will never allow it." Then, smiling warmly, she adds, "But I would love dinner."

Before I can stop it, my lopsided smile makes its appearance. "I promise to make less of a mess at dinner than I did here today."

"That is if you can convince him to give his approval. And that's a big if," she raises her eyebrows as though she finds some humor in the challenge. "I should go."

With a wide smile, Krista bashfully waves her good-bye. Her coyness makes her seem more human than she should and makes it harder for me to remember that this is doomed to failure.

I hear the front door open when I notice her Walkman still lying on the counter, "Krista," I call after her.

I hurry down the hall to the doorway being sure to stop in the safety in the shadow of our porch roof.

As she spins, her feet crunching the gravel beneath them, I toss the Walkman toward her gently and almost perfectly into her hands. "I'll come by around eight," I add as I lean against the door frame.

Her cheeks flush, "See you then."

She opens her car door and I ache to be able to go into the sun and hold the door open for her like a real gentleman would.

Just before she gets in, she adds, "And um... good luck. You're gonna need it."

Then with a giggle, she gets in her car and drives away. Even after she is out of sight I linger in the doorway. It is some time before I realize that Julia is standing next to me, smiling.

"I like her," Julia states innocently.

"Me too," I nearly whisper. My eyes drift to the side, feeling guiltier than I should. I technically have not done anything wrong.

There is no unwritten law about vampires dating werewolves and flirting with a werewolf certainly is not against any rule. While I am not ignorant enough to actually believe that pursuing her will not have repercussions, I am pertinacious enough to do it anyway.

"She kind of reminds me of Tara. Strong will but soft heart." Julia pats my shoulder as she leaves, "Don't blow it this time, yeah?"

I smirk to myself. I will certainly try not to 'blow it' but mostly I am just going to try not to get myself killed.

*　　*　　*

I drum my fingers over my lips debating with myself. I really should not see her again. My family would not approve; no vampire anywhere would approve. Her family certainly will not approve. The list goes on and on, but would she approve? That is the important question. Currently, she does favor dating me but she is still naïve to the fact that I am not what I seem. What will happen when she inevitably does discover me?

Stop it, I tell myself. Stop entertaining ideas like that. Even if I do earn a second date, Krista can never ascertain what I really am. The entire purpose of lying is to ensure just that. I should not even be seeing her again as it is. There is no disputing that. We are too different. It will only cause pain and problems for everyone around us, and death. So much death.

I have seen the casualties a simple friendship between a werewolf and a vampire can cause. My friendship with Tara led to the murder of an entire pack in Alaska. Granted, it was my idea to attack, but all that death was due to us being merely friends. Imagine the escalation of emotions and fatalities if Krista and I did become romantically entangled. Particularly, if there were any hint of deceit or trickery involved. Even something as trivial as Krista not realizing I am a blood thirsty menace to existence could be misconstrued into a deception. Okay, so that is deceitful and definitely not trivial, but still.

The darkness swallows me as I descend into the fusty air. I do not bother to turn on the light as I step inside my room. This section of the house had been 'off-limits' to Simone as she cleaned. No reason for anyone, even a human, to realize that our basement has more bedrooms that most two-story homes.

The smell of dust masks the mustiness and encases me as I pull the sheets from the furniture. I pull the linens from the bed and add them to the pile of sheets that is forming on my floor. I should have done this menial task as soon as I got here. Luckily, though, vampires do not have to sleep so I had not been obligated to rush into making my bed. This is not my first time living here and seeing the worn furniture stirs up more than just dust.

The last time I lived here, my family was still a family- and long before they added the electrical system to this house. I admit I was happy to stop using candles completely. Nothing is more worrisome than a sheep capable of accidentally setting your house on fire, especially during the day.

That seems so very long ago and I am not in the mood for reminiscing. Grabbing the pile of linens, I go upstairs and dump them in the washer. Laundry is not my favorite task, but it is one of the easier ones and can be done with very little effort or thought.

However, even the tediousness of chores cannot stop me from thinking of Krista. Part of me knows that I should be attempting to talk myself out of seeing her. It is the sensible thing to do and sometimes a prudent thought or two does cross my mind. But a bigger part of me knows it is futile. I have already made up my mind and no amount of persuasion will change it. I want her. It really is that simple.

I stop by the hall closet on my way back to my basement bedroom and take out some fresh blankets and linens that I specifically asked Simone to wash this week. Judging from the smell of them, she did. Yet, even the pleasing floral scent does not distract my mind from the way Krista's aroma carried me off. Sure, she had that less-than-ideal wolf muskiness that she had tried to cover it with Chanel No. 5. The two scents did mix more delicately than I would have believed if I had not experienced it for myself.

Chanel No. 5- I believe that is what Marilyn Monroe wore and I find myself beginning to wonder about the possibility of Marilyn being a werewolf too. She would have had to fake a death to escape the limelight before the public noticed that she could not age. Perhaps Chanel No. 5 is a werewolf thing. As my mind drifts away on this absurd tangent, my foot misses a step in the dark and I tumble down the final two stairs.

Landing with a thud, I lie on the cold basement floor with the bedsheets scattered over me for a moment, contemplating how distracting infatuation can be. I have said before that women will be the death of me but this time, I might be right. No, not from a simple fall down the stairs, but Krista could quite literally kill me. Werewolves are not to be underestimated and definitely not to be trifled with. Still, with every blink I see her face.

Finally, I rise, dropping everything on my bare bed, and flop down next to the pile of sheets, unable to stop my thoughts. I can see her dark hair swaying, her olive shirt twisting with her movements, as she searched for her elusive Walkman. Then she turned to me, and despite her eyes being wide and startled for a moment, they were the most spectacular brown I have ever seen. Encompassing darkness with flakes of honey to light the path of anyone lost within their endless grasp. Her eyes could trap even the most determined soul. Her voice melted her words to the point that she could have called me a leech and I would have thanked her.

As I lie there thinking of her, my smile fades. I am not supposed to see her again. That is what everyone will say. I could keep her a secret for a while. My own tantalizing conundrum, stacked like a dangerous house of cards ready to collapse at any moment. But if I chose to hide her, I would not be able to ask for the help that I desperately need. I am not used to needing advice but there is an even bigger issue than dating her. How do I get permission from an alpha?

Krista did not seem to know what I am, but what if her alpha does? I definitely will not get a date if he so much as suspects I am a vampire. And I will not win her heart if I have to kill her alpha either.

I let out a heavy sigh. This was not well thought out. At least, I know *who* to call. I need someone who could lend real advice that will actually be useful, not just laugh at my predicament. I need someone who understands the alpha mindset. I need a werewolf. Honestly, I need Tara, but any werewolf is better than nothing at this point.

Grabbing the phone, nervousness washes over me. I dial quickly and impatiently wait while it rings in the receiver. This is it. The moment of truth.

"Hello."

"Roddy, listen, don't hang up. I have a dilemma."

"Imagine that," he says sarcastically. "Nicolas, you *are* a dilemma."

"I'm serious."

"So am I." He groans as though I woke him up and knowing that he works the night shift, I probably did. "Alright. I doubt I can help much. I mean, I don't really have experience with 'I just killed *another* person' scenarios but... shoot."

I start to speak but the words stop on my tongue. I already know what his advice will be and I do not really want to hear it. He will tell me to avoid Krista; that I have already gone further than I should have allowed myself.

So, instead, I ask something that has been weighing on my mind, "How's your mother?" Tara, my best friend, still has not spoken to me. I had rather hoped that she would have seen the logic in my actions and forgiven me by now, but I am still waiting on that day.

There is a sigh on the other line, "Is this really your 'can't wait another second' dilemma?"

"No. But I still want to know."

"She's fine, Nicolas. She told me that if you called, I am to hang up immediately and I have a huge stack of letters you wrote that I am supposed to get rid of."

Well, he certainly did not listen very well since we are still on the phone and he is willing to offer advice. Most likely it will be a warning instead of advice. But still. I am grateful for his disobedience just the same.

"Did she read them?" Please say she did.

"They're still sealed so, no, I don't think so."

I sit quietly for a moment, trying to think of my next question but not really sure which ones I want an answer to.

"She asked about you," Roddy starts.

What? "Me?" About how to kill me? Or how to forgive me? Either way, at least I'm still on her mind.

"Yeah, you. She knows I don't listen to her and keep talking to you anyway. I mean, it is sort of my fault. I did ask you to keep my location a secret and you doing me that favor is what led to her hating your guts. But anyway, yeah, she asked how you were and what you've been up to. And I told her."

"What did she say?"

He laughs lightly before he replies, "Well, she said, and I quote, *'Same old, Nicolas. Still being a selfish ass.'*"

At least she did not make another threat to murder me in some irrationally complex and obscene way. "Another decade or so and maybe she'll say that to my face again."

Roddy laughs, "She can't stop caring about you, Nick. No matter how much she tries. Her wolf chose to care about you, and the wolf always wins. They're loyal to a fault; even if we don't want them to be. Love, hate, it's forever. She'll come around. Just give it time."

Forever, he says. Then I will have to extra careful about how close I get to Krista and how quickly.

There is a short pause. When he continues, his voice is soft, "So, what's your crisis?"

I shift into a more comfortable position pushing an old pillow under my head. "Okay, so, hypothetically, what if a vampire wanted to date someone other than a vampire but also not a human?"

"Does Mr. Hypothetical have a name?"

"No, he's hypothetical." What is so complicated about that? Does he not understand what hypothetical means?

"Okay, so, hypothetically, a vampire is searching for something but not a vampire and also not a human? Like what he is looking for exactly, like a moose or something?"

For heaven's sake, this is like talking to Luther. "No!" I snap. "Look, I'm Mr. Hypothetical." I might as well do this quick and to the point. Like ripping a Band-Aid off. "Roddy, I asked a wolf on a date today."

"I know you're Mr. Hypothetical, Nick. I'm just giving you a hard time," he chuckles lightly. "And what do you mean a wolf? Like a *real* wolf? Like, live in the woods canine kind of wolf?"

"Worse," I mumble.

"A werewolf! Are you serious?" he stammers out disbelievingly.

Almost defensively, I blurt out, "Yes. Her name is Krista and she is impeccable. Honestly, I am hoping I can find a flaw in her on our date but I doubt I will."

"Holy shit! Mom is going to love this."

"Focus, Roddy."

"Right, sorry," he says. "So, what's the problem? I mean, other than the obvious." He does not try to hide the humor in his voice. "She's in a pack, right? Oh no, who did you kill? Her brother? Her father? Wait… was it her alpha?"

I suppose if I was him, I would assume I had killed a pack member too. "I haven't killed anybody." Not yet.

I let a long sigh, almost embarrassed that I need to ask. "How do I get permission from her alpha?"

Seriousness enters Roddy's voice, "You don't. If he knows what you are, you definitely will not get permission. You might not even make it out of there alive. And even if he doesn't know what you are… hell, even if you were human, once an alpha gives an order to ask before dating outside the pack, it's over. Short of enthralling him, you don't stand a chance."

Silence settles over the phone as I contemplate his words. Enthrall him. That could work. It is risky though. If he does not know I am a vampire, enthralling him too soon will only make him suspicious that I am not human. Plus, I doubt he would like me much after he did realize that I tricked him into giving consent. That kind of deception is punishable by death. Or I imagine so anyway.

My thoughts are broken by Roddy's voice cutting in, "Enthralling would be a bad idea," he says as though he is talking to a child.

Not surprised that he knew what I was thinking, I lie, "I know that. I wasn't going to." He knows me too well. He surely hears the lie but does not call me out on it. He knows my own self-interest supersedes almost all of my actions.

"Look, my advice is to ask. Be told 'no'. And move on with your life," he says plainly. "There's not much else to it."

When I picked up the phone to dial, I already knew what advice he would give but I suppose I did not really want to admit it to myself. "Alright. Well, I will let you get back to sleep then. Talk to you later, Rod."

"Yeah. Let me know how it goes. And whatever you do, do not enthrall him."

"Sure." I hang up the phone and stare at the ceiling. The advice he intended to give is sensible but instead he accidentally gave me something better. A back-up plan. Enthrall the alpha. Easy. Risky, but easy.

I do not lie there long before dusk settles outside and I can make my escape into the night. Sliding on my jacket, I go to the garage. I press the button and the garage door lifts, letting in the dim light trickle in. My reflection glistens in the gunmetal gray of my Ducati 916 Senna. My birthday present to myself a few weeks before I decided to come here, I was not about to leave it behind in the move.

I ride down the streets lined with older brick buildings that give a charming, rustic feel to this town. Before the werewolves were exposed, Stevensville had been ideal for vampires. Not many wolves lived here. It is close enough to Missoula to give us an adequate supply of food yet nobody looks for a killer to live in such a picturesque town.

However since the living restrictions were issued, the wolves gathered in small towns, joining packs to form larger, stronger alliances. Some did have to give up a little bit of their authority as the hierarchy of command was shifted by adding so many new powerful wolves, but it was a small price to pay when a pack could increase their numbers from twelve to fifty or even more like the local pack did. Krista's pack is, unfortunately, one of the biggest which will make this that much harder.

I take the side streets to the edge of town where the gated wolf retreat is located. As I ride alongside the perimeter, I look at the high stone wall that encircles it, separating the wolves from humans who still fear them.

As I approach the gates, I scan the area. There is a forest directly across from the community and a small booth with a single human manning the gate. Not much security but I suppose the lone human is still more than the werewolves actually need.

I notice a small clearing in the forest nearby. It is not wide but still looks out of place in the dense tree line. As I slow my bike to stop, I realize what the clearing really is. A small, dilapidated cemetery. There are only a few small tombstones, and they are worn to the point that no names can be made out.

Even though it is small, I will have to remember the location of the cemetery. If I need to escape into the forest, the little clearing would stop me in my path. So a mental note of its location, it is. Just in case.

I stop at the security booth near the gate and slip off my helmet as a round, little man flips off a tiny TV and leans toward the window enough that I can read his name tag, LARRY.

"A little lost, are ya?" he asks.

I flash him a warm smile, "I don't think so. I'm looking for a werewolf that lives here. Her name is Krista."

Crossing his arms, he laughs as though he heard a joke in my words, "Krista Hartley. I know her. What kind of business do you have with her?"

"I- Well, actually I need the alpha."

Knowing my intentions, Larry drapes his arms in the window sill, "You're wasting your time with that one. The alpha doesn't let her date humans."

I smile to myself. I have not been human for a long time. Not that Larry needs to know that. "It's my time to waste."

Thinking for a moment, a slow smile spreads across his face, "Alright. You have half an hour. You get in, get your denial, and get out. And the next time you come here, you better have been invited by the alpha himself."

Oh, I plan to.

He reaches under the desk and the iron gates begin to open. I can see the rows of houses, just over ninety homes are located in this wolf community, most belong to werewolves but their human families are permitted here as well, pushing the population to close to two hundred residents.

With seventy-six werewolves and one hundred twenty humans, this community is by far the largest I have ever seen. Above the iron gates is a wooden archway with the name "Lockwood" engraved for all to see. Etchings of little flowery vines weeding across the arch attest to the craftsmanship and to the devotion to the pack inside those walls. This community is more than a town to them. It is a safe haven, allowing them to transform their bodies freely without gasps and ridicule from the humans.

Looking at the streets in Lockwood, I am not so much worried about finding her as I am about finding the rest of her pack. But still, I glance over at Larry, "Any chance you could help me out with directions?"

Mistaking my hesitation for being overwhelmed, Larry smiles, "You know being Friday, neither Krista nor the alpha are going to be home. They're too much alike. If they're not running around as wolves, they'll be down at the tavern. Its two streets down, take a right on Sycamore, Joel's Tavern is on the left. You can't miss it."

Smiling at him, I nod, "Thanks."

I slip my helmet on again and start passed the gate. Driving through the neighborhood, I watch the houses with their lights shining on the street, children playing inside, and teenagers holding hands on the porches. It looks like a normal town because it is one.

I make a right onto Sycamore. The houses on this road are smaller than the ones before but just as nice. Very quickly, I notice the pattern of the five styles of houses that repeats the farther I ride. Just where Larry had said I notice the large, lit sign for Joel's Tavern.

Pulling into the parking lot I see the first of the many wolves I will meet tonight. The tall, lanky man with an Osprey jersey and cap does not exude much authority, but the stocky, dark-haired one beside him definitely does. I park the bike and lay the helmet on the seat as they watch me with stern expressions.

I walk toward the tavern door as though I belong there, hoping that I pass for a human. The stocky man waits for me to get close then pushes off the wall and steps in front of me, blocking the door.

"Can I help you, son?" he asks sharply.

"Doubt it," I tell him then look over at the other man and add, "Nice shirt. I pegged you for more of an *Icedogs* fan though."

Hearing the derogatory implication of my comment, the lanky man steps forward but stops when the stocky man puts his hand up, "I'll handle this, Kent."

The stocky man crosses his arms over his chest, irritably, "I don't think you know who you're talking to."

Apparently, neither does he. I shrug lightly, "I don't think it matters. You wanted to know how you could help me, try getting out of my way. That would help."

I do not want a fight. Not this deep into wolf country, not with wolves that believe vampires are extinct, and definitely not with Krista's pack. You cannot win over a woman by killing her family. Well, not usually. But there is something about his arrogance that grates against my own and my annoyance spills out into every word.

I start passed him but he shoves me back. Before he speaks, my sarcasm whips out, "You're not trying to intimidate me, are you? Cause, last time I checked, I'm not a little pig and I'm not exactly afraid of the big bad wolf."

Kent's mouth drops. I suppose he is not used to hearing a human talk back to the stocky man. To be honest, I probably should not have since he seems to hold a high rank among the wolves and I may need to use his authority at some point. But it is too late to change it now and back-pedaling would only make me look weak.

The dark-haired man just shakes his head, holding back most of his irritated laugh. I start toward the bar again, but he puts his hand on my shoulder stopping me beside him, "Boy, your lack of self-preservation is either impressive or stupid and I'd rather not find out which. So, if you won't watch your words, you need to watch your back. Especially around my wolves."

He has a point. My arrogance does seem to get me into trouble but I do not really need him to tell me that. Pushing his hand off of me, I smile sarcastically, "Thanks for your input."

The heavy smell of werewolves slams into me as I open the bar door and step inside. In an instant, the talking, the dancing, and the laughter stop abruptly as everyone turns to stare at me. Wolves do not normally make me nervous but the size of this pack makes me swallow hard. If even one of them realizes what I am, I will not make it out of here. That much is obvious.

Of the limited humans inside the bar, I recognize one scent quickly as she pushes through the crowd. I have smelled her rose perfume on my sheets. Her dark eyes light up with her smile, "You must be Nicolas."

I reach my hand out to shake hers, "You must be Simone." I scan the room, not for the potential dangers like I should be, but for Krista.

"That's right. Krista said you might show up tonight."

Simone's words seem to fade into the musty air when my eyes find Krista sitting at the bar biting her lip to hide her smile. In that moment, I no longer care about the risk of being here. She is worth it.

"Excuse me," I tell Simone without looking away from Krista. The crowd watches me as I make my way to the bar, but I barely notice them.

The man sitting beside Krista shifts towards her but does not move close enough for me to believe he is anything more than a friend. A territorial, werewolf friend.

With my lopsided smile, I say, "I told you that I would be here."

Her cheeks flush as the blonde man beside her slips off of his stool, "I'm Warren."

I reach my hand out despite not wanting to shake his, "I'm Nicolas."

He looks at my hand a moment then up at me again. "Do you have permission to be here?"

I can tell he is powerful, not alpha but high in the ranks, nonetheless. Still, I give my answer to Krista instead of him, "I will."

She smiles as though my answer was humorous just as Simone approaches and takes Warren's hand, "Buy me a drink, babe."

He lets out a heavy sigh indicating that he really does not want to leave Krista alone with me but when he looks at Simone, his eyes soften and he nods toward the bar, "Okay."

Before he steps away, he leans close to Krista's ear. If I were human his words would be difficult to hear. But I am no human and can hear him easily as he whispers, "Look, I'm not trying to interfere, but you know what Bryant would say."

His subtle mention leads me to believe that the one named Bryant is also the alpha. Now, all I have to do is find this Bryant and coax him into agreeing with me.

She nods slowly as Simone pulls Warren's hand, "Come on," she says impatiently.

At least *she* wants me to have my moment with Krista. If I ever feel the need to massacre this pack, I will have to try to make sure that Simone lives.

Warren nods once at me as he walks away. Sipping her drink, Krista leans back against the counter, "You have to ignore the wolves in here. They're just being protective."

Not protective; they are being territorial. Female wolves are rare and they do not want to run the risk of not producing more wolves but I do not correct her, "I understand it. I came in here uninvited which is frowned upon."

"Yes, it is," she tells me without losing her smile, "But if you knew that, why did you come?"

Because I do not think about my actions before I do them. My lopsided smile shows itself as I say, "Because you're here."

She blushes lightly and I continue, "Besides, I promised you that I would be here to ask the alpha at eight o'clock and it is now...," I look at my watch briefly, "eight eleven."

As she turns toward the counter to hide her smile, her hair slides off her shoulder. Her curl bounces but she does not seem to notice it the way I do. Her brown locks appear soft and weightless, making me wonder about how her strands would feel grazing over my skin ever so lightly.

I lean against the counter so that I can see her face. I nearly cannot find my words but somehow manage to say, "You do still want to go out with me tonight, right?"

Without gracing me with her eyes, she says quietly, "You'll never convince him to say yes."

"Let me worry about that," I tell her.

Looking around the room, I try to figure out which of the wolves would be Bryant.

He will be arrogant and smug but still have an allure about him that draws people to him, making them want to obey.

She spins around toward me again with a stare that is more intense than I was expecting, causing me to stop thinking altogether. However, her words bring me back from my temporary distraction, "Well, here's your big chance," Keeping her eyes on me, she adds, "He's by the door."

My eyes move to the door quickly but who I see there is not who I want to see. Leaning against the wall with a smirk is the stocky man from outside.

"He's the one in blue," she finishes.

For a moment I am hopeful that maybe I'm wrong but I'm not. The dark-haired, stocky man from outside is the only one at the door in blue. "Of course he is," I mutter to myself.

Hiding the angst of going to talk to the alpha which I already had words with once tonight, I look over at Krista and tell her, "I'll be right back."

Making my way through the crowd, I walk toward Bryant. My words to him will be hard to undo. Why did I have to open my big mouth outside? I should have known he was the alpha when he told me to be careful around *his* wolves.

"Come to apologize?" he taunts. Pushing off of the wall with his foot, he gestures at a table nearby.

As we sit down, Kent and two other wolves stand near us, trying to project an intimidating atmosphere. It would work for a human but they are not the reason I am nervous. He needs to say yes. He has to. She cannot go against an order, even if she wants to. He is my only chance to spend more time with her. I need him. Because I want her.

"I think we got off on the wrong foot," I start. I reach my hand out toward him, "I'm Nicolas."

"Listen, kid," he starts, nearly making me smile at being called a 'kid', "I'm not interested in letting some arrogant, two-bit punk date my daughter."

Daughter? Well, this just keeps getting better.

"I'm not saying no because of your personality, which frankly, needs work," he adds.

I could protect myself. I am not some weak, fragile human but I cannot explain that to him and still expect him to allow me to be here.

Bryant continues, "And I don't really care that if she phases against her will she will rip your head off. I don't like you enough to care about your death."

He is lying but I do not interrupt him merely to tell him that he does, in fact, care about protecting me as well as Krista.

"I only care about the distress murdering you would cause my daughter." His eyes drop to the table as a sullen look spreads on his face, "It's not something you ever forget."

His tone makes me believe that he knows that from experience and I wonder who it was that he killed and why, but I do not have time to be personal with him tonight. The only thing I want to hear him say is yes.

He leans forward, resting his elbows on the table, "So my answer is no."

"Bryant," I start discouraged, "I just want...-"

"I said no," he snaps. "Now you can do us both the favor of leaving."

Realizing that he is not likely to change his mind tonight, I look across the room at Krista sitting at the bar where Simone has rejoined her and tapping her toes to the music. Her eyes meet mine. Soft and kind, they hold mine with warmth and fill me with a longing to hold her not just with my eyes. But in my arms. And in my heart. For all time.

Yet, I cannot. Not now and possibly not ever.

Without looking at Bryant, I quietly ask, "Could I at least say good-bye?"

"Of course." He smiles sarcastically, "We're not animals."

I walk toward her more slowly than I need to, hoping to extend the minutes of my life that would have her image in them. But even slow steps cannot keep me from losing her forever.

Her eyes hold a pity in them, "He said no."

"Unfortunately," I say simply, unable to form any other words to sum it up any more thoroughly.

Setting her glass on the bar, she continues as though she has had this conversation before, "But you want to still be friends, right?"

Friends. Such a harsh sounding word. Friend is never the role I want to play in her life.

"Quite the contrary," I start solemnly. "I'm afraid that being merely friends would never suffice me." Taking her hand, I bring her skin to my lips gently, "I hope that one day it will not suffice you either."

She looks at me with wonder in her eyes at my sudden formality. I realize that a human my age would not be so formal, not these days, but I cannot escape my upbringing. Besides, if this turns out to be the last time I see her, I want to at least have kissed her hand.

I could say goodbye but I refuse to let myself believe this is the end. Instead, I simply say, "Until our paths cross again."

She does not say anything and she does not need to. Her eyes grow soft making it that much more difficult to convince my feet to begin moving. But I must go.

As I make my way across the bar to leave, my eyes find their way back to Krista one last time. Her beauty takes my breath but she does not seem to notice her effect on me as she smiles softly.

I walk back into the night air, passing the lingering werewolves outside the door. They say something but I ignore them. My mind is elsewhere, mulling over a plan to see Krista again. I am Nicolas Rider and Nicolas Rider does not take 'no' for an answer. There has to be a way to change the alpha's mind. Bare minimum, there has to be a loophole I can exploit.

Driving through the streets, I begin to consider what I want and the risks I would be putting everyone in if I should get my way. Perhaps I should stop my pursuit while I still can. However, I cannot help but to push those thoughts from my mind as I picture her standing near the bar, smiling at me. No, this is not the end. I refuse to let it be. The risks involved are a small price to pay for the change to make her smile not just at me, but because of me.

Chapter 3

In *no rush to go home*, I drive around the town looking at all of the things that have changed and thinking of a new plan. I could enthrall Bryant but that really should only be used as a last resort. Any suspicion that I am not human would be detrimental to dating Krista, not to mention detrimental to me continuing to live at all. I am good in a fight but not even I believe that I could escape a pack that size.

Knowing that I will be cooped up most of the day in my home makes me use most of the night to contemplate my predicament and daydream of the way Krista's hand had felt in mine. The way her skin spilled warmth onto my lips when I kissed her hand. And the way her hair cascaded over her shoulder.

Thinking of Krista brings a smile to my face and the welcome thought that nothing could ruin my night. Then, just like that, my night takes a turn for the worse. As I pull into the garage, I see the moving van that I have been dreading. My family. They are here. For a moment I consider just sitting on my bike in the driveway for another hour or so. The sun would come up and take me. Burning into ash may be more bearable than seeing them again.

A moving van may not be the most comfortable way to travel but it does offer an inconspicuous way to transport coffins. While I do realize how cliché it is for vampires to use coffins, I cannot think of a better solution. They are easy to come by and although I have never enjoyed the cramped space or stale air inside a coffin, they do seal out the daylight impeccably well. And that is of great importance when you are a vampire traveling during the day.

I look into the back of the moving van as I make my way toward the door into the house. The space in the back is a small, mostly empty space. Other than a few suitcases the only things inside are the caskets stacked two high, like personal vampire bunk beds.

Grudgingly, I open the door to the kitchen. I might as well get this over with.

"Hey, Nicolas," I hear.

Looking toward the voice, I see who I assume is Marcella's sixteen-year-old sheep standing near the sink. Obviously, a teenager would not be my first choice for a sheep but Marcella is not as fastidious about meals as I am. "Hi, Andrew."

Even though I am not pleased by having a teen for feeding purposes in my home, I honestly am pleased that it is Andrew I see first. I am in need rush to see either Marcella or Luther but I know it must be done. And soon.

"Can I get you something? I'm sure you're famished after such a long drive," I suggest. There is a part of me that hopes he is, just so I have an excuse to cook something and procrastinate meeting my family a little longer.

"I'm fine. But are you?" he asks, leaning his head to the side slightly, exposing his neck.

My mouth waters with his offer but I ignore the way the burning in my throat rages and smile softly, "No, thank you." I have my own sheep for that. Speaking of which. "Have you seen Julia?"

He nods, "Marcella sent her to the grocery store."

I hide the grimace his words cause. There is something about Marcella bossing around my sheep that makes my skin crawl. It would not have bothered me before but things have changed. Julia is mine and Marcella will not be taking anyone else from me.

"Did anybody go with her?" Hopefully, Marcella at least sent somebody with her. Julia has never been in this town before and sheep are notorious for not understanding proper social interactions. In a new place, it is imperative that someone accompanies them outside of the house. At least until a rapport with the locals has been established. There is nothing like trying to break your sheep out of a mental hospital.

Andrew shrugs, "I don't think so."

Of course. "Well, please let Luther know that I went to escort Julia at the store and that I will be back before sun-up," I tell him.

With a wide smile, he says, "Sure thing."

It is not really necessary to notify Luther of my whereabouts but, like children, sheep enjoy having a job and responsibility that they know they are capable of doing. It pleases them to follow our commands and it would be easy to indulge too much with too many orders; after all, it is nice to have someone who wants to see you happy.

It is a short drive to the grocery store which is good since I am literally running out of nighttime hours. Assuming Julia has my car, I take my bike. Despite the short ride, I try to enjoy the cooler night breeze. The evenings have been so humid lately; the hot air has pressed on me nearly as much as my reservations about joining my family again. The change in weather is welcome and, hopefully, a precursor for the relief my impending reunion might also bring.

As I walk across the parking lot, I get the feeling that I am not alone. It is not a wolf. It is definitely a vampire I have felt before but it is not one of my family.

I look around but do not see anything. For a moment, I begin to consider that it could be one of Levi's friends. I start toward the store again but I cannot shake the feeling that this vampire is not friendly.

Within easy view of the humans in the store is not a place for a vampire fight. So in hopes of dissuading whoever is lurking in the shadows, I hurry toward the store until the voice I hear stops me in my tracks, "Long time, no see, Nicolas."

I turn abruptly and stare at a face I have tried to forget, "Salem."

My eyes change to solid black instantaneously and I feel my fangs press against my lips.

He laughs, "Now, now, Nick. And here I thought we could be friends but you're always so eager to fall back into our old roles."

Yeah, I am. The role where he ruined everything I had and everything I was going to be.

Although he was taking orders from Marcella, it was him in the alley that night. He could have told her no instead of submitting to her every whim. Merciless, he took the life of my fiancé and turned me into this monster.

"How long do you think covering this parking lot in your blood is going to take?" I shrug lightly, "There are other things I need to do tonight."

He smirks, "I'm here to deliver a message. Nothing more."

"Plans change." Message or not, what he is getting is a fight.

He chuckles to himself, "They want you left alive. They didn't say anything about maimed."

Before I can contemplate who, *they*, are, his eyes change to black and he bolts toward me. I stand still, counting the seconds it takes for him to clear the distance. When he nears me enough, I grab a cart and slam it into him, sending him flying into the metal supporting pole of a cart return bin. Before he can bounce off of it, I am in front of him. I wrap the cart around him, bending the metal, letting it cry out into the night air and pinning him to the pole.

With an angry hiss, he struggles to get free but I kick his knee hard enough to slide the return bin back a few feet. I hear the bones snap even over his painful scream and it makes me smile.

He pushes against the cart and it crashes to the ground as he finally releases himself. Between furious, pained pants he punches me in the stomach but I follow with a sharp uppercut that makes him double over. Grabbing his head, I bash his face into my knee.

He steps back with blood pouring from his nose and a look of confusion and frustration on his face. I kick him in the chest, pushing him back further, then follow him with a slew of kicks and jabs, most of which he does manage to block but I can tell that the ones that do make contact hurt worse than he lets on.

I kick him back across the parking lot. Sliding to a stop, he starts after me again. It is time to end this before the humans see us. I grab a small car by the fender. Swinging the small car, I slam it into Salem, smashing him between it and another car. As I toss the car aside, he slinks to the ground.

My fist drives into the side of his skull and I feel his bone crack and separate. He shakes his head, but that will not clear the massive headache that we both know is present.

I flip over him, grabbing him by the hair. I pull him into the air and slam him to the ground between the cars. I jump onto his back. With one hand on his jaw and the other on his face, I open his mouth as wide as I can and then some. He screams in pain as the skin in the corner of his mouth begins to tear when we hear the sliding doors of the grocery store.

Stopping what I am doing, I cover his mouth with my hand to silence him. He struggles beneath me so I pinch his nose as well, blocking his air. His fighting increases but I am stronger than he remembers and can keep him on the ground.

I can hear the loose wheel of a cart squealing as it comes closer and slowly his fighting begins to decrease. I know suffocation will not kill him but if he passes out, perhaps this human will not notice us.

The human slows its pace to a near stop, probably just noticing the mess I have been making. After a very brief moment, the human hurries toward their car again, I assume very nervous and a little scared of what they imagine could have happened here to flip a car on its side and smash the cart bin.

As his body grows limp, I pull him behind the car and out of view just as a woman pushes her cart past us. It only takes her a moment to fearfully load her car and drive away.

Looking at Salem's limp body lying on the ground, I consider killing him while he is indefensible and how that would not be the way an honorable man fights. Is it really winning if he cannot fight back?

Watching his chest rise with each relaxed breath, I think to myself, *ah, hell with it.* I want him dead more than I need my honor. I snap the muffler off of the car closest to me, making the edges jagged and rough.

Leaning over him, I tell him, "Goodbye, Salem."

But just as I raise my arm in the air, I feel a cold hand wrap around my wrist. Everything goes white and I am overcome by the most peaceful feeling. A warmth cradles me, wrapping its comfort around me.

It only lasts a moment before it begins to fade. An obnoxious brightness floods my eyes and I blink quickly to help me focus. Slowly, I gain the understanding that what felt like mere moments must have been much longer.

The haze clears and I realize I am sitting in a white room. There are no windows and despite the room's large size there is not much furniture to speak of. Stranger yet, I do not see a door in to or out of the room at all. The lack of windows or doors does not help my still-muddled brain to construct an escape plan.

In the corner and still unconscious, Salem lies on a white sofa that is shorter than him forcing his legs to hang over the end uncomfortably. Near him, perched on the back of the couch, is a small, fragile-looking vampire watching me with a child-like grin. Her large eyes are set oddly close together helping her slender nose give her a distinct countenance. Her red hair is piled on top of her head in a desperate attempt to control the curls spilling out. Wild and unruly, her heavy rings of curls poke out and dangle over her, adding an odd sense of craze to the eyes peering out from behind them.

Unsure of what happened or how I got there, I look to the vampire in front of me. She stands behind the white desk separating us. Beautiful and elegant, her sharp features give her a hard appearance. She taps her fingers together in front of her lips impatiently. Given her demeanor and position in the room, I am going to assume that she is the one who sent Salem with a message for me.

She lowers her hands when I look at her, "Good. You're awake."

"What just happened? Was that some sort of enthrallment?" I ask.

She half-smiles, "You're lucky you can remember that much. Humans never do."

Vampires cannot enthrall other vampires. We have never been able to. It is a natural survival tactic. It is impossible. But I have no other explanation, so I simply ask, "How did you do that?"

"Is that really what you want to know?" she challenges.

She is right. There are more important things at hand. With a fog still lingering in my mind, I ask, "Why am I here? What is it that you want?"

"You." Stepping closer, she replies, "I am Amelia. This is Casiana," she says, gesturing to the tiny woman beside Salem- "and we have been looking for you and vampires like you for quite some time."

"Why me? I'm nothing special."

"But you are different."

Amelia walks around the desk and reaches out her hand. I look at her for a moment, trying to gauge the situation I seem to have awakened to. Still unsure, I slide my hand in hers and notice the thin faint-gray crescent tattoo on the thenar region of her hand between her thumb and index finger.

"You're with the Genesis," I say matter-of-factly.

Genesis. The only vampire-specific religion that I have ever heard of. They worship Lilith, the child-stealing demon credited with creating vampires in the first place. Legends vary; some paint her as an enchantingly beautiful demon, and others portray her as a witch with the wings and talons of a beast. She was said to be Adam's first wife. Once she turned against the angels, she was banished from ever entering heaven and her own children were cursed to die.

Her anger was said to have pushed her toward seeking revenge on God's children by feasting on their blood, stealing their souls, and other imaginative things like that. Noted for stealing newborns from their mother's and defiling men, Lilith was more of a heartless monster than any vampire will ever be. But that is the thing about myths; they are not limited by the truth.

The Genesis follows the lead left by the legend. They are eccentric, volatile, and vicious. More like a cult than a religion, they accept only the best and dispose of the weak. I suppose I should feel honored that they would want me, however, I do not.

"Good, you have heard of us," she smiles. "That will help speed things up."

Leaning back, I rest my arms over my chest, "You still didn't say what you want with me."

Amelia sits back on the edge of the desk, smiling gently, "Why, nothing much. You see, we are looking for someone and we just need to be sure that you're not that someone. We will start with a blood sample. Most candidates do not advance to further testing."

Just a blood test. Sounds like there is a catch.

Noticing my hesitation to ask more, Casiana gracefully flips off of the back of the couch the way an acrobat might if they had spent centuries practicing. Her footsteps are quieter than any vampire I have heard before. Her flip does not look as though she is attempting to boast her skills in any way. Instead, it seems natural, as though walking on her hands is just as acceptable and easy as walking on her feet.

Just as she gets close, she methodically flips onto the desk as a gymnast climbs onto a beam. Casiana takes a few steps on her hands before cascading down into a seated position on the desk facing me.

With her large eyes and long face, Casiana's features are odd, almost bird-like and the way her toes curve around to grip the edge of the desk only adds to her animal appearance. Somehow, despite her feral attributes, Casiana is still beautiful in her own way. Not someone I would be tempted by but beautiful just the same.

"Casiana, here, is the lead on our Nexus project," Amelia tells me.

"You do know who the Nexus is, yes?" Casiana says with an accent that I cannot discern. A mix of several intonations dances across her voice, almost as though she has created her very own ambiguous accent.

"No," I lie.

I have lived long enough to have heard bits of the legend. The supposed link between worlds. The Nexus is capable of our salvation or our destruction. Some stories say the vampire will start a great war and bring the destruction of werewolves. Other stories say the vampire is immune to the sun and brings the end of our kind. Salvation, destruction, special abilities. The story of the Nexus is no different than any other myth, really. Just different characters in the same old story. I am surprised that a group as large as the Genesis even puts much conviction in a story so fantastical.

Knowing I am lying, she raises her eyebrow.

Smiling widely, I add, "And neither do you. If you did, I wouldn't be here."

Keeping her tone buoyant yet condescending at the same time, Casiana informs me, "We have been testing people for centuries, Nicolas. And while it is true that nobody has met our needs yet, you can rest your pretty little head that we will find the Nexus. Even if we have to test every last aberrant vampire on earth." She taps my nose with her finger playfully with her last word.

"What if I refuse?" I ask.

Amelia smiles, "We do want you to be on board for this, Nicolas. It's easier that way."

Casiana cuts in cheerfully, "But make no mistake, while we want your cooperation, we do not *need* your permission."

For a moment, I consider simply allowing them to take a sample to be done with the whole thing. What is the worst that could happen? I will not match whatever they are looking for. Nobody will because the Nexus is not real. Besides, perhaps they would be willing to trade my blood sample for Salem's life. That would be a win-win for me. I would get to kill Salem and be done with the annoyance of the Genesis all in one fell swoop.

Before I can announce my offer, Casiana speaks again, "We already know that there are things that affect you that do not affect other vampires." Drugs, I am sure that she means drugs. However, I am not sure how they are aware of it. "Perhaps something that affects us would not affect you in the same way. Maybe even the sun. Have you ever noticed anything different about yourself? Anything at all?"

I can eat human food, sort of. Normal vampires regurgitate immediately when ingesting food but I can hold it for hours without feeling nauseated at all. It is not anything special, though. Choosing when to purge my stomach contents does make pretending to be human at a dinner party a lot easier, but it is not something worth mentioning or bragging about. My body does not digest human food and I will have to regurgitate it eventually just like every other vampire.

I only discovered that ability by accident. I have never really tried to figure out if there is anything else that I can do, probably because I do not believe there is anything different. Being able to hold food longer does not make me different enough to raise any concerns. Besides, holding food and being affected by drug use are not all that useful alterations.

"No," I lie.

Casiana smiles at me. "You are lying but I applaud your attempt to dissuade me."

"Vampires evolve after they have lived long enough," I say simply. "Everyone knows that."

"True," Amelia starts, "we do adapt to a degree. But it is not simply your adaptation and abilities that caught our eye. There is something else about you, something specific to your past which makes you an especially good candidate."

"Like what?" Me and my past? I am a pretty typical vampire living a fairly boring life, given the circumstances.

Before either of them can answer I throw my hands up, "You know what, it really doesn't matter anyway. You can't change the fact that I don't want anything to do with your Nexus hoax. And I think your little cult has wasted enough of my time."

Amelia's lips press into a tight thin line as her anger starts to get the best of her. I stand to walk away though I still do not know how to exit this obnoxiously achromatic room.

I stop, however, when Amelia snaps, "We are a religion, not a cult."

Turning to face her, I tell her irritably, "You worship Lilith, right? And she was evil? Your stories say she couldn't bear children, only demons. That's what your deity and your religion call you; *demons*."

"Because they didn't have a word for us."

I let out a small chuckle and say under my breath, "Yeah, keep telling yourself that." Then louder, I ask, "Now, which way is the door?"

Casiana folds herself into a flip off of the desk, landing her feet directly in front of me. "I urge you to reconsider."

There is something hiding in her eyes and a chill to her voice that tells me she is right. I should reconsider. But as Amelia walks to me, I tell Casiana, "Look even if Lilith had existed, she was vain and empty. You would be a fool to think Lilith would have cared about you more than she cared about herself. She wouldn't have. But more importantly, Lilith couldn't have. Because she's a myth. Nothing more. And frankly, being a myth is one of her better qualities."

Amelia's hand stings my cheek in a quick slap. "Watch your words carefully." She grabs my chin forcefully, "Keep in mind that this 'cult' is bigger than you think. And we are not above killing you for blasphemy."

She turns toward Casiana, "Take what you need. I am done here."

As Amelia walks over to the desk, Casiana tells me softly, "We're not crazy, Nicolas. We are searching for answers, just like you. We could be an ally, you know?"

Handing me a card with only a phone number on it, she continues, "We could help you, if you let us."

Exhaling forcefully, I toss the card on the floor, "Thanks but don't hold your breath. I don't need your kind of help."

The kind that comes with a price. A debt owed to a group that will take repayment whenever they want and however they see fit.

Casiana adds, "A warning then. Watch you back, Nicolas, because we will be."

Her tone is more eerie than I would have thought possible from such a tiny woman and it sends chill along my spine. She does not wait for my response which is good because I do not have one.

She steps beside me, leaning close to my ear, "Oh, one more thing: you were wrong before. Amelia did not enthrall you. I did."

I look over at her quickly. I catch a brief glimpse of her cold smile, then everything goes white.

*   *   *

My eyes open but I lie still allowing them time to focus again. Even before the fog has lifted from my mind, I can recognize where I am. I am home. In my own bed. I can hear my family moving about above me. I do not hear Marcella but I do hear who I assume is her youngest vampire, Vanessa, laughing.

As I lie in the still air listening to my former family above me, I smile slightly. There is a part of me that has missed having a group. Missed having a house full of sounds. Missed the safety. The belonging. It is in that moment that I realize just how lonely I have been and just how much I have missed having, not just a group but having, *my* family.

Sure, my family has its flaws. Luther is an imbecile. Vanessa is inexperienced. Marcella is cruel. Kate was banished due to my reluctance to forgive. Despite their many, many flaws, they are my family. They always have been and forever will be, whether I like it or not. When I really think about it, it is no wonder why I became so self-absorbed.

In the darkness of the room, my black eyes begin to make out the dust floating above me. The specks swirl with each forceful breath. But as my eyes clear, my mind begins to grow anxious. How long have I been in this enthrallment trance-like state? How did the Genesis get into my home, put me in my own bed, and who would have granted them permission? If they can enter my home so easily, is there really anywhere that is safe from them? Is Krista safe?

There are too many worries to consider any of them fully. Perhaps a shower would do some good to clear my mind. Besides, I will need one anyway. I can still smell Krista on my clothes along with an odd mix of the other werewolves that were in the tavern. And ideally, I do need to smell less like a den of wolves before I meet Marcella. That would only lead to more questions. And right now, I have enough of my own.

Using twice the soap I would normally, I attempt to remove the wolf smell from me. Even with the extra soap, I can still smell Krista and part of me does not want to remove every bit of her. I stand in the shower far longer than I need to, postponing my next task of greeting my family.

The water runs over my body but it does not take my troubles with it. I cannot remove the image of Krista's smile at the bar. The gentleness of her eyes when she looked into mine. The blood rushing to her cheeks. While the simple thought of her pushes me to smile, I cannot shake the reality that I may very well never see her again.

I have to find a way around her father.

As I turn off the water, I can hear Luther thump against the floor upstairs as though he is jumping. I smile to myself knowing that even though I do not particularly enjoy Luther, it will be nice to have the distraction of other vampires. Being alone with Marcella is not something I am ready to embrace. Not yet.

I hear the voice of our newest member, Vanessa. She has only been a vampire for fifteen years. She is passed the most difficult cravings but still has much to learn. Even though I have never actually met her, I have spoken to her on the phone and part of me is eager to help her on her path to being a capable vampire. Undoubtedly, she will be a better pupil than Luther ever was. A tree stump could be a better pupil than Luther.

As I make my way quietly up the stairs and into the kitchen, I decipher that the noises are coming from the garage. I press my ear to the door to confirm my suspicions. A vampire can never be too careful about opening a door that leads to the outdoors. During the daylight hours, even a garage door being left open accidentally can end your day rather abruptly and rather painfully.

Just then, I hear a loud crash in the garage. Opening the door, I lean against the door frame to the garage to watch Vanessa with Luther.

"Keep your hands up, elbows in," Luther says as he pushes her elbows close to her ribcage.

I have to smile to myself. Vanessa does not look like a boxer, not even with the correct stance. It is obviously not her fighting style and if Luther was any kind of teacher, he would notice that too.

"Are you honestly taking lessons from the worst fighter in the house?" I ask Vanessa, making her look at me and smile.

"Well, you looked busy napping. I didn't want to interrupt," she says.

I was busy, lost in a strange sleep-like trance. Trust me, the interruption would have been welcomed. Although, I am not certain whether I could have been roused or not.

Luther crosses his arms over his chest as though he does not appreciate my intrusion but I am only stepping in for the good of Vanessa. I would never interfere for the sole purpose of irritating Luther. Okay, maybe I would.

"I'm not napping now," I smile at her.

As I step into the garage, Luther huffs, "I don't need your help, Nick."

With a light, sarcastic laugh, I tell him, "Not even I am vain enough to assume that my help alone would be quite enough to solve your issues."

I walk over to Vanessa, "But she does have the potential that you are lacking. Besides, she doesn't need my help either."

Putting my hands over hers, I lower her fists, "Boxing is not for you. If you want to know your fighting style, follow *your* heart, not his."

With his heavy sigh, I can practically hear his eyes roll but still I continue, "This new body of yours is designed to inflict pain. It knows your strengths better than you do. Just do what feels natural and watch how easy it is to win."

Luther claps his hands lightly, "Compelling speech. Really, just wonderful. But don't you think she should first learn how to fight before you bet on her winning?"

Without taking my eyes away from her, I answer him, "She does. Marcella told Yen all about the 'human' Vanessa. And, naturally, Yen told me."

"Naturally," Luther grumbles.

"You are a black belt, aren't you?"

Vanessa rubs her arm nervously as she glances at Luther with pity in her eyes, "I'm sorry Luther. You just seemed so excited to teach me; I didn't know how to tell you."

Despite the way it obviously bothers him to know that she is not the helpless child he assumed her to be, he shrugs, "That's okay. So, you took some classes in karate."

Something in his words sparks an annoyance and her eyes light up with anger, "Not karate," she says sharply, "Taekwondo. And I was an instructor. I have been undefeated in every competition since I was twelve. My whole life was in that dojo and if I hadn't been tricked by Salem, I'd be kicking someone's ass right now."

Pushing past me, she stomps out of the room. I knew that my maker, Salem, had tried to get back in Marcella's good graces by offering Vanessa to replace me but I have never understood why he thought it would work. It must be terribly sad for him to be shunned so completely by his maker and all of his creations. Marcella claims that she has had no contact with him since I returned but I know better than to believe her.

Luther looks at me with narrow eyes and I cannot help but to smirk, "Guess you're back to being the lamest vampire in this house."

"That's it." He puts his fists up, "I hope you have your dancing shoes on."

I laugh to myself lightly. This being our first battle in a long time, I will try to take it easy on him. Well, maybe. "I thought you'd never ask."

He stays back, waiting for me to advance since he knows too well that rushing toward me is a mistake. After all, I have beaten him in every tussle we have ever had. Ever.

However, I do not need him to be close to win. Moving more quickly than a human can process, I kick the heavy-duty trashcan at him. It crashes into him, knocking him back and distracting him enough for me to hurry toward him. Grabbing his face, I slam my head into his nose. I can feel the bones snap under my forehead and smell his blood pour from his nostrils but that only makes me crave killing him more.

With a quick blow to his sternum with my palm, I drive him into the wall. Before he hits the ground, I am there with an upper-cut to his abdomen.

He manages to claw deep gouges along my ribs amidst the array of punches I deliver to his face and chest. The sudden pain makes me back up a step and rethink my approach as I hold my side, feeling the warmth of my blood staining my shirt.

He has gotten better.

The crimson on my fingers smears as I snatch the pitchfork from the back wall. I spin it once, knocking his feet out from under him. Twirling the pitchfork over my head, I slam the handle down across his ribs. With a groan he rolls onto his side and spits blood onto the cold floor. Using this brief break, I pull the middle two tines apart, creating a wider space between them then plunge the tool over his neck, immersing the tines into the concrete and pinning him to the floor.

With my hand on the handle, I push my weight on it enough to keep him from freeing himself.

"What was that? Thirty seconds? I think that's a new record," I goad.

"Shut up, Nick," he says irritably, pushing against the pitchfork.

Resting my arms on the top of it, I push the tool further against his neck until it becomes difficult for him to breathe. The concrete cracks and splits around the tines as they sink further into the cold floor.

"If we keep doing this, I'm afraid I might get tired of winning. Seeing your blood and hearing your cries just doesn't hold the same pleasure it used to," I tell him casually. Then laughing to myself, I add, "Who am I kidding? This is the best part of living with you."

He tries to respond but only chokes on the limited air. I do not intend on killing Luther but it is fun to watch him squirm.

The sound of the garage door motor kicks on, pulling me from my pleasure. Quickly, I pull the pitchfork out of the floor as the garage door begins to open and the sunlight inches its way toward us.

Grabbing his hand, I jerk him to his feet and we run inside the kitchen. I shut the door, protecting us from the sun and sigh. I suppose I should have explained to Julia that she needs to honk the horn before she opens the garage during the day.

Turning around, I see Luther smiling at me widely, holding back a burst of laughter. Only vampires can be fighting to the death one minute and saving each other the next. That is how it has always been for me and Luther, me beating him then me saving him. Never really the other way around, though.

I start laughing and he follows my response but I am sure we are not amused by the same thing. It is funny to me that he could not kill me. He could barely even scratch me. But Julia, a weak human, could have killed us both.

Marcella walks in the kitchen, giving us a curious look. I suppose it is unusual to see us laughing together and not at each other.

"Did I miss something?" she asks.

Seeing Marcella stops my laughing short, "It's a long story." It is actually not that long but I do not feel compelled to explain it either. Somehow, it would not seem as funny if I said it out loud.

Marcella takes a deep breath before she starts again. "How have you... been?" she asks me, as unsure about our first face-to-face conversation as I am. The last time we were in the same room, I stormed out after discovering that she killed the child I wanted to adopt. It was nearly thirty years ago and I have not seen Alaska or Marcella since. Until this moment.

As I speak, Luther begins slinking out of the kitchen but is less discreet than he intends to be, "I've been good."

It is strange looking at her. In some ways she has not changed at all, like I just saw her yesterday. But the Marcella I knew would not be so anxious around me. I suppose a part of her is worried this reunion will not work and I will disappear again. That she will lose another son permanently. Again. Her worry hangs in her eyes, hoping that I do not bring up our past. I am not used to seeing her walls lower, leaving her so exposed.

I focus on small talk, avoiding topics that might culminate into an argument. No mention of Punzi, Kate, or any other differences we have had. None. Not today. Not this soon.

"Your hair looks nice," I say in an attempt to continue the conversation. Small talk is still talking, right?

Flattered, she smiles softly and touches the tips of her pixie cut with her fingers. "I just wanted something different. Do you really like it?"

The short hair accentuates the hard edges of her face, emphasizing her stern jawline and sharp nose. It does make her appear more austere and callous than her bob did. However, Marcella is austere and callous so I tell her with a small smile, "It suits you."

She smiles widely with my words. I am sure, however, that the smile is not because of my pragmatic compliment. Instead, I believe she was nervous about seeing me again. Just as I was. Her smile is more of relief than happiness as she is simply pleased to not be arguing with me any longer. I must admit, I am relieved to find a peace between us again as well.

As Luther slowly slips around me trying to awkwardly avoid Marcella and myself, there is a knock on the door and everyone is grateful for the interruption.

"I'll get it," Luther snaps, using the distraction as an excuse to see himself out of the kitchen.

As soon as Luther is out of sight, Marcella begins again, "Nicolas, I just want to say that I am really glad that you asked us to come here with you. I want to make this work. I want to be a family again."

She brings her hand toward me and I fight the reflex to pull away. Placing her hand gently on my shoulder, she adds, "I have missed you more than you can imagine."

There is a sadness in her eyes that I have only seen a few times over all these years. Marcella does not usually allow herself to be vulnerable and is even less inclined to allow herself to show it. While she may believe that exposing her weakness is a liability, it is the only way I know that she is being honest.

Marcella is a most convincing liar. After all, she is the one who taught me how to lie so smoothly. Silver-tongued and conning, she forces the appropriate emotion to cement her deception. However, if you really know Marcella, you recognize that her forced emotions are too convincing, too perfect, and too believable.

An honest Marcella struggles to hide and control her emotions. So much that when she does show something other than her cold, callous demeanor, the emotion spills out of her like a cup overflowing, messy and muddled. When she attempts to conceal her feelings is when I know to trust them.

Smiling softly, I tell her, "I'm glad you came, too."

Just as my sentence is finished Luther peeks into the kitchen and stares at me with a large, childish grin sprawled across his face.

My smile disappears with his asinine expression, "What?" I ask.

"There is a lady in the study for you," he teases.

A lady here? For me? Maybe it is Krista. My heart nearly stutters with both excitement and dread. I am more than impatient to see her again but, at the same time, I am also not keen on exposing her to Marcella.

Watching me, Luther smiles more widely. Surely, he can see the chaotic racing in my mind even though my face remains calm. Gauging my response, he adds, "And she's hot."

My eyes snap to him before I can mask the anger in them. He sees it there and in that moment we both know I am hiding something. Something that involves a woman.

Unsure if Marcella saw it too, I bury everything, my feelings, my confusion, and my concerns, to look at Marcella and shrug, "Hm, I should see who that is. Excuse me."

As I brush past Luther, I replay the past few seconds. It all happened very quickly. If Marcella did not see the instant of panic in my disposition, it is likely that she bought my oblivion to who this mystery lady could be. I go quickly while also trying not to appear too eager to reach the study.

As I enter the room, my eyes do not fall on Krista. Of all of the women in my life that I might have imagined, I did not foresee her. The lady standing quietly with her back to me is Simone. Her eyes scan across the books along the wall before she notices me and smiles warmly, "Nicolas."

"Hi, Simone." I walk toward her enough to close the door. Even though I realize that the door will do nothing to make my conversation more private in a house of vampires, it does help me pretend that secrets might not be so easily discernible.

"I was not expecting you. Is everything okay?" I ask, abstaining from asking if Krista specifically is okay.

"Yeah, everything is fine." Despite her smile, she fumbles her fingers over her hands anxiously. "Look, I'm not supposed to be here. And it's important that the pack, especially Warren, *never* finds out that I came here today."

Nodding, I say quietly, "Of course." Walking toward her, I gesture toward the chairs by the desk, "Do you want to sit down?"

She does not start toward the chairs; instead, she pulls out a folded paper from her back pants pocket. Breathing heavily, she stares at the paper for a moment longer then pushes it toward me suddenly without looking up.

Her words rush out just as hurriedly as her arms did, "Tonight is the first night of the fair if you're interested."

As I take the paper she had thrust at me, I look at it more closely. It is a hand-written address with the words 'FAIR 8 PM' above it.

"You want me to go to the fair?" I ask curiously.

Finally, she looks up at me, "I just thought that you might like to see what Missoula has to offer. The daytime is mostly families, but there are a few of us who are planning on going later tonight." She raises her eyebrows impishly, "And you never know who you might run into."

I smile softly at her implication. Krista's alpha did not ban us from bumping into each other at a public place. He simply said 'no dating'. If it is just two people being in the same place at the same time, it is not a date. Well, not technically.

"I am sure that I would love the fair. Thank you." For the offer and the loophole.

"Her dad wants what's best for her. And so do I. So don't make me regret this," she says soberly.

As her friend, Simone will undoubtedly regret this moment. There will undoubtedly come a time when everything will culminate and my façade comes crashing down. One or both of us will undoubtedly be hurt by my pursuing. Knowing this, I choose not to lie and instead use the only words I can honestly say, "I will definitely try my best not to." Although I am not quite sure how.

She nods once then starts toward the door when I speak again, "Hey, Simone." I wait for her to turn to face me to continue. "Really... Thank you." I tell her genuinely.

A small smile spreads across her face while she nods lightly. "Hey, do me a favor? Tell that big guy that the next time I come over, he better not check out my butt. It's creepy and I don't appreciate it."

It would be my pleasure to tell Luther that he is 'creepy'. I laugh to myself, "Sure thing."

Her smile spreads into a full grin with my laugh. "See ya later," she says simply then shows herself out.

I stand in the study for a moment considering what to tell my family, where I am going, what I am doing, and why I want to go alone. Thinking about what I might say to Krista when I see her, how did I know to find her there, and since we cannot date where does this go passed tonight?

There are so many things to mull over but first things first. I need to eat. I need that human, fleshy glow that only blood can provide. I need to look as human as possible tonight. I have a date. That thought alone makes my stomach twist with excitement. A date with Krista.

The same loophole I am so grateful for will enviably be a thorn in Bryant's side. That does not matter to me, though. I thoroughly intend on exploiting this loophole to my fullest capabilities before he implements a new rule to close it.

As I walk out of the study to find Julia, Luther pushes himself off of the wall where he had been waiting for me.

"Well, well, you waste no time. You've only been here, what, a day and you already have a little cutie chasing after you," he taunts.

Just as predicted, Luther would miss the mark and be inept at deciphering the obvious. An imbecile could have heard any part of that conversation and realized that Simone is not the lady in question. Furthermore, it is quite clear that Krista is not chasing me. I am most certainly the pursuer here.

Rolling my eyes at his incompetence, I say simply, "You have no idea what you are talking about." Continuing to walk toward him, I lie despite knowing it will be ineffective, "Simone is the maid. She just stopped by to get paid. I forgot to write her a check the other day. That's all."

"Pfft, no clue, eh?" He taps toward his ears, "You might not think I'm the brightest but you do realize that I'm not deaf, right?"

Well, the lie was worth a try. "Look Luther, I am not interested in Simone. What I am interested in is finding Julia so I can have a decent meal."

"Okay. Well, if you're not interested in Simone then I call dibs," he jokes.

Dibs. What a juvenile notion. But regardless of my opinion or his on the matter, I use the opportunity to inform him of her opinion. "No, you don't. You cannot chase after Simone. She thinks you're creepy. And she was adamant that you be made aware of it." Then, smiling, I tap toward my ears and add, "But you heard that, didn't you?"

Huffing, he mutters more quietly than a human would be able to hear, "Well, there is no law that says I can't enjoy a fair too. Maybe I'll just stop by and check it out myself."

His whispering seems as though he does not want Marcella to hear us either. As though he understands my desire to keep Marcella out of my relationships as much as possible. Considering this, I do not say anything rash or abrasive even though I would like to.

"Luther," I start with a sigh. "Why do you even care who I might be interested in?"

"Because, Nicolas," he says almost harshly. "Unlike you, I have been stuck with women for decades. Just women. Women talking about men *nonstop*! You left- and I get it. I completely understand why you had to leave. But- you left me with Kate, and Marcella, and Vanessa, and even Yen for a while, for the past *thirty* years. Do you know how many gossipy, man-hungry conversations I have had to listen to? Do you? Because I lost count."

A smile spreads and I chuckle to myself. I do understand. More than he realizes. I have lived with Marcella most of my life and I fully comprehend how exhausting it can be to live in a house full of women. Craving the night almost as much as blood just for an escape and a few minutes of quiet time, alone.

"It's not funny, Nick." Luther misreads my laugh but continues anyway. "I need some dude time. I want to talk about boobs instead of bra sizes. I mean, seriously, I don't care what size a bra is. I only care that I can take it off."

My laughter bursts out, "Okay, okay. That's enough." I place my hand on his shoulder, "I am not taking you to the fair but I will make sure you get some dude time. I promise."

Luther sighs with relief, "Thank you."

"I'm supposed to go for drinks in Missoula with Levi soon. You can come with us. I can see if he wants to go tomorrow night, okay?"

"Thank you. Really Nick, you're a lifesaver," he half-jokes.

Dropping my hand, I attempt to end the conversation, "Okay, now I need to eat so I can get a shower and get ready. I have a busy night ahead of me."

As I start to walk away, I hear, "You already had a shower."

Turning around, I see the smirk that has spread across Luther's face. There is only one reason to take a second shower after feeding. A human would never smell the blood from a feeding still clinging to clothing but a non-human would. I had inadvertently given away something I never intended to. And surprisingly, Luther caught it.

Knowing that at this distance anything I say to Luther would be heard by every vampire in the house, I simply raise my finger to my lips, indicating the secrecy I want Luther to keep. Intrigued, Luther's eyebrows raise. I know that he will be asking for more information but that will have to wait.

I continue my search for Julia and once found, I take her to my room to feed. My mind races and my heart pounds simply thinking of my would-be date with Krista. Luckily, Julia's blood helps to begin to soothe my anxious nerves. Before my shower, I load a CD, hoping the music will distract me. I sing loudly with the band simply because Luther loathes my singing and soon gets his attention.

Luther bangs on door to my room, "Stop that, Nicolas, or I swear, I will end you!"

I smile to myself but keep singing anyway.

"Nick, I'm not joking," Luther insists, "If I hear one more syllable, I will murder you in your sleep."

Of course he could not, even if he did try. But I pull the curtain back slightly and call out, "I'm sorry, what? Did you say something? I couldn't hear you over the incredibly less irritating sound that wasn't your voice."

"Ha ha," he says flatly, "I bet you have been working on that comeback for the past thirty years."

I shake my head to myself. This would be more fun if he could at least come up with something good. But it is still nice to have someone who enjoys playful banter again. Well, he might not like it but, at least, I enjoy it.

"Actually, I am surprised that you caught the insult. I thought it might be a little over your head," I tell him.

"Keep yapping and I'll make sure there is a whole lake of water over your head," Luther tries but I can hear the smile in his voice.

As she walks past him in the hallway, Marcella snaps, "Luther, be quiet."

"He started it," Luther whines like a child.

"I said, quiet!" she orders and to my surprise, he listens.

I hear his footsteps grow quieter as he leaves but I sense Marcella still standing at my door, listening.

Even though Luther hates my singing, I actually do have a nice singing voice so when the next song begins, I start singing again. Marcella has always enjoyed my singing and I do not doubt hearing me in the shower after these last few decades is a bit nostalgic.

As the song approaches the chorus, I call out, "Marcella. You're on backup."

As I suspected, her voice is close. She was still by the door. There is a smile in her voice as it matches mine and to my surprise, she knows the words as well as I do. We continue through the chorus and for a moment, my troubles are far from my mind. My hunger is appeased, I have my Krista, and I have my family. There is nothing more I could want in this moment. But that moment is brief.

As the chorus ends, our moment of reminiscing ends just as quickly as it began. Reality washes back over us both as I shut off the water. Marcella's voice fades into the emptiness, consumed by the bitterness still lingering between us. I could call out to her. Tell her that I am trying to forgive. Tell her that I understand her actions all those years ago. Apologize for my part in our severance. But I do not.

The dripping water taps on the floor as Marcella's steps carry her away from me, allowing me the liberty of immersing my thoughts completely and wholly onto someone much more pleasing. I smile as I see her face in my mind. Soon, I will see her face not simply in my mind, but physically in front of me. Soon my Krista will be close enough to touch.

Chapter 4

Humans love fairs. They love the food, the rides, and they even enjoy having the excuse to dress like trollops. I rub my fingers across the stamp on my hand, smearing the ink. The fair is not a pleasing place for me. Sure, there are ample options for food here. Humans with reduced inhibitions make easy prey. But the overpowering scent of grease makes the air heavy and sticky in an uncomfortable way.

I have killed at a fair but I found it more preferable to kill in the parking lot away from the stench of cooking oils and sweat. The parking lot proves to be distant enough to enjoy sinking my teeth into a struggling human. The crowds walking to and from their cars, add a more than enjoyable heightened risk of getting caught which only makes my snacking more satisfying. But I am not here searching for a meal. My eyes scan the crowds for Krista or Simone, anybody that could justify my being here.

Waiting on the sunset had made me later than I wanted to be. Finally, I see her. Standing in line for the Ferris wheel, Krista smiles at something Simone has said. The heat has caused her to pull her hair back but her large curls still fall over her bare shoulder gently. The humidity has dampened her skin, causing the fair lights to glisten on her.

Her rose-colored tank top is not expensive or elaborate. Just a simple material without any image or design to speak of, yet it accents her figure wonderfully.

While I do not like that Warren is with her too, I do enjoy watching her eyes light up when she sees me across the grass. Her radiant smile draws me in, coercing me to go to her and making me ignore the dangers yet again.

Warren grimaces as I walk toward them. Most likely, he is internally groaning about the conversation he will inevitably have with Bryant about me being here. However, I ignore his discontent concerning my presence. It would be imprudent of me to not speak to her now that she knows I am here; and I care very little about how much distress this might cause him.

She smiles widely as I get closer, searing in my need for her that much more. "Are you stalking me?" she jests.

I shrug and reply jokingly, "Maybe a little."

Warren interrupts with a reminder aimed at me, "You know you don't have permission to date her, so why are you here exactly?" He keeps a neutral demeanor and tone, contrasting his territorial behavior on the first day I met him and I wonder briefly what made him change his disposition. Perhaps it was Simone.

I glance at Warren, "That's the beauty of it. This isn't a date." Then looking back at Krista, I continue with a smirk, "Just two people coincidently bumping into each other at a public place and then deciding to spend the rest of their time at said public place in close proximity to one another."

He lets out an irritated chuckle. "Sounds like you really thought this through, haven't you?" Warren says dryly.

"This moment is the only thing I have been able to think of all day," I tell him without taking my eyes from Krista.

Krista's cheeks redden as she peeks over at Warren sheepishly, "Definitely not a date."

He forces out a heavy breath and mumbles to himself, "Fine, but just tonight. Bryant will have my hide as it is."

Krista grins excitedly and lips the words *'thank you'* to Warren.

"Okay, now that we have that settled, you two should get on the ride before that guy has a coronary," Simone says, gesturing toward the Ferris wheel.

Krista and I both turn and find that while we had been talking the line had moved without us. Standing next to an empty seat, a man waves towards us irritably, "Next!" he calls loudly.

Krista grabs my hand subconsciously and pulls me toward the ride.

She slides into the cart and pats the spot next to her. The lights from the ride dance across her skin, making me unable to take my eyes from her as I slide in beside her.

Krista either does not notice or does not mind my staring because as the ride moves to allow the next riders on Krista says simply, "So. Go ahead. Impress me."

I shift in my seat, turning my body toward her, "Okay. Um..." Unsure of what she is asking for, I let out a light chuckle, "Do you want me to, like, bench press a bear or something?"

She laughs lightly, "No. Just tell me about yourself." She grabs the end of a curl and twirls it in her fingers aimlessly, "What's your story?"

Tell her about myself. Now that is a novel idea. I mean, I do want her to know everything. Every secret, every vulnerability, every inch of me. However, it is not likely to go smoothly if I say, *'Hey, I am vampire. Here is a stake. Feel free to plunge it in my heart.'*

The ride moves again prompting me to give an answer, "It's kind of a downer. Are you sure you want to hear it?"

She looks at me briefly, gauging her own response in her mind before she replies softly, "Yeah, I do."

"Okay." I let out a heavy sigh, organizing my thoughts quickly. The most believable lies are the ones that stay as close to the truth as possible. While that is my typical reasoning for attempting to only halfway lie to the unsuspecting about my past, there is a different motive I stay so close to the truth. With Krista, I actually *want* to be honest. It is a feeling I am not familiar with. And there is a part of me that is frightened by it.

"I never knew my mother. She died during childbirth. And it's strange that even though I never met her, I do miss her. I don't have any pictures of her, or much else, really. But I have been told that I resemble her quite a bit."

She touches my hand gently. The warmth of her fingers nearly causes me to lose my place in my prevaricated narrative but I continue just the same, "My father blamed me. I was a constant reminder of what he had lost. And as such, he was not kind, or loving. Not towards me. We weren't very close and I eventually went to live with some cousins. I heard a while back that he died but I didn't attend the funeral."

My father died *'a while back'* is vague enough to be true, and, honestly, my vampire family could be considered my cousins in a weird dysfunctional sort of way. Overall, there are not many stretches to the truth in my backstory which fills me with an odd sense of pride. However, being proud of being *mostly* honest is a wretched thing when one really stops to consider it.

"But on a positive note," I continue, "I love the family I do have. My cousins are actually here visiting right now so you might get to meet them. They're..." Vampires. Murderers. Sociopaths, "odd. But they are..." Good people? Nice?

"Family," Krista finishes.

"Exactly."

"Well, I'm sorry your childhood was not so great. It sounds pretty terrible, actually," she rubs the back of my hand comfortingly.

I could use her pity against her- use her kindness as a means to my gain. I have been known to use similar methods before, but manipulating Krista would only leave me feeling empty and alone.

"It was horrid at the time, I would have traded anybody for any other life but," I place my hand over hers, stopping her fingers from trailing across my skin and look into her eyes, "I like who I am. When women hear about my past, they see a project. And I do realize that some women like fixer-uppers but I don't want you to be mistaken in that. I am not broken. Good, bad, this is it. This is me. No amount of TLC is going to correct my flaws. And trust me, there are plenty of them."

She raises one eyebrow curiously, so I add lightheartedly, "But those are, more like, fifth date proclamations."

"Oh, so you think there's going to be a fifth date?" she asks playfully.

"Well, I certainly hope so. I just have to convince your dad that I'm a better catch than I am."

She laughs lightly, "Tonight isn't going to get you any brownie points with him. Sneaking around behind his back never does."

"Yeah," I nod. "That fifth date is probably going to be postponed a little."

"Probably."

She smiles warmly so I seize the opportunity to change the direction of the conversation and ask, "What's that like, anyway? Having an alpha who is also your dad? Because, honestly, he is a pretty intimidating obstacle for me."

Intimidating may be a slight exaggeration. I find Bryant more of a daunting inconvenience than frightening. However, if I were human, I am sure that intimidating would have been the correct word to describe him.

Smiling, she begins, "I don't know. Um, it's different for me, I guess. To me, he's just my dad. I mean, yes, he can give orders that I do not want to follow and, yes, I do have to obey. But he only makes rules that he thinks will protect the pack, just like any other dad would do."

I shrug, sarcastically, "Right. I mean, he is still just one man, right?" Though, that's not exactly true. He comes with a pack. A rather large one at that.

"Yeah, just one *werewolf*," she corrects. "A werewolf who also happens to be the sole reason this is a fake-date and not a real date."

I nod and joke, "There's that."

"My dad's rules are meant to protect the pack and the humans from each other. Humans accidentally kill other humans all the time. But inevitably it will be a werewolf that accidentally kills a human and when that happens..." she shakes her head thinking. "Everything is about protecting and preserving our pack. Everything."

She shifts in her seat, "Look, you said that you have flaws, well, so do I. Don't be fooled into believing that I am not dangerous. I mean, for the most part, I'm not; but given the wrong scenario, I could really hurt you. Possibly even kill you. It's important that you understand that right upfront. Don't ever forget that. I am not like other girls."

No, she is definitely not like other girls.

I know wolves can be volatile. I have felt their teeth in my skin. Their phases must be voluntary in order to remain in control of their wolf. Anger, pain, and fear can overpower them enough to force a phase which is dangerous. She does not know what I am, therefore does not realize that the risks involved for me are very different than for a human.

"I am well aware of *what* you are. I'm trying to find out *who* you are."

Exaggerating a fake stretch, I lay my arm behind her on the back of the cart. "So, it's your turn to talk. Tell me everything. I want to know if you have any siblings. What your favorite movie is. What kind of music do you like?"

She smiles at my excited rambling, but I cannot stop myself, "How old are you, physically *and* actually? What kind of job do you have? What's your favorite food? You know, do you prefer kale or pizza?"

She snickers, "Well first off, nobody likes kale."

Chuckling under my breath, I shake my head, "No, I suppose not."

She smiles at me briefly before continuing. For a moment, I wonder what it is she is thinking of but my thoughts do not stay there long. The lights from the ride reflect in her eyes, drawing me in. Just as I begin to lose myself in their enchantment, she begins speaking again, pulling me back to the moment at hand.

"It's always just been me and my dad. I do have an older brother but you don't really need to worry about him just yet." She looks over her shoulder, "It's me you need to impress."

I do not know if it is the challenge in her eyes or the sultry tone of her voice but my skin warms in response.

"And where is he ranked?"

"Third in command. Right under Warren."

"Are you two very close?" I hope not. My experiences with older brothers have not been good ones. For some reason, they do not like me. I cannot imagine why.

She shakes her head, "Not really. He's older than me and lived with his mom so I didn't grow up with him much. But he is still my brother so he likes to throw his opinion around *a lot.*"

Great. Perfect. Just what I need. A brother who will undoubtedly try to make up for lost time by being overly protective and intrusive now.

"I would have thought Warren might be your brother or something," I tell her.

"More so than Mitchell but no, I grew up with Warren. He actually owns the shop I work for now. So, he's my boss and dating my best friend so I pretty much see him all day, every day."

Her light giggle at the end of her sentence leads me to believe that while she does not dislike seeing Warren so often, she still longs for some time without wolves hovering over her every move.

"Shop?"

She smiles warmly at my change of direction, "Yeah. An auto shop. I used to run my own garage when I lived in Missoula. But then the wolves came out, and everybody freaked. My friends hated me, my business went under, and then to top it all off, they passed those stupid living restrictions."

Restrictions that would have made her leave the city. It is still illegal for a wolf to live within the city limits but that will probably change in the next few years. Humans are still adjusting.

"I didn't really have anywhere else to go," she continues. "So I joined my dad's pack and I'll probably be here forever because my dad will not sever my ties voluntarily. I would have to break the bond myself but that's," she shakes her head, thinking of the right word, "unlikely. But um, yeah, I started working at Warren's shop. We restore classics and we get some real beauties come through our shop, too. Hands down, it is the best job out there."

Seeing the excitement in her eyes, I ask her, "What made you get into cars so much?"

"Same thing that got Warren into them. My dad. Growing up with a single father, I spent most of my childhood in his garage. Just me and my dad. Warren lived down the street so he was there all the time."

She sighs quietly and my thoughts linger around how her breath would feel on my skin. "I don't know. I guess I'm just more comfortable in a garage than anywhere else, even my own house."

Resting her head back on the seat, she bats her eyes but something tells me that she did not realize that she did it at all. "So what about you? What do you do?"

Hm, what do I do? That is a loaded question. I lie. I manipulate. I murder freely for any reason that I deem acceptable in that moment.

"I actually dropped out of nursing school to write." I mean, I did work in a hospital when I lived in Alaska. "And despite the statistics, I was able to luck into a pretty good gig."

"Really?" Half-turning in her seat, she lights up with interest. "What kind of books do you write?"

True stories. Stories about death and violence. Stories considered to be fiction by the humans. Stories about me.

"I write short stories and articles for a science-fiction magazine."

Excitedly, she reaches out and grabs my forearm and my stomach rolls with nerves, "Which one?"

It takes me a moment to answer but finally say, "Asimov's."

"You do not," she shoves my arm playfully. "We have a couple of those in the lobby at the shop. I read them on my breaks all the time."

My lopsided smile slides across my face, "Then you might have read some of my stuff. I use the pen name, Haddox Pierce."

Her jaw drops but I only notice the way her grip tightens on my arm, "That's you?" she nearly squeals. "You wrote this one, um..." She snaps her fingers several times, thinking hard, then starts again, "Well, I don't remember the name of it but it was about a vampire."

Yeah, that's definitely mine.

Her words roll out on top of one another, "It was incredible. I remember reading it alone in my room and it gave me chills. I don't know how you think stuff up like that." Mumbling to herself, she trails off, "What was the main character's name again?"

"Vincent Rider." The same name I always use.

She smiles widely. "That's right. Rider. You gave him your last name," she says, connecting the dots of my limited honesty. "That's so neat."

And my real first name. My human name but she does not need to know that yet.

"Yep, neat." Not only my name, I also gave him my stories, my experiences, my regrets.

"He's my favorite so far. You're a really good writer, you know that?"

I know she had a compliment in there but I only heard that I, well my fictional self, am her favorite vampire and that makes me smile.

"Thank you. Not a lot of werewolves like vampires. I'm kind of surprised you find them so interesting," I say, all too aware of how little werewolves care for vampires. I have felt their bite too many times to doubt their opinion of my kind in general.

She rests her hand on her knee, making circles with her finger, "I know, it's weird. My pack thinks I'm crazy. Everyone is so convinced that they're extinct but, I don't know. Maybe they're not." She leans close and whispers, playfully, "Maybe they're all hiding." She giggles to herself as she leans back into her seat.

The fact that she does not believe the façade we have painted for them proves to me that she is one of the smartest in her pack. It is a shame that despite her intelligence, she will rank at the bottom of the pack until she marries someone higher. It is an outdated dogma and one of the many reasons I do not often associate myself with wolves. Well, that and the fact that they always try to kill me.

"I don't think you're crazy. It wasn't that long ago that humans thought you weren't real either," I tell her.

She smiles softly and it captivates me. I should not be here. I should not be dating a werewolf. It could, no, will, get me killed. But that does not seem to be a good enough reason not to.

She shrugs playfully, "Well, either way, they do make interesting stories."

I can feel the nervousness creep in. Here it is: the opportunity to probe her real feelings about what I am without revealing myself. I focus on my breathing. Why am I so nervous? I am never nervous for a date. Maybe it is because if her family learns my secret, I will definitely be killed. No, that is not it. It is her.

Something about her makes me anxious. Something about her makes me want to say the right things and be the right person, but without lying more than necessary.

Here goes nothing. "What do you think you would do if you ever met Vincent? I mean, do you think you would even want to meet a vampire if you had the chance?"

"Of course not," she laughs. "Vampires are murderers, Nick. I'd kill it."

Disappointment tugs at me. Despite the fact that her answer is the most logical response, and I did anticipate it, I still had hoped for something else. I had hoped for some tinge of inclination toward vampires that I might build on.

Regardless of how she feels about vampires currently, I do savor the familiarity in her voice as she called me 'Nick' instead of 'Nicolas' and choose to focus on that as I continue, "Of course, you would most likely be natural enemies anyway." Then, changing the subject, I redirect, "So, I did notice that you avoided telling me how old you are."

Crinkling her nose in the most endearing way, she says, "Successfully avoided, I thought." There is a brief pause before she continues, "I'm twenty-five."

Her eyes drifted as she said her age, avoiding eye contact. She just lied to me. And she was terrible at it.

I smile to myself, "Yes, physically, I'm sure you are. But maybe this time, you could tell me how many years you have been alive."

Seeming slightly embarrassed, her cheeks blush, tempting my hand to feel the warmth her rush of blood brings to them.

"Promise it won't weird you out?"

"Trust me, I can handle it."

I am no petty human who would compare her age to their own. A human might hear her age and become bothered. They would begin viewing her as an elderly woman, someone older than their own mother, perhaps. But immortals do not view time in relation to those around them. Age truly is just a number, a number of little relevance to maturity, skill, or capabilities. Immortals are not old; they are not young; they just are.

She grimaces slightly as she answers, "Forty-two."

Forty-two. She is just getting started with her life. Pursuing her will undoubtedly leave her consumed by guilt, anger, or pain once she knows what I am and discovers my grand betrayal. It is shameful of me to be selfish enough to swallow her innocence so completely and so early in her life.

I try to answer as I believe a human might, "Well, you look great."

She laughs but I am sure it is not the first time she has heard such a lame jest.

The Ferris wheel comes to a halt with us near the top and for the first time, I realize that we missed the entire ride. I had not noticed when it began nor did I pay any attention to the views the ride offered. I had been much too absorbed in watching the lights illuminate her vivacity, aching to touch her warm skin, and hearing her voice strum the air between us.

I step out of the cart and hold out my hand to help her out as well. "What about your mother?"

She smiles delicately before she answers, "She passed away. It's not uncommon for werewolves to die during childbirth."

As she steps off the platform, I do not back up causing her to step down close to me. Looking in her eyes, I say quietly, "I'm sorry."

I am sorry. Not because I asked but simply because she had to lose her mother before she really knew her. I am sorry because I understand. To be aware that despite all efforts, you will never fully know how much you are missing and there is nothing to be done about it, is a lamenting cognizance to carry.

She stares at me longer than necessary, the air vibrating between us. I realize that kissing her would be imprudent and out of place, particularly since I barely know her. However, that knowledge does not slow the crushing urge growing inside me to glide my fingers along her cheek, lifting her chin toward me. My lips on hers... I can nearly taste her just thinking of it.

As Warren and Simone step off of the ride forcing us to move aside, Krista drops her eyes from mine. Biting her lip, she shoves a loose strand of hair behind her ear, causing my heart to beat that much faster.

Sucking in a sharp breath, Krista fumbles with her words, "Um, do you want.. uh..., some, like, cotton candy or something? Or we could get on another ride. Whichever."

Although Krista had been asking me, Simone is the one who answers, "Definitely food. I need grease and sugar in my stomach in the next few minutes or I might lose my mind."

Shaking her head, Krista smiles and rolls her eyes, playfully.

Without taking my eyes from Krista, I nod towards Simone, "Sounds like she needs an elephant ear."

Simone touches my shoulder matter-of-factly then, looking at Krista, she adds, "He's a genius."

They both giggle as Simone takes Krista's hand and pulls her toward a sugary smelling food truck.

Watching them trot off, Warren leans near me, "Are we supposed to know why that was funny?"

"If you ever meet a man that does, tell him to write a book for the rest of us," I joke.

Warren laughs, lightly. "Come on. I'll let you buy Krista some sugar since you can't give her any of your own," he says and then laughs harder at his own joke than he had at mine.

Admittedly, his joke is clever and it makes me smile as we rejoin the ladies. They both order an elephant ear and we pick a picnic table nearby. As Warren and Simone sit on one side to share her elephant ear, I choose a spot next to Krista.

She picks up a piece of the sugar-coated treat, "Want some? We could share. I'm not going to eat it all anyway," she offers.

"No, thanks. I don't eat sweets." Or anything else solid if I can help it.

Simone cuts in playfully, "You don't know what you're missing."

I am sure I do. By not eating the sticky-smelling dessert, I am missing the heavy, nauseating feeling of food waiting to be expelled and then I will be missing out on purging my stomach contents after I leave here. I know exactly what I am missing.

But instead of saying that, I simply smile.

As I look back to Krista, I realize she is smiling at me and I begin to wonder how long she has been staring.

"How come you don't eat sweets? Are you, like, a diabetic or something?" she asks, just before taking another bite.

I start to shake my head when Warren chimes in, "I bet he's watching his boyish figure."

"Yep, that's it, Warren. I'm watching my figure." A goofy smile spreads on his face as I continue, "Because not all of us are as good as you at impressing women with grease smeared all over our chins."

Simone looks over at him and laughs at the greasy sugar she somehow had not seen before. She grabs a napkin and begins wiping his face off, smirking at his inability to cleanly feed himself.

Krista says to me quietly, "If you don't eat sweets, we could have gotten something else or we could have rode something. You don't have to just sit here just because I wanted to." She says it almost as an apology; as though she could ever be an inconvenience to me.

Smiling to myself, I stare at her briefly before I answer. "Krista, I think you misunderstand why I'm here. I'm not here for the fair. I'm not here for the food or the rides. I'm here for you. So whether we are sitting at a picnic table or the top of the Ferris wheel, it really doesn't matter; just as long as I'm sitting next to you."

Blushing ever so slightly, her cheeks warm and her eyes grow soft but she does not look away from me. I can feel the air between us sizzling across my skin, causing the hairs on my arms to stand at attention. The look in her eyes tells me that she can feel the energy swirling around us too. Knowing that her alpha's order would cause her physical pain if I indulged myself in a kiss that we are both longing for, is the only reason I remain still. Silently, I wait to press my lips to hers and drown ourselves in an ocean of passion that neither of us dares to resurface from. For that I would wait an eternity.

I am thankful when Simone interrupts, unwittingly but imperatively, bringing us both back to the moment at hand, "Come on, you're getting cleaned up," she says to Warren as she pulls him from the picnic table. "I'm pretty sure the elephant ear had less sugar on it than you do."

Then, looking at us, she adds cheerfully, "We'll be right back." We watch them walk toward the restrooms on the other side of the fairground.

Once they have disappeared into the crowd completely, Krista takes my hand, "Now's our chance."

Before I can respond, she pulls me in the opposite direction Warren had gone, leaving our mess of plates on the table.

"What are we doing?" I ask curiously.

She smiles back at me over her shoulder with mischief in her eyes, "Ditching the babysitter."

Something in her words, or perhaps it was in her tone, sends a fervent rippling of heat through me. Despite my attempt to hold it back, a sudden rush of desire catches me off guard. I can only hope that my unbridled eagerness does not show on my face as she drags me through the crowd towards the parking lot.

"You have a car, right?" she asks, looking over her shoulder for any sign of Warren.

"Yeah, of course." In that moment, I have never been more pleased to have brought a car instead of my bike.

Once we get into the parking lot, she stops me, "Which one?"

I scan the lot quickly, despite knowing exactly where I parked. It simply seems like a human thing to do.

"There," I say pointing.

Deep oxford blue, my MG RV8 shimmers in the moonlight. It is not a common car on this side of the hemisphere so it is no wonder to me why she asks incredulously, "For real?"

She smirks as she continues, "I pegged you for more of a Honda Civic kinda' guy." She glances over at me, raising her eyebrows, "You know, cute and compact."

I was not expecting her blatant flirting and, for once, I cannot think of much to say.

Walking over to my car, she runs her fingers over the round headlight and along the fender, "Do you know a lot about cars?"

Yes. Yes, I do.

I shrug, "Just what you learn in high school auto shop."

"Mm-hm," she says, not really believing me, then looks at the car again. "But you are aware that this car is pretty rare, state-side, I mean. I never thought I'd even see one."

Staring at my RV8, her eyes hold the same greed and desire that a child's eyes possess in a candy store. Her eyes roll over every cold metal curve. She clearly realizes that this one is not an original 1960s model, not with the updated more masculine and stout body panels. The upgrades in the newer models did not stop at aesthetics though, which I am sure she already knows.

"And it's a right-hand drive. Neat," she says more to herself than to me. Watching her study the car, I am glad that I had left the top down so that she could easily see the interior.

She brushes her hand over the beige leather seat slowly despite being pressed for time. As much as she clearly wants to continue inspecting my car, Krista looks up at me and smiles softly, "Well, how about you kidnap me now?"

I do not want to kidnap her, though. What I want is something else entirely. She is not doing anything in particular to tempt me, but I am tempted; so very tempted. Her skin looks human enough to make my mouth water and my heart race. The way she leans against the fender makes me want to lie her over the hood, grab her knee, pulling her leg to my ribs, and... Stop, I tell myself.

My cheeks warm as blood rushes to them and I look away to keep her from seeing the yearning in my eyes. "It's not kidnapping...," I hold the keys up, letting them dangle between us, "if you're driving."

Her face lights up, "Are you sure?"

I open the driver's door for her and notice her bite her lip, holding back a smile. "Most men don't open doors anymore."

Most men do not drink blood or kill humans mercilessly either. I doubt she has ever been on a date with anyone retaining even a fraction of my past sins. "I'm not like most men."

"I've noticed," she says softly. "Now, let's get out of here while we still can," she adds, playfully, snatching the dangling keys from my hand.

Closing the door, I hurry around the car, being sure not to go more quickly than a human would. I jump into the passenger seat without using my door, flashing a lopsided grin at Krista as she turns the key.

The engine rumbles to life. "Ooh, 3.9-liter V8. Much better than the original B-series."

She smiles widely at me but before I can offer any input on the improvements made from the earlier models, Krista peels out of the parking lot.

The wind rushes past me as Krista speeds down the road, darting through the slower fair traffic. Her hair whips wildly behind her as the sugar-laded scents grow farther from us.

"Have you ever drove the 60s models?" she asks me.

I shake my head even though that is not exactly true. I did drive one once but it was brief and I did not own it.

She nods, deep in thought. "I was wondering how they compared. The newer ones, like this, are supposed to have a wider track and better suspension," Krista tells me, loudly, trying to overcome the roaring of the wind on my ears that would obscure her voice if I were actually human.

"The salesman said it improved the handling and that the manufacturer kept the wooden dashboard to maintain its quintessential British feel," I tell her with a smile.

She looks over at me briefly and I cannot read the expression in her eyes. "Where did you get it?"

"I picked it up when I was in London last year." Admittedly, it was more difficult than I expected to get the car across the American border but humans can always be persuaded to make irrational decisions. You just have to figure out what to use to convince them.

Her eyebrows raise slightly, interested. "You went to London? That's so neat. I want to see Europe someday."

"Why don't you?"

She smiles softly, the way an adult smiles when they attempt to explain Santa Claus to a small child. "I was going to. I saved up my money and everything. I even booked the flight. But then werewolves were exposed and there were a whole bunch of new laws, so, you know," she shrugs with her last words.

Laws that said she could not board a plane.

She does not look away from the road as she continues, "I joined the pack and, I don't know, even after the flight restrictions were lifted, I just stayed."

As she takes the on-ramp to the highway, I shift in my seat, "I don't think I could ever be part of a pack. At least, not as a wolf. I don't really enjoy taking orders."

Taking her hand from the gearshift, she lays her hand on the edge of the seat between us and my fingers ache to touch hers. My heart picks up its pace as I think about how easy it would be to take her hand in mine. I could lean in slowly, taste her lips, and run my fingers through her hair.

"Nobody likes taking orders," she says, simply. Then shrugging, she continues, "There's something about being a werewolf that makes you need a pack. It's like something pulls you towards it. I tried to stay a free wolf as long as I could; but once werewolves were revealed, I started running out of friends. I was suddenly alone, and I needed my pack more than ever."

From the corners of her eyes, she looks over at me and smiles warmly, "So what about you? How come you are so persistent about trying to date me when you keep being denied?"

As I stare at her flawless beauty, taking it all in, I contemplate her question. Why am I so persistent? Why can't I walk away when I know I should?

She misinterprets my delay in responding and assumes I did not hear her question. Smiling, she jokes, "I asked you something. Try to stay focused."

But I am focused. On her. Because, right now, she is the only thing I want. I decide to tell her honestly, despite it being too forward. After all, this may be my only opportunity. "I think it's because you're the north to my south. It would have been easier to simply avoid you, but I let myself venture too close. And something about you pulled me in. Now, I honestly don't think I could escape your hold even if I wanted to try."

She smiles bashfully without looking away from the road. I could continue. Tell her how I do not fully understand what it is like to be drawn to a pack, but I do know what it is like to feel alone. Say that when I am near her, all that emptiness is gone. Make her understand that I cannot comprehend how a werewolf could make a vampire feel so human.

Instead, a lump forms in my throat. It is not my thirst that makes it difficult to swallow. Worry creeps into my mind, telling me that I have said too much already. If I continue, I will surely frighten her away by giving the impression that I am nothing more than a clingy, stalker type of guy.

I clear my throat in an effort to begin speaking again. My words are more rushed than I anticipate but I do manage to say, "So yeah, I will be persistent in finding loopholes until I have permission to date you because, right now, that's the only thing I can do."

The traffic light changes and she slows to a stop. The wind swirls her scent around me as her hair dances over her shoulder. The crimson hues of the light casting down on her illuminate her skin, bringing out the contours of her cheekbones and smoothness of her full lips. When she looks over at me, her soft brown eyes invite me in and I begin to understand why she hijacked us away from the fair. Just like me, Krista only needs one justifiable reason to be here tonight. And for a moment, I let myself consider that perhaps she craves me as much as I need her.

A slow smile spreads across her face, causing my heart to race. I know she can hear it almost as clearly as I can but that is a good thing. The nervousness makes me seem more human. But what is she thinking? Was I too forward? Does she realize I am being honest for a change? Or does she think my words are just that? Words. Said by a player? Or worse? She could think I am the possessive, jealous type, bent on making her mine so that I can control her.

As I further contemplate ridiculous scenarios that I cannot stop from entering my mind, the traffic signal changes to green once more and she speeds off. She switches through the gears quickly, getting to a speed in which she no longer needs to shift. Then without any words, she lies her hand over mine, sending a surge of heat through me. Her fingers curve around my palm and delicately thread their way between my own fingers.

I bite my lip nervously as my heart pounds even harder, distracting me from my trembling hands. I should not be so anxious about this. It is simply holding hands. I have done a lot more than hold hands with a lot more dangerous beings. There is no logical reason to be jittery about her touching my hand. Yet, here I am, lost in a cascade of confusing emotions.

I can barely move as impatient excitement and restless apprehension struggle to be the more prominent sentiments. These are unusual feelings for me. I do not get nervous, doubt myself, or even consider I might not get what I want. I tend to lead in a relationship, first to make a move, always knowing what to say and do. But I do admit that despite the uncertainty, the thrilling eagerness of her simple touch forces my lopsided smile out and for the first time in a long time, I truly blush.

She holds my hand most of the drive, only letting go to shift gears. We talk a little, but, mostly, we merely enjoy riding next to one another. Our scents mix in the night air as the wind from the road rushes past us. I am not sure where she is taking us but I am also not sure that I care. As long as she is beside me, any place would do.

About twenty minutes is all it takes for her to transport us somewhere else entirely. It is true that, geographically, we are not far from where we started, but, somehow, it feels different. There is no more fire raging in my throat, no werewolf versus vampire risks, and no impending daylight- nothing standing between us. There is only her and I.

When she stops at an overview, there are a few other people in their cars but I do not pay much attention to them. My mind is elsewhere, wrapped in a passionate embrace. As I stare at her, I am lost in an image of her fingers tangling themselves into my hair, just to be a little closer. Her pulling my face to hers. My tongue tracing the same path hers had before...

Her words bring me back to the moment as she asks, "Are you okay?"

"Uh... yeah. Sorry," I tell her. Krista chuckles lightly in the most endearing way as I finish. "I was daydreaming."

Krista smiles softly for a moment before nodding toward the overview, "Come on."

Walking over to the edge of the shrubbery, she looks at the far-off scenery, admiring the picturesque view of the mountains, "I come here sometimes when I need a break from the pack. It's beautiful, isn't it?"

The mountains are peaceful and calming but I am not looking at them. I find that I cannot pull my eyes away from her face. The moonlight dances across her skin, softening her already flawless features. Her eyes cannot hide the smile in them and I let myself fantasize that I might be the reason for it.

If I could stop time in this moment, I would. I would pause everything just to watch her gazing over the mountains as the cold light washes over her, highlighting every perfection her face possesses. She will forever be more beautiful than she will ever know. Part of the perks of being a werewolf. Her flawlessness was forever captured that day she first phased and her aging stopped.

To avoid being cliché, I do not say my thoughts about her beauty aloud. Instead, I look out over the mountain-view and mutter quietly, "They're lovely."

But our moment is broken by a strange voice, "Since when did they start letting people bring their pets here?" Standing between two other arrogant looking men, the light-haired man crosses his arms over his chest.

"This isn't a dog park, you know. So where's your leash, pooch?" he continues.

I look over at him sharply as he smirks at Krista but she does not even glance at his snide expression or his inadequate muscle tone to boast such an insult.

"Wouldn't you be more comfortable at home drinking from a bowl?" he goads.

She calmly refuses to look at them, patiently waiting for the men to leave.

But I am not so tolerant. "Excuse me," I blurt out as my heart races and I fight to keep my temper in check.

He looks over at me nonchalantly, "I wasn't talking to you."

As he takes a step closer to Krista, I step quickly between them. "But I *am* talking to you," I snap.

Krista grabs my arm, "Nicolas, don't."

Her eyes show a sadness in them but something tells me it is not from the comments. It is more of a pity for their ignorance. "Please," she whispers.

I know what I want to do. I want to grab him by his hair, slam his face into the hood of my car, shattering bones and sending blood pouring over his chin. I want to feel his fear in the air around me. I want to taste his blood until his body goes limp and his pathetic life leaves him once and for all.

However, I am on a date with someone who thinks I am human, so fighting him is not an option. At least, not in front of Krista.

Smirking sarcastically, I ask him, "How exactly does your tiny mind fit inside that big head? Does it just rattle around in there?"

He starts to respond but I cut him off by saying, "I wouldn't worry too much, all that extra space will quickly fill with your inevitable failures and shortcomings. It's just part of having such a wretched personality. Now if you don't mind, I'm going to get back to my date, because, unlike you, she is worth my time."

His eyebrows come together while his mouth tightens into a thin line. I can tell his mind is rolling over a petty comeback for me but all he manages is, "Yeah... well...-"

I cut him off before he embarrasses himself any worse. "That's your cue." I nod him away as I tell him, "Start steppin'."

One of his lackeys hits his shoulder, "Come on, man. Let's go."

His friends walk away, back to the truck they came from. The light-haired man stands still for a moment, glaring at me, before he follows them. I want so badly to go after him, show him what a real animal is, but, instead, I lean back against the car next to Krista.

With the bed of the truck full of immature, hooting humans, the truck pulls away, leaving dust hovering in the air.

Krista half-smiles at me and says softly, "Nicolas, people say things like that to me all the time. It doesn't bother me. I'm used to it."

But she should not be. She does not deserve to fall victim to their callousness. They see her as a werewolf, a tame dog, nothing more, but they are wrong.

When I look at her, I see a beauty that the world is lacking. In her presence, I feel a warmth that I have searched for but have not found anywhere else, not even in me. There is not a second of the day when she is not on my mind- what I should say and do; how she will respond; when I can see her again.

"Sorry I let them get to me. I just, um... I don't know how you get used to people like that, you know."

She smiles warmly as she stands in front of me. She leans her head towards me kindly to emphasize her words, "Trust me, it's not a big deal."

Reaching towards her, I rub my fingers along her arm towards her wrist simply to feel her skin against mine. "But you're a big deal to me,"

I whisper to myself.

As my hand reaches her wrist, she takes my hand gently, asking quietly, "What did you say?"

I look over at her, expecting to see her uneasy with my words, but the way she smiles at me, tender and half blushing, makes me believe that maybe she feels the same.

My lopsided smile graces my face. "I said, 'would you like to dance?'" But we both know that is not what I said.

"There's no music."

"Are you sure?" I say, pretending to listen to some faint sound. "Do you hear that?"

I walk over to the side of the car and lean over the door to reach the stereo. The low hum of a slow song that I do not recognize flows from the speakers.

Krista giggles lightly as I reach my hand towards her, half-bowing in front of her, "My lady, the question stands."

"With you, sir? I could want nothing more," she jests.

She slides her hand in mine and I lead her just steps from the car. A few humans take notice of us. Their grins and hushed words only help to remind me of the flames in my throat. However, none of that matters right now, not when she puts her arms around my neck, moving her hips to the beat in front of me.

My hands rest on her hips, following their swaying. Her body feels natural under my grip as she strums her fingers along the base of my hairline. The light brushing of her fingertips sends chills along my skin. Slowly, she looks up at me from the tops of her eyes, making her appear more tempting than I could have imagined on my own.

She watches me warmly, without speaking. In those few silent moments, her eyes are full of thoughts. Thoughts that I long to hear.

When she does speak, her words are soft, "You're a very different kind of man, Nicolas Rider. Not like the men in my pack."

"No," I tell her as the song on the radio changes. "I am the exact opposite of a werewolf in a lot of ways."

Werewolves are hot-tempered, possessive, and head-strong. Vampires are much more calculated than wolves. But for all their shortcomings, werewolves do not murder freely. They are not liars. And they will always put others before themselves. So no, I am not like the men in her pack.

Thankfully, the next song is also slow. I continue to hold her close, dreading any up-tempo song that could come and risk ending our embrace.

"Yes, but you are also the same in a lot of ways." She smiles at me as she adds, "Somehow you are very foreign and yet very familiar, all at the same time."

Her hand slides down to my chest and the music becomes background, distant and quiet compared to the sound of my pounding heart. As she lays her head along my collarbone, I slide my hand along her arm to her hand on my chest. Holding her hand, I keep it there against me, feeling the heat of her skin through my shirt.

The songs play, one after the other, but I am not about to ask her to stop pressing her body against mine. As the hours advance, the humans become exhausted. The dew begins to set, causing the air around us to become sticky and uncomfortable. Yet even as the humans leave, she does not seem to notice the weight of the humid night air.

Eventually, all of the humans are gone, and we are finally alone. Not just in my mind. No, at long last, we are actually alone. Standing in front of my car, with the mountains to bear witness to a night I do not want to end.

Our hearts beat a melody that keeps a warmth surging through me and for a moment they seem to pound simultaneously, perfecting the moment. The lust-filled tension thickens the air between us as my lips beg to touch hers.

Moving under its own will, my hand cradles her face, feeling the heat of her skin melt on my fingers. I gently lift her face.

As I lean toward her, she pulls back. "I'm sorry. I-," she mutters.

I understand her hesitation. Violation of any standing order from the alpha would cause her physical pain. Not just any pain. Severe, excruciating pain even from something as simple as a kiss.

To spare her from trying to explain, I whisper, "I know. Leaning my forehead against hers, I glide my fingers along her cheek, adding quietly, "Causing you pain is not my intention."

Her hand slides from my chest and along my arm, stopping to hold my wrist near her chin. Closing her eyes, her breaths grow heavy with jagged, sharp exhales. I am not sure whether it is the anticipation of coming pain, or, possibly, just possibly, it is my touch that takes her breath.

With a gentle smile, I tell her softly, "Trust that I will not try to kiss you."

Grazing my nose along hers, I can feel her body begin to relax. As I glide my cheek along hers toward her ear, I let my breath warm her jawline and exciting her skin. With one hand still cradling her head, I let my other hand make its way to the small of her back. I hear her breath catch as I curve her into me.

"This is enough," I whisper close to her ear. I let my breath course over her earlobe. Her grip on my wrist tightens as she exhales sharply. Then staying close to her ear, I add, "For now."

I drag my cheek back across hers and place my forehead against hers once more. I glide my fingers over her smooth skin on her collarbone and along her neck until both of my hands are cradling her head. As I brush the tip of her nose with mine, I feel her chin lift toward me and I lean away.

I want nothing more than to press my lips to hers. Let her pull my shoulders closer as my tongue caresses hers. But it cannot happen that way. Not in this moment. The alpha made sure of it with his orders.

As she opens her eyes, I do not hide the sadness in them. "I don't want to hurt you," I tell her, honestly.

Her eyes are not sad, but they remain muddled with an emotion I cannot pinpoint. "Then don't," she whispers.

Her words are simple, but their meaning is substantial. The vulnerability in her voice indicates that she is leery of more than my kiss and the pain I might cause her is not exclusive to tonight. And she is right.

I should tell her. Let her endure the pain of discovering that I am a vampire. Now. The longer I wait, the worse it will be for her. But I cannot. I will not. I merely want one perfect night with her. One night to look back on and remember warmly, long after she has learned to hate me.

So instead of doing the right thing, I brush her hair away from her face and press my lips to her forehead. Her arms wrap around me so that as my lips leave her forehead, she nuzzles into me, hugging me tightly.

"I should take you home," I tell her. "They're probably getting worried about you."

Taking her hand, I start toward the car. As I walk around to the driver's door, Krista slides onto the hood. Smiling at my confusion, she lies back, looking up at the stars. She pats the hood beside her, lightly.

Then as I lie down next to her, she says almost as a question, "Just a little longer."

Relieved to not be taking her home just yet, I lean my head against hers and take her hand in mine. "Okay," I say smiling my lopsided grin.

We lie on the car hood, looking at the stars and learning oddities about one another. Facts such as her out-right despise of mayonnaise, and how she broke her femur by falling out of the back of a truck when she was ten. That she graduated near the bottom of her high school class but only because she cheated off a dyslexic girl, who is now, surprisingly, a lawyer.

It is not until she rolls toward me, draping her arm over my ribs, that I realize how late it has gotten. Despite the evitable sunrise, I linger there. I let her breaths calm until they are slow and even, being careful not to disturb her as she slips into a dream.

I could sleep as well but I do not want to. I do not want to miss a single moment of her body trusting mine to protect her from the darkness of the world, the scent of her hair so near to my nostrils, or miss the heaviness of her arm holding me next to her.

However, all perfect nights must come to an end. I wait as long as possible but as the daylight nears, I nudge her softly, "Hey."

She moans quietly, "What time is it?"

"Time to go home."

"What?" she says, sleepily. Krista sits up, attempting to clear the fog in her mind. "Oh, I didn't mean to fall asleep. I'm sorry."

Sitting up beside her, I shrug, "Don't be." I slide off the hood and hold my hand out toward her, "But I do need to get you home."

She smiles widely as though my sentence is an understatement, "Yeah."

As I drive her back to Lockwood, she lets her fingers strum through my hair. Distracting as it is, I do not ask her to stop playing with my hair as I race through the streets in order to beat the sun home.

Her fingers caress my concerns and doubts. Her tender touch beguiles me so much that I do not even consider asking why she wants me to drop her off at the entrance gate instead of the front door of her home. I simply stop at the gate as she instructed me. But as I stop near the security booth, she bites her lip nervously.

"Walk me to the gate?" she asks.

Here it is, the moment at the end of every first date. The moment when questions and uncertainties flood the mind. But this is a *fake-date* and there are rules answering all of my usual questions of whether we should kiss or if we should even stop there.

However, I still find myself rubbing my hands together nervously which is ridiculous considering that we have quite literally spent the entire night together already.

"I had a really nice time, Nick," she says, hiding her smile.

I start to respond when a werewolf howls in the distance. My nerves have me on edge causing me to jump a little at the sound.

Taking my hand in hers, she tells me gently, "You don't have to be afraid of the pack."

"I'm not afraid of the pack," I say quickly without thinking of my answer at all.

"Then what are you scared of?" she asks, teasing.

Deciding to be honest, I tell her softly, "You."

Krista smiles at my response and raises her eyebrows, waiting for me to continue.

"I want you to like me, Krista. So much that it frightens me. I worry that you might not feel the same or that I might not have made a good impression tonight or what if this was my only chance. Usually, I have a pretty good pulse on a situation but with you... It's the uncertainty of it all, I suppose, that scares me the most."

As Krista listens to my words, she darts her eyes to the side, trying to hide the fondness that fills them. Smiling widely, she waits until I finish completely to say, "That was a very thorough response. You're really not afraid to just say whatever is on your mind, huh? You just lay it all out there."

Not waiting for my response, she lets out a long exhale and adds, "You are one of the strangest people I've ever met, Nicolas Rider. And that is not a bad thing."

She steps towards me, closing the space between us. "I want to try something," she tells me. "But you have to stay very still, okay?"

Sliding her hand to my chest, she leans close and does something I am not expecting. She kisses my cheek, making me suck air in sharply. I continue to hold my breath until her lips leave my cheek, afraid that somehow my breathing will only contribute to any pain she may be feeling.

It is only when she leans away slightly with a wide grin and touches her lips to hold back an excited giggle, that I realize that kissing me did not hurt her. Even though I am relieved that it did not cause pain, I cannot understand why she would risk it.

With her fingers still covering her lips delicately, her eyes dart wildly from my eyes to my lips and back again. She leans close again, but this time hesitates, letting her lips hover just in front of mine. "Don't move," she says quietly, in attempt to hide the doubt in her voice.

Closing her eyes, she presses her lips to mine. A heat surges through me, starting deep in my core and rushing upward until it spills into every inch of my being. Her kiss only lasts a moment, but it is long enough to secure my resolve in pursuing her.

As she pulls her lips away her face remains mere inches from mine. The doubt in her eyes is washed away, leaving only exhilaration in its place.

"What was that?" I ask, still confused about why she would attempt kissing me in the first place.

I understand that if the alpha's orders were not to date a *human*, I would not fall into that category and therefore, the order would not apply to me. However, she does not realize that I am anything more than human. What her motives are to risk pain for a kiss is beyond me.

She smiles widely. "A loophole. And I can't believe it worked," she says, more to herself than to me.

A loophole? "What loophole." Before I give her a chance to respond, I ask an even more important question, "Wait. Does this mean I can kiss you now?"

She simply continues to smile at me. "Goodnight, Nicolas."

She starts to turn and walk back toward her house, but I am not done with her. If my kiss is not going to hurt her, then I am giving her a real kiss tonight. This night is not ending with a peck, not if it could be our last.

I grab her hand. Jerking to a stop from my unyielding body, she looks back at me. My face must express my desire because her breaths quicken as I close the distance with intention.

With both hands, I pull her face to mine. This time, however, I do not hold back. My lips express my craving for her as another wolf howls far off. She pays no attention to the pack in the distance or the security guard gawking at us in disbelief. As my tongue rolls over hers, her hands slide along my ribs until she is using my shoulders to pull me closer. Her breaths grow jagged, narrowly escaping our lips.

The wind shifts, bringing with it the sweaty scent of the security guard and calls to my inner monster. Even though the sweet bouquet of his blood causes a torrent of fire to rip through my throat, the monster in me cannot answer. The man in me will not stop this for something as trivial as a meal.

Keeping my hand on her cheek, I glide my thumb over her bottom lip, feeling her hot breath on my skin.

When she opens her eyes, I smile, "Just in case I never get the chance again."

Smiling bashfully, Krista pushes her hair behind her ear, "Well, like I said before, goodnight, Nicolas."

As she walks towards the gate I call after her, "You know it's morning?"

I can hear her laugh lightly, but she does not turn around. So I ask, almost shouting, "What loophole, Krista?"

This time, she does look back. Her hair spills over her shoulder and

I get one more glimpse of her smile before I have to go home and hide everything about her from my family.

"Goodnight, Nicolas," she says simply, just before she slips in the gate and out of my view.

Letting out a heavy breath, I look over at Larry, the security guard. "I still don't have permission."

Larry laughs, "You might not have permission, but you sure do have some brass, boy."

Running out of time, I get in my car and drive home as quickly as possible. For a moment, I even contemplate parking my car and running home. It would be faster. But as fate would have it, I pull into the garage with thirty minutes to spare before sunrise.

I dash downstairs and to my room, dodging the vampires who might smell Krista on me. In the safety of my room, I do not worry so much about my family smelling the wolves. I collapse on my bed, feeling pretty good about how the night went. I rest my hands behind my head. I still do not have permission to date Krista but I did have an amazing night with an amazing woman. To top it off, I did get to kiss her which is more than I hoped for.

Just as I begin to let myself doze off with the sweet thoughts of Krista lying next to me, I hear a pounding on the door upstairs. My eyes dart open when I hear an angry, yet familiar voice, "Where is that little twerp?"

My gut knots instantly. Not now. Not here. Not Bryant.

Chapter 5

Rushing upstairs in attempt to beat Luther or Marcella to the very angry werewolf in our entryway, I slide to a halt a few feet from Bryant and Warren.

I smile nervously but it does not change his hard expression. "Bryant. I was, um.., I was just about to call you."

Ignoring my quite obvious lie, Bryant snaps, "Save it, you little shit."

Bryant steps towards me as he continues, "I gave you very clear advice to stay away from Krista and instead you kidnap her?"

Kidnapping is a bit extreme since it was her idea but I decide to skip the technicalities of it. "With all due respect Bryant, you didn't leave me much of a choice."

"No, you're right. I didn't leave you a choice. Because I chose for you. Leave Krista alone. It was really simple instructions, but, apparently, still too complex for you to comprehend." Bryant starts to step towards me again but Warren grabs his arm. Warren shakes his head at me, urging me not to provoke Bryant.

I get it. Krista is his only daughter, and I kept her out all night without his blessing. However, understanding his frustration does nothing to stifle my own.

"I can't do that," I tell him defiantly.

He snorts, "Oh, please. Why the hell not?" Then adds with a mocking tone, "You can't live without her? You think she's the most beautiful woman you've ever seen?"

The satirical tone of his voice grates against me, and I step towards him, blurting out, "No, I don't."

Bryant stares at me briefly, either taken aback by my words or by the fact that I do not seem to fear him the way I should.

Using his momentary silence, I backtrack slightly by adding, "Krista is not the most beautiful woman I have ever seen." Or even been with, but I choose not to disclose that part. "Some women pay a lot of money to be the vainest creatures in the world. And they are gorgeous. But that's it. That is all they have in their bag of tricks. Their beauty. But not Krista."

I cannot read Bryant's expression but I continue more calmly, "The way Krista's inner beauty is matched by her physical attributes is unparalleled by anyone else I have ever met before. And that makes her the most *desirable* woman I've ever seen and that is so much better than being merely beautiful. So, no, she isn't the most beautiful woman in the world, but Krista is by far the most beautifully complete woman I have ever met. And you cannot expect me to walk away from that."

Bryant's face softens, but his response remains short and brash, "That's exactly what I expect you to do."

"No," I tell him but my words sound weaker than I intend them to.

Warren looks around uncomfortably behind Bryant but I cannot tell which one of us he feels is wrong about this.

"Please, Bryant," I say quietly. "I know it would be a lot simpler for everybody if I could walk away right now. You don't like me. My family doesn't like you. Trust me, I get it. I have tried to stop thinking about her. It's not that I won't. Bryant, I can't."

Knowing what I need to say next, I drop my eyes. Nearly choking on them, the words are harder to produce than they should be and, yet, weak enough for him to hear the vulnerability in them. "Bryant, I am begging you to reconsider letting me date your daughter."

Pitying me, Bryant's eyebrows relax, "Look, kid-," he starts. He lays his hand on my shoulder and my eyes snap up to his. He adds, "It's nothing personal," but I am not listening.

His eyes are on me and his hand is on my shoulder, this is my chance. It is risky to enthrall in front of another werewolf but I do not believe Warren will understand what he sees. Plus, I do not care about the risks. If I am ever going to enthrall him, now is the time.

Before he moves his hand, I lock Bryant's eyes into mine and tell him matter-of-factly, "We both want the same thing. You and I just want her to be happy and safe. *I* can make her happy and *I* can keep her safe. I just need you to get out of my way. And you need to. For Krista."

I can see Warren's confusion having witnessed what, I am sure, he believes to be a very odd exchange in conversation. Letting Bryant go from my control, I add softly, "Please, Bryant. Please reconsider."

Bryant's eyebrows come together as he tries to process the thoughts I placed in his mind as they conflict with his own convictions on the matter. He rubs his forehead for a moment before looking at me, still troubled, and adds, "Just stay away from her, kid. Okay?" but his words are not as strong as they once were.

As they turn to leave, I call out, "Hey, Warren, can I talk to you?"

Warren stops in the entryway but does not seem happy about listening to me.

"You could have talked to me last night," Warren begins. "Maybe told me where you were sneaking off to. I'm supposed to protect her from insignificant peons like you. Not just because I'm her superior but also because she's like my little sister. And I happen to take both very seriously."

He starts towards the door again when I speak up, "She's also a wolf. You and I both know that means she could kill me."

Well, if I were human.

Warren nods and crosses his arms over his chest as I continue, "Humans dating wolves, there's always a risk. But you overlooked that risk when you started dating Simone."

His jaw clenches but he lets me finish, "All I'm saying is that Krista isn't the same little girl that was holding a wrench alongside you in her daddy's garage. She can handle this too. You just need to give her more credit and give me a chance."

Warren lets out a forceful exhale and steps close to me. Being taller than me, he is compelled to look down at me as he continues talking. I am sure that his height gives him an added sense of leadership with the pack. Yet, his natural dominance does not seem to provoke me the way other males do.

"Look, Nicolas," he says gently. "You seem like a good kid. But being a werewolf is kind of like being in the military. There's a hierarchy.

There are rules. The alpha is our leader and everyone obeys him. There are obligations to the unit as a whole. And because Krista is female, she has different obligations than I do."

I cross my arms over my chest and do not attempt to hide the disdain in my voice, "What, breeding?"

"Yes," Warren says bluntly. His eyes tighten but he does not seem angry, only smug, as he continues, "Females ensure the survival of our species, not males. The pack expects her to marry a werewolf. We depend on it to survive."

Hearing his words, I realize that there is no hope for me to convince Warren that I should date Krista. Not today, anyway. All that is left is to hope that my enthrallment on Bryant will be adequate to soften him just enough to finally consent.

Warren is wrong, though. I do understand werewolves better than he realizes. Being friends with Tara has opened me to a world I only ran from. Females are rare. Females have different privileges and protections. As a female, Tara cannot be challenged by a male for power and position. Not because she is weaker than a male, but because she is more valuable than him.

I understand that females have specific obligations to the pack that men do not. Continuing the species, survival of the pack rests on their shoulders. I am aware of that. But what about Krista's obligations to herself? What if she would choose to be with me? Is that such a terrible thing?

I let out a sigh but let Warren speak, "Bryant doesn't prohibit her from dating humans because he hates them or because he's old fashioned. Bryant understands how a pack functions. If you were one of us, you would understand her duty to her own kind first. All of us are second to our wolf. The wolf always trumps our wants. But you don't understand that, and that's the real problem. No matter how much you try, you will never comprehend Krista as a wolf first."

Warren's words are soft but firm. I could tell him that he is wrong. That he does not know what he is talking about because he does not know what he is talking to. I am fully aware of carrying something inside you that controls more of your actions that you would like it to. But now is not the time for that.

However, there is one thing I do want to know. If I am not getting permission today then I will need to know how to exploit the rules again.

So as he reaches for the doorknob, I say tersely, "Well, then help me to understand this: last night when Krista kissed me, she said there was a loophole that allowed her do it. What was she talking about? What loophole?"

Warren turns back toward me quickly but his eyes do not meet mine right away, instead, they dart from side to side with his thoughts for a moment. Finally, he asks, "Wait … she kissed you last night? With standing orders in place?"

"Yeah; I mean, I guess the orders were in place. It was like an hour ago."

Warren rubs his face along his jaw and over his mouth, exhaustively, and lets out a stressful sigh.

"She said there was a loophole," I say.

"I should have never let you get that close," he mutters to himself.

"What exactly did she mean?" I ask, urging him to answer me instead of forcing on the inner conversation he is having.

When his eyes meet mine again, they hold a subdued perplexity in them. "It means you're gonna' get your way."

He walks outside. Following him quickly, I stop the door from closing completely as he nears his car. The porch roof protects me from the sun and I can see Bryant sitting in the passenger seat, rubbing his temples as though the invasion of my enthrallment has given him a headache.

"Warren!" I call after him. "What loophole? I still don't understand."

"That's the problem, Nick. You don't." Warren says as he gets in the car and they drive away.

*   *   *

The wind rushes past me, mixing the scents of the night wildly as Levi speeds passed yet another housing complex. I am far too distracted to focus on the conversation happening around me. Busy replaying the events from earlier today in my mind, I do not notice when we stop at a gate until I feel a hard slap on my shoulder.

Levi's accent is thick when he asks, "Nick? You alright?"

"Uh, yeah, I just-," I fumble through my words with no real answer. I am not about to say that I was just thinking about the werewolf consuming my mind and her father who happens to be standing in my way. Not to mention the fact that I am completely at a loss as to what the loophole Krista referred to means. Or, that foolishly attempting to date a werewolf is bound to reveal how many vampires actually live here, including Levi, who has a considerable guise already in place.

"Sorry, I was just... thinking."

Luther leans forward, flopping his arms over the edge of the front seat, "Nicolas got yelled at by his girlfriend's daddy today."

I look at him sharply, "Sit back, Luther. Nobody asked you."

"Girlfriend?" Levi smiles at me.

Luther does not lean back but he does answer Levi for me, "She's a wolf."

Levi's smile fades. "A wolf?"

His fingers flex over the steering wheel, not as though he is angry, simply mulling over what was said. Somebody opens the gates for us and Levi drives passed them slowly. I do not recognize the man standing in the dark night but he is definitely not human.

Reaching back to put my head directly on Luther's forehead, I shove him into the back seat. He lands with a thud and I mouth the words, *'Stop.'*

It is not that I do not trust Levi but the fewer vampires who know about Krista, the safer my secret is. Vampires have a knack for ruining lives and I do not want my secret being exposed to her simply because a vampire wanted to rain on my parade. I may not be willing to tell her what I am just yet but I do already feel obligated to keep her as removed from my world as I can. Accepting something like me is easier if she never has to see what I am. Not the part of me that stalks its prey and indulges in their screams.

Levi drives up a driveway long enough that the house remains hidden. He drums his fingers over the steering wheel, thinking quietly.

"And her daddy came to yell at you. Hm," he finally mutters to himself then resumes drumming his fingers.

I let out a long exhale to begin explaining my unwavering interest in Krista, even though I do not quite understand it myself. "Alright, um-"

Levi interrupts me by putting his index finger up, "Nope."

He adjusts the rear view mirror to see Luther better, "Hey, Luther," Levi begins, smiling widely. "Do you know why a werewolf's daddy would come and yell at a puny, little human?" Looking at me, Levi adds, "I'm assumin' that's what you told her seein' how you're still alive and all."

He looks in the mirror again and continues before Luther can offer any answer. "It's 'cause he's also the alpha."

Levi looks at me again and adds confidently, "That's it, ain't it. Her daddy's the alpha."

There is no point in lying to Levi. He would not believe me now anyway. "Always the detective."

Luther leans forward again, wedging his face between us, "Are you serious?" He bursts into laughter, cutting me short before I can answer. "You might as well stake yourself because her dad's gonna! Ain't nothing like pissing off a papa-alpha."

"Thanks for those words of encouragement," I say dryly.

As Luther flops back into his seat again, I meet Levi's eyes. He is not laughing. We both know I am pursuing a pleasure that will only cause pain. But Levi realizes that has never stopped me before.

"You don't need encouragement, Nick. You're already incorrigible," Levi says more to himself than to me.

Levi lowers his voice that Luther may not notice him over his own relentless and asinine laughter.

"I'm sayin' this as your friend, Nicky. Get what you need from this girl and get out of there. If they discover you, beatin' you seven ways to Sunday will be the most merciful thing they do. You hear me?"

His solemn tone tells me that his advice is prudent. The problem is that what I need from her is not a one-night stand and is not something I can just walk away from.

Refusing to lie but unable to explain that I will not be taking his logical advice, I simply nod.

Luther leans forward again, flopping his arms over the seat, "Sorry," he apologizes between chuckles. "It's just. You should have seen it. Her daddy came all fire and brimstone. And Nicolas just had to take it."

"That is a gross exaggeration," I chime in. Looking at Luther in the rear-view mirror, I add, "But I suppose the simple-minded can only see things in the most basic of ways."

Bryant had actually been very calm considering I disappeared with his daughter. And I did not simply stand there and take it. Nor did I have to. I merely chose not to expose myself as a vampire just yet and continue my human guise by remaining complaisant.

Sounding chipper, Luther adds, "Yeah, well, this simple-mind thought it was hilariously spectacular to watch you get your ass handed to you. *Basically*."

Levi shoves the gear selector into park and turns off the engine, saying cheerfully, "Well, y'all know what I think's spectacular?"

He smiles widely, insinuating his answer, which only causes me to smile in return as I answer for him, "Murder."

"You're darn tootin'."

Looking out of the window at a small two-story house, I ask, "Where are we anyway?"

Levi laughs loudly. I suppose he is relieved to have the change in subject as I am. "You really weren't listenin' at all, were you? It's a Manor, Nick."

A Manor: simply a nice way of saying a slaughterhouse. It has been a long time since I have been to one but I am sure the premise has not changed. Multiple families of vampires agree to crash a human party. Pretty simple, really. However, now that it is harder to explain away an entire houseful of dead humans, Manors are not as common. Undoubtedly, the network of vampires Levi has established helped to organize this feast.

"Are you sure you want to do this?" I ask Levi. "You know, you are a cop now."

He smiles, the moonlight glistening on his exposed teeth. "I'm off the clock, Nick. Besides, ain't my jurisdiction, anyhow."

I look again at the house, tucked away from the road and without a neighbor in sight. Convenient. The obnoxious music saturates the night and vibrates the windows in an unnatural way but I can still make out the laughter from inside.

"Y'all wanna do the honors?" Levi asks.

"Sure." Somebody has to let all of the vampires in. It might as well be me. "Come Luther, I'll show you how it's done."

As we walk toward the house, I can hear the conversations inside are the standard arrogant, self-satisfying, and complacent babble that stereotypical teens are eager to cling to in an attempt to seem like an adult. In reality, adults look at their behavior as evidence of their immaturity and lack of real-world experience. Still, every year more mindless, teenage drones are introduced into a cycle that creates regrets and excuses for the remainder of their life, which for these teens is not much longer.

Judging from the cars parked without any logical pattern, several of the teens here are indulged and spoiled but most look as though they paid for their car with pizza money. Most of the teens here are probably good kids in the wrong place at the wrong time. It is shame that the majority of victims attending are so young. I would have enjoyed a slightly older crowd. There is less risk of guilt when killing adults.

I walk up to the door and knock firmly. Luther stays a few steps behind me on the porch, unassuming and, more importantly, silent. During all of the years of attempting to teach Luther something, or anything, really, he did apparently learn to let me do the talking.

It is not long before a slim blonde girl opens the door with a drink in her hand. Before she can begin to wonder if I am a cop, I say, "I'm delivering a keg. Do you mind if I come in and see where I want to put it?"

"Awesome." She smiles widely and steps aside, "Sure, come in, set it up, do whatever you got to do."

She steps aside to let us in as she adds, "If you want a beer, that's cool too."

"No, thanks. I'm on the clock." As I step inside, I ask, "Is it alright if some friends of mine come in and help me?"

"Yeah, sure. Whatever you need." There it is. Permission to slaughter her friends.

Despite her obviously glazed over eyes, I can tell she is normally a sweet kid; definitely not one that deserves my fangs.

Grabbing her arm, I lean close to her ear, "You will not remember my face. The beer is making you sick. So sick that you are going to go straight home and rethink your life."

Making my way through the crowd, I watch her long enough to see her confused face look down at the cup in her hand, set it on a table near the door, and leave. She may not understand her sudden nausea but tomorrow she will be glad she left when she did. She will say how lucky she was, how blessed to be alive, and she will thank God for *my* mercy.

My eyes scan the room for anybody else that I might let free but find none that persuade me to make the effort of sparing them. Clearly a college party, there are a few people dancing in the crowd but most stand with one or two other teens and early twenty-somethings holding plastic cups of whatever cheap alcohol they could afford.

The house holds a sweaty scent along with yeast from the beer and body spray from the clearance rack at the mall creating an odd mixture in the air. A group of friends in one corner blow smoke in the dog's face and laugh at its' obvious disdain for it. The room is thick with shifting glances featuring sarcastic and arrogant smirks.

The girls, undoubtedly, are insulting and picking apart every other girl in the room while the guys are talking only of the girls as well. Their conversations differ though. The boys here are mostly concerned with finding their next conquest tonight.

I realize that most people would say that the raging hormones and desperate need for freedom are to blame for their conduct. It is just typical adolescent behavior and they will grow out of it. They would eventually become functioning adults who contribute to society.

However, my centuries of observation have given me a different theory. This "typical teenage behavior" is merely a construct of having an adult body without responsibilities or even the slightest expectation that they would behave in any other manner.

When I was a teenager, I thought like an adult and was expected to behave like an adult; because in my time, I was an adult. Current youth act like they enjoy being irresponsible, sex-starved hooligans with no repercussions to any of their actions because today's society does not expect them to be more than that. It is sad, really, when you think about it. The youth today are so limited by their freedom to be useless.

If I was not the only person in the room that seems disturbed by or even notices the couple having sex on the couch, perhaps I would not be at ease with killing an entire room of youth. Yes, their parents will be heartbroken and, no, I do not like to kill children, but at least their behavior is making me feel less conflicted about killing these ones.

I see Levi and two other vampires slip in the front door as Luther leans against a wall. I know there are others outside; I can feel their hunger as they watch and wait there until the killing begins.

Only a few humans even seem to notice me and the ones who do see me do not care that I am there as I walk into the kitchen. Less people are in here, although there is a cluster of kids playing beer pong on the island. Beyond them, I can see the door to a basement.

Opening the door, I step into the darkness and the monster inside me stirs, knowing the slaughter that is about to ensue. My mouth begins to water at the anticipation of blood running down my throat and coursing over my skin. Fire burns through me as I crave the way the scent clings to everything, allowing me to take reminders of the massacre home with me.

I find the breaker panel near the stairs and open the cold, metal door. My eyes do not need to adjust to read which breaker will turn off power for the entire house. Just as my fingers touch the switch, I am made aware that an eager vampire grows impatient when I hear a loud thump above me followed by a piercing scream.

Footsteps begin to scatter in an illogical and rushed pattern. More screams cut through the night and I do not wait any longer for darkness to blanket the humans above me. I flip off the power and rush up the stairs. As I reach the door to the kitchen, my eyes go black. I open the door just as the body of a boy flies past me and something, no, someone jumps over the island after him.

His scream transforms into a gasping, gurgling sound and the intense scent of blood slams into me. I know what makes those wet, slurping sounds coming from the other side of the island. A vampire. Given the scent of her, it is a vampire I have never met.

A girl runs past me and I grab her wrist. Mechanically, I yank her back and snap her neck, letting her body collapse to the floor. Not all of these humans will feel fangs tonight but there can be no witnesses.

Drinking is not the only way to enjoy blood. The smell of it wraps around me, caressing my nose delicately. The sight of it tantalizes my inner monster. Hearing their screams only adds to the satisfaction of their demise.

I step over her body to look around the island but only find the dripping remains of the young boy that had flown past me. I focus on the chaos around me as the humans panic, running through the pitch black of the house. They trip over one another and everything in their path as their eyes try to focus on the black shadows all around them.

I grab a human by the hair and slam their back into the wall. Putting my hand over her mouth so the others around us do not realize how close they are to death, I sink my fangs in her neck. Her tears roll over my fingers but these tears are not from pain. They are from fear.

I do not take my time nor drag out her suffering. Quickly, I drink my fill and toss her to the ground. A boy runs past, tripping over a chair and landing on his back. His eyes grow wide when he sees my silhouette and he slides away further.

Leaning over him, I snap the leg off of the chair and bury it deep inside his chest. His blood pools around the chair leg and my monster rages inside at the sight. His eyes lock with mine although I doubt he can actually see me very clearly. Choking, he coughs up thick blood which rolls over his chin. He will die soon but not soon enough to escape feeling the fangs of two vampires as they pounce on his struggling body. They pull and tug at him wildly. By the time they leave his dead body there on the cold tile floor, little of him will be recognizable.

Standing up, I see another boy scrambling through the kitchen. As he nears me, I slice his throat with my sharp fingernails leaving deep lacerations. The slashes open his airway and his lungs begin to fill with his own blood as he drops to his knees. However before he touches the ground, Luther catches him. He lifts the boy to his lips, biting through the remaining pieces of tissue with ferocity. Luther leaves little room for doubt that by the time the boy is drained his neck will no longer be intact.

I move into the living room and can see the blood streaked over the walls. There is a vampire in the corner smashing a teen's head with a book. Judging by her scent, I can tell that she is the same one from in the kitchen earlier. She licks the cover of the book and hits him once more before she stands up.

Looking at me, she watches me for a moment curiously, then drags a human boy to his feet. The vampire keeps her eyes on me as she bites into his neck. A slight amount of moonlight sneaks in where the drapes have been torn down.

Her long blonde hair is pulled back in a tight ponytail but still glistens in the dim light. Her thick bangs cover her entire forehead with no gaps in the hair and are cut bluntly across her eyebrows giving her a classic, disciplined appearance. Meticulous and calculating, she is definitely not a woman to be trifled with.

The moonlight makes it easier for the humans to see us in this room. One boy raises up behind her, ready to stab her in the back with an envelope opener. Reflexively, I pick up the fishbowl and throw it at him. The water makes the bowl heavy and much too difficult for a human to throw with the force that I do. The bowl hits him in the cheek and slams his head against the wall, crushing his skull.

The fishbowl falls to the floor with a loud thud and rolls. The blood and brain tissue prevent it from going far, though, as it stops on a sizable chunk of tissue not far from where it landed. The vampire drops the body she just drained and smiles at me before she grabs another teen.

Excluding the blonde woman, I have been too consumed with my own slaughtering to have paid much attention to the other vampires in the room. By my very rough, and very vague, estimation, there are no more than fifteen vampires in the house. Fifteen vampires do not need much time for killing a houseful of humans. As the screams begin to dwindle, the thick scent of fresh blood floods the air which only contributes to the need to finish the remaining supply of humans once and for all.

I reach into the fireplace where one girl is hiding and pull her to me. Despite her fierce struggle, she is easy to overcome and my fangs are in her neck quickly.

I purposely open my mouth slightly while I am drinking from her to allow the blood to run down my chin and stain my shirt. Knowing my skin and clothing are painted in crimson makes my inner darkness rage even more. I pull her closer as my hunger turns into greed. Chomping into her neck again, I sink my fangs even further into her than I had before. Her scream becomes filled with pain and panic as I drain her quicker than I normally would.

Tossing her aside, I grab another teen to supply my growing need. I sink my fangs into his neck and listen as his gasps become gurgles. As I hold him by the upper arm, my greed causes my grip on him to tighten and I feel his bone crack within my hand. Soon, his body goes limp and hangs over me. His raspy, desperate attempts for air no longer distract me from the screams.

A girl runs by me but trips over one of my victims. I grab her ankle and sling her over my head and down onto the ground hard enough to break most of the bones on her right side. She whines loudly, unable to scream because of the pain it causes. Her body twitches even though she tries to lie as still as possible. Mercifully, I step down on her head quickly, feeling her skull pop under my foot like a juicy bug.

A small group of boys make it to the door and rush outside. I cannot risk letting people escape and tell others about what happened here. I start after them but a firm grip on my wrist stops me.

"Don't," the blonde vampire says with a faint Russian accent. "The others are out there. Those boys won't get far."

Her eyes are not the black I expected to see. Instead they are icy, pale blue, nearly white in appearance. Then, right on cue, a scream echoes across the night and stops abruptly. She smiles pitilessly at the sound, "That girl you let go didn't make it to her car either."

Honestly when I let her go, I was not sure if she would make it or not. I had hoped, however. She did seem like a nice enough human. Such a waste.

"Who are you?" I ask.

She shrugs lightly, "Your friend. Your enemy. You decide."

Her answer is not what I expect. Her words tell me very little but before I can ask more she rips through the house. She moves quickly, painting the walls in human blood until every last one is silent.

I can hear the scattered, shuffling of feet above us slow until it stops as well. Judging from the living room, I can only imagine the equal mess that is sure to be upstairs. Even though there are several other vampires in the room, I cannot help but to watch her. Something about this blonde vampire seems all too familiar.

When Levi comes downstairs, I approach him quietly, "Do you know who that is?" I ask him, nodding toward the blonde.

His eyes find her sitting on the floor, among a pile of humans, blood glazed on her face in a delicate way. Fondling the charm on her necklace, she appears almost lost in thought.

"Oh, that's Mila. I actually invited her 'cause I thought you two might hit it off. But that was before I knew ya had a girlfriend. And I know how you feel about monogamy, so I reckon' I'll just, uh, take her on home myself," he says with a wink.

Unable to think of much else, I smile at him. "I guess so," I tell Levi as Luther makes his way to us.

Before either of us can acknowledge Luther, a vampire shoves a body off of the karaoke machine in the living room. With singing sure to follow, Levi nods toward the kitchen. Even though vampires do have naturally good singing voices, it is quite distracting while you are attempting to have a conversation.

Luther and I follow him into the blood saturated room and sit down where someone has hoisted a body above the kitchen island. Still groaning, the boy's blood makes a tapping sound as it drips to the counter.

Levi sifts through the shattered alcohol bottles on the floor and picks up three shot glasses that had somehow survived the chaos.

Wiping them out with the corner of his shirt, Levi continues speaking, "You boys should be aware that they's some nomads nosin' around. There was a murder last night. Now, it's being dubbed as a hit and run, but I ain't no fool. I know fang marks when I see 'em."

Nomads. Just what I do not need.

If any vampire could blow my cover to Krista and her pack, it would be a nomad. Impulsive and primeval, nomads are unpredictable, loose-ends that nobody wants invading their territory. Nomads make co-habituating with humans problematic, at best. More often than not, nomads only serve to murder enough humans that the local vampires have to relocate in order to not be discovered.

Occasionally, killing a nomad is easier than actually uprooting your home as a vampire. With my increasing interest in Krista, I am hoping the nomads do not stay long. If they bring too much attention, I may have to hunt them down myself. I refuse to let a nomad drive me away from Krista so soon.

"I know it wan't you guys." Levi sets the shot glasses under the quick dripping from the boy above us. "And it certainly wan't any of Amelia's vamps. They're killers but they got more sense than that."

Despite the scenarios populating in my head about the nomads, Levi's casual mention of the leader of a vampire group who happened to, essentially, harass me just one night ago, takes precedence. Levi might know why the Genesis targeted me in the first place or how to get them off of my back. Regardless of the help he might offer, one thing is for sure: Levi knows something. Question is, how much does he know?

"I didn't realize you were on a first-name basis with Amelia," I say with a tone insinuating that I want to know more.

"Of course, I am, Nick. This is my town. I'm on a first-name basis with everybody who crosses that county line. Since I took over, the crime rate has dropped thirty percent. Course, we don't do everythang by the book. Cain't get a warrant? Doesn't matter. They don't live to see the inside of a courtroom anyway. But still, legal or not, thirty percent is a hell of a good number."

"Who's Amelia," Luther asks.

"Hell, son, don't look as confused a cow on Astroturf. Try to keep up," Levi jokes. "Amelia runs the Genesis, which is a cult, more or less. Crazy Lilith-fanatics. But I tell you what, there sure is some pretty ladies ridin' that cuckoo train."

"You know a lot of ladies with the Genesis?" I ask playfully, still prodding for answers.

"Just the important ones," Levi says with a wink. Then looking toward Luther, he adds, "There's this one, Casiana, she's a snake of a woman but, boy oh boy, if she ain't a looker."

Levi slides the now nearly full shot glasses toward us and we each take one. Before they can pick up their shots, I laugh lightly, "You actually think that bird-looking chick is hot?"

Levi simply smiles, but Luther chimes in, "You don't have any room to talk, Nick. You're dating a dog."

There is no animosity in his tone which is why it does not rile me. He only attempts to goad me with his use of the word, *dog*, to describe my beautiful Krista. Knowing he means no actual disrespect, I smile at his comment. After all, it is one of his more clever comebacks. Perhaps he has learned something from me.

"Touché," I say simply. Then raising my shot glass, I add a toast, "To the ladies we can't have and the friends we don't want." I look at Luther with my last words and he narrows his eyes back at me but there is no real anger in them.

His false anger only makes me smile as we down the drinks. Our full bellies cannot quiet our torrent gullets completely. The soothing qualities of the blood, even just the small amount in our glasses, is always a welcome attribute. Like a shark, a vampire's hunger is never truly satiated.

We slam our little glasses on the counter hard enough to make a loud bang but still not risk breaking the very limited supply of intact glasses left in the house. I slide the glasses back under the dripping body. His struggling only causes his dangling limbs to speckle blood on and around the shot glasses, but I do not attempt to stop his awkward, weak swaying motion. There is enough blood falling into the glasses to be sufficient.

Sitting at a bar with friends, drinking shots, reminds me of what it was like to be human for a moment. Sure, the bar is part of a stranger's kitchen and my friends are murderous sociopaths, but still there is some nostalgia to it all.

Then, Levi disrupts the moment by doing one of the most human things. He looks over at Mila and waves her toward us, "Mila!" He interrupts our guys' night for the sole purpose of copulation.

I start to protest but it is already too late. She is already too close. I did not want *her* to come over. I would not have minded somebody else as much but something about Mila seems familiar. And for a reason I do not understand, the sentiment I feel is not a wistful nostalgia or comforting in the least. This familiarity has an unsettling, nearly ominous aura to it.

As she makes her way to us, he adds, "Watch out for that'n. She's a hired gun for 'em. She could rip the soul right out the devil himself."

Her ties to the Genesis make my leery inclination to avoid her altogether seem that much more prudent. However despite my reservations, I smile when she approaches. My predisposition about her is no reason to be impolite. Being rude to a beautiful woman is never wise. Especially when she happens to be an assassin.

Reaching out to shake her hand, I introduce myself, "I'm Nicolas."

With her hand in mine, she says bluntly, "You smell like dog." She pauses for emphasis a moment, then smiles at me before continuing, "But I suppose you would. Your fondness for them comes naturally to you. But I assure you, it isn't. Natural, I mean."

Dropping my hand, she adds, "Still, it is nice to meet you after all this time."

Her words are like a riddle. However, despite the significant questions forming in my mind, I am even more perplexed as to why Levi would think I would have been interested in Mila. Petulant, querulous women are only good for one thing and I have Yen for that.

"I'm sure the feeling is mutual," I say.

Levi grabs her quickly around the waist, pulling her against himself and causing her to let out a playfully squeal.

Her icy demeanor melts into a chuckle. Even she cannot resist Levi's southern charm. She kisses him on the cheek, "How are you, Levi?"

"Better now that you kissed me," he smiles and I nearly roll my eyes at how ridiculous his statement is.

She lays her hand on Levi's shoulder, letting her arm drape down his back. There is a tender intimacy to the way she leans against him, leading me to conclude that this is not the first night Levi will be taking her home.

"That's a nice necklace," I lie, merely to keeping the conversation polite. The necklace that she wears is actually not even all that pretty. The medallion-styled charm looks too bulky to compliment her figure, and the darkness of it makes it difficult even for my vampire eyes to make out the etching.

Despite the weighty, somber appearance, she touches it delicately with my words as though it is fragile. It is clear that the necklace means more to her than I realized.

"Thank you," she says. "It was a gift from Casiana."

Levi looks over at her, "Oh yeah, Cass has one just like that."

A thousand thoughts race through my mind. I knew Levi knows who Casiana is but is he really close enough to her to call her, *Cass*? Does he know that she can enthrall vampires? Is he helping them? What about Mila? Is it even a coincidence that we are all here together at the same time?

Stop it, I tell myself. I must force myself to ignore that trail of thoughts. Levi would not manipulate me for the Genesis. He is much too honest to swindle anybody for a woman. Copulation is not a viable motive to deceive your friends. At the very least, it is not a justifiable incentive for philanderers, such as Levi.

"Who's Cass?" Luther asks, still playing catch-up to our conversation.

Mila answers him simply, "My boss."

I slide my glass from under the slowing dripping of blood as I add, "And Amelia's number two."

I lift the glass toward my lips but before I can take the first sip, Mila reaches over and takes it from my hand. She downs the crimson drink without removing her eyes from me. Her expression and cold stare cause me to believe that my words invoked a challenge of some sort, though I cannot understand what about them was abrasive to her.

So despite my better senses, I prod her a little further, "I am surprised that she needs an assassin though. Casiana seems perfectly capable of deranged carnage all by herself."

Mila sets the glass down gently and smiles. The white of her teeth contrasts against the crimson staining them, making her smile seem that much more unnatural and crazed.

She adds with an icy chill, "Make no mistake, Casiana *is* capable of anything."

Mila leans over the counter, toward me. She studies my eyes as though she is looking for secrets in them. Although her peering is brief, I grow uneasy by it. When her eyes soften, I realize she has found the answer she was looking for.

Her words are softer than before as she adds, "You think Cass is wrong about you? You believe the Nexus to be a hoax?"

She says it as a question though her tone that more of a statement and she does not wait for my response before she adds her own, "But you are a fool."

I lean toward her and say condescendingly, "I think the Nexus is drivel. Just some bit of nonsense crafted up for the feeble minds."

Her eyes tighten slightly but I do not wait for her response before I continue, "And quite frankly, I am surprised someone like you still believes in such fairy tales."

"Mockery does not make you right," Mila says flatly.

She climbs onto the counter slowly and sits facing the dangling human. Grabbing his hair, she spins him so that his face is near hers.

She speaks softly at the boy but her words are for me, "An unnatural creature like the Nexus is not born. It is made. Whether you believe you are a Nexus or not, Casiana has a plan for you Nicolas. And her plan is no more escapable than this boy's death."

She slides her hand along his arm and takes his hand. Keeping her eyes locked on his, Mila puts one of his blood soaked fingers in her mouth. With his consciousness fading, the boy's eyes are barely open. If he were not dying, I am sure that he would find her intense gaze and gentle suckling on his fingers quite arousing. However, he is dying so I am sure that her actions are more tormenting than pleasing for him.

"Didn't your mother ever tell you not to play with your food?" Luther asks, causing me to smile.

Smiling coldly at the boy, Mila brings his hand to her cheek and rubs her face with his fingers, smearing fresh crimson over the dried flakes of blood from her previous killings.

I look away but I can still hear the way his skin snaps quietly as her fangs pierce his wrist. I can hear the sloshing of his blood in her mouth, his holding back the weak whimpers as the scent of his blood fills the room.

Her breath catches as she pulls her teeth from his flesh. I know that feeling. Intense satisfaction unlike any other. If I had to make a comparison that a human could comprehend, it would be the moment just after an orgasm with someone you did not deserve but tricked into bed anyway. It is an erotic sense of power and ownership, coursing throughout your entire body. Every inch of you excited by the simple act of taking what you want and being completely unstoppable. Every cell strengthened and alive once more.

The stillness of the air is unmistakable; the boy is dead. Mila looks over at me as she tosses his arm away from her. His body sways with the momentum.

"There are others like you, Nicolas. Vampires who have been altered and improved by us. But the results have always been lacking. We still need to find *the* one. The one who can do what only our Nexus must."

Mila slides toward me, allowing her bottom to push a pool of blood over the edge of the counter. It spills onto my lap but I do not look away from her. Placing her hand on the back on my chair, she leans her face mere inches from mine.

Mila rubs her hand across my face tenderly. "Cass will discover if you are *the* one or just *another* one. That I am sure of."

She shifts back slightly, allowing me to see her face better as she continues softly, "You have already been tampered with, Nicolas. The damage was done decades ago. You cannot escape it now."

Mila smiles mischievously as she adds, "But perhaps you did not realize that."

I grab her forearm, stopping her hand. I do not understand what her scheme is nor do I want to. Her words make little sense and offer even less answers. Like a twisting trail, you believe it will lead somewhere fruitful but following it you only become lost to its deception.

I lean to the side into clear view of Levi and tell him, "Thank you for the drinks, Levi, but I think it's time I go home."

"Yes, Levi, take Nicky home," Mila says derisively. Then rolling onto her stomach, she looks at Levi with a mischievous smile, "But hurry back."

She tiptoes her fingers through the smeared blood and up his chest. Then pulling at his collar, she shifts herself onto her knees in front of him, "I want you inside of me before the sun rises," nodding toward Luther, Mila adds,-"And I suppose the big guy will suffice as a time waster until you join us."

I slide my chair back. I have heard enough. There is no part of me that wishes to continue listening to any of the drivel coming from her. Conversation with Mila should be considered a form of whiplash; sudden jerking from topic to topic and mood to mood. Her abrupt transitions and flip-flopping only leaves you with the knowledge that all that jerking is simply going to end up becoming the root of one giant, nagging pain. All you can do is hope that the pain will leave of her own regard and quickly. Just like whiplash.

I leave their prattling behind me and start into the living room to make my exit when a warm hand wraps around my wrist. I turn to see which freshly-fed vampire has me and see Mila. Her expression is much softer than it was in the kitchen, almost timid, as though she is about to apologize.

"Wait," Mila says with a hushed tone. "Look, I know how I come across. I'm abrasive, I know, but you need to hear this. If you are truly going to pursue a wolf than I must urge you to watch her back."

I pull my hand loose from her grip, "Is that a threat?"

"No. Not a threat exactly. More of a warning." Mila steps closer, leaning toward me to hide her words from any who might be reading her lips. "You are right, Nicolas, Casiana is capable of deranged carnage. And if Cass thinks you are the one she needs, she will stop at nothing to make you play your part. You need to consider what you would be willing to do to save your wolf, because there will come a time when you are asked just that."

There is an honesty to her tone that leaves me unsettled. Casiana is demented enough to come after Krista for her own gain. That I do not doubt. But what would I do if I could not save her? That I do not know and that is what disturbs me.

A pity hangs in Mila's eyes as she continues, "And a second warning, if I may: be careful. Not just with Cass but with these wolves too. If they find out what you are, they'll come after you. Then Casiana will have the reason she needs to destroy their entire pack and your wolf will die with them."

Mila looks around briefly before she continues, "You are the only thing Cass wants right now. She will eliminate anyone that stands in her way. Marcella, Krista, me. Even you. Either you help her or you help no one."

She rubs my arm gently. "You're a decent enough guy, Nicolas. Last thing I want to do is scoop up your ashes. I really hope I do not have to kill you." Sincerity laces her tone more than it should. Perhaps, she does not care to hide it; or perhaps she is simply better at faking integrity than Marcella.

Whether Luther was paying attention to our conversation or not, he speaks lightheartedly, as though he has heard very little, "Looks like you're riding home with me, Nick. You ready?"

Ready to leave Mila and her Genesis ties behind? Always. I smile at him with a simple nod just as Levi scoops his arms around Mila's waist. She smiles widely and lets out a light squeal. With his teeth grazing her neck, he lets out a playfully growl causing her to laugh. For a moment, Mila looks like an ordinary girl and more innocent than I would have thought her capable of. Unable to hold onto her hard exterior against Levi's boyish charms, Mila does not fight him, instead she only giggles as he heaves her body over his shoulder, pretending to groan under the strain the way a human would.

"You boys have fun, 'cause I'm gonna." Levi chuckles at his own words as he carries her up the stairs.

I wait until they are gone before I ask Luther, "Are you sure you don't want to stay? I don't actually need someone to drive me home. I am quite capable, you know?"

Luther lays his hand on my shoulder and nods toward the stairs they had ascended moments ago, "I have dated enough crazy to know that I'm not interested in even one night with that nut-bag of a bipolar conundrum."

I laugh at his not-so elegant, yet surprisingly accurate way of describing Mila. "Come on, let's go get you laid by someone just as wild but less psychotic."

"Oh, you think I need your help snagging a lady?" Luther asks, noticing my reference to his ineptitude in my offer.

While I am sure that he would have no issue finding a woman to suit his needs, I still choose to pretend that I do not believe there is a human or vampire with so little intelligence. As we start towards the door, I add, "I am feeling generous and I just so happen to make a great wingman."

"Oh, I bet," Luther says unbelievingly. "Nobody as self-centered as you is ever the wingman."

Luther is right. I do not often persuade ladies to entertain my friends. It might seem selfish but, in all honesty, most of my friends do not need my help to begin with. They are all more than capable of ascertaining things they seek on their own. But I choose not to enlighten Luther to this fact at the moment.

Instead, we leave the Manor on that note. The note of seeking a lady to entertain Luther since I am spoken for; albeit, I am not *technically* spoken for. Yet.

The night progresses surprisingly easy. Luther and I exchange banter but the irritation and contempt I once held for him seem to have subsided for now. Perhaps, he has become a competent vampire. Or perhaps, I simply do not view him as dead weight holding me prisoner in a septic pot of misery. Either way, I must admit that it is nice to have him as a buffer between myself and Marcella.

After making our way into town with Levi's car, we rummage through a few local bars until we find a girl sitting alone, presumably waiting for a group that has not yet arrived. Convincing her to join Luther in a nearby alley is disgustingly not difficult.

The bar is not a place I want to stay in. The smoke is heavy and the scent of alcohol is not as intoxicating as it seems to be for the humans.

Besides, I do not want to be a recognizable face should something horrific happen to a certain local girl who just so happens to be in a disreputable embrace with a vampire in a dirty alley at this very moment.

Eventually, I find myself waiting outside, trying to focus on my own thoughts and ignore the moaning coming from the alleyway. I do not have to stand there long before I see a group I do not intend to see, and my plans for the night go a direction I did not intend them to go.

There, across the street, exiting the back of a truck, are the three boys that insulted Krista. Despite all three boys standing alongside the gas pumps, only one boy seems to be going into the gas station. The same smugness rolls from them now as it did the other night. A smugness that I will put an end to.

As they walk around, presumably stretching their legs a bit, I call to Luther, "I'll be right back. Don't do anything stupid."

He does not answer but I do not expect him to. I do not need his response. I know Luther heard me. Hopefully, he will not accidentally kill her until after I come back from my own endeavor.

I cross the street quietly just as the boy who paid for the gas walks back out of the gas station. It is the ring leader, the one with the biggest mouth that sees me first.

"Can I help you?" he asks.

It is obvious that he has already forgotten me so I will be sure to remind him before he dies.

Keeping my eyes on the ground, I walk across the rest of parking lot to them. I stop near him and keep my voice flat to ensure that he realizes I am looking for a fight, "I'd like to have a word with you. All of you,"-pointing to the alley-"in there."

A smirk forms on his smug face as his arrogance coaxes him into believing this will be an easy win. After all, it is three to one. "After you. But, uh, what's this about?"

"When you insult someone I care about, you leave a debt to be paid. I am here to collect. It is that simple," I tell him plainly as we descend into the dimly lit alley.

I allow them to surround me as we walk. If I were human, corralling me in the center would make me easier to overtake. But it will have little effect on the outcome tonight.

Finally, the ring leader realizes what offense I am here about, "Oh, I know you. You're the guy that was with that bitch the other night."

My anger rages with his nonchalant derogation of Krista but, externally, I remain unchanged by his words, "You should have learned to fear the werewolves when you had the chance."

He laughs, "Why? They're mutts and just like all dogs, they won't bite the hand that feeds them. They could do something but they're cowards."

"Fear would have taught you to show respect even when you don't have any. If you had learned to fear them, I wouldn't have to teach you now," I tell him bluntly.

He chuckles to himself, "You're going to teach us, huh? How? Are you a big, bad wolf too?"

My eyes change to black as they foolishly follow me far enough into the darkness. Letting malice smother my words, I tell him quietly, "Oh, I'm much worse than that."

I hear the man behind me on my left inhale, but it is the last time he will. I slam my forearm into his throat, collapsing his trachea and preventing him from exhaling. He grabs his neck as he drops to his knees, strangling on the quickly staling air trapped in his lungs.

The ring-leader stands frozen in fear at the sight of the hollow abyss in my eyes. Urine streams toward his shoe while the other sidekick steps toward me, blocking the light-haired ring leader from me. The sidekick draws his fist back in attempt to protect his friend. I step toward him and grab his face with my entire hand. Flexing my fingers, I crush the bones together, feeling the fragments snap under his skin.

He is not dead; however, I am sure he wishes he were. I toss him aside into the brick wall and step toward the last man. The one who brought this on all of them. Unable to move, he looks around frantically while his breaths become shaky and forced.

Stepping toward him, I grab his throat and slam him into the building.

"I'm sorry. I didn't mean it," he mutters from his quivering lips.

But no apology will suffice me now. I lean close to his face. "What was it you said? *'Wouldn't you be comfortable drinking from a bowl?'*" I ask, nodding toward the faceless body starting to tremor on the ground as shock sets in.

"Because of your ignorance, he will spend the rest of his life eating through a straw. He will be put into a straitjacket for telling people exactly what happened here tonight. But he will not care. Not once they start the meds and he begins to drool from the distorted crevices he once called lips."

I lean close to his face to let my words sink in, "And all of this is because of you."

As his tear drips onto my arm, he asks, "What are you?"

Letting the darkness inside seep out in my voice, I tell him coldly, "Retribution."

Without any more delay, I sink my teeth into his carotid and his blood floods my mouth. His body shakes under my grip as his raspy breaths become slow and less frequent.

Ripping my fangs out of his cold neck, I let his body slide down along the wall. I lick the blood from my lips as I step over his trembling friend and walk out of the alley.

I could have taken my time, taken pleasure in their deaths, but an alley is not the place for a slow murder. I do not wish to draw attention which would only lead to more bodies. I hurry back across the street, knowing that we do not have much time before somebody goes looking for the owners of the truck which is still idling at the pump.

I call into the darkness, "Luther. Wrap it up. I made a mess and we have to go."

I do not need to clarify anything more. Luther is fully aware of what a vampire considers a mess. It only takes a few moments and I hear him zip his pants.

That is when I add, "And Luther," I pause for moment considering my options but there are not many, so I concede, "No witnesses."

There is a muffled scream from the alley but it is brief. When Luther emerges from the alley, he does not ask what I did or why. He merely nods toward the car and we begin leaving just as the gas station clerk takes notice of the truck still in the parking lot. However, I do not believe the clerk paid any attention to the car we are driving which is good considering that it belongs to Levi.

People like Levi and his vampire officers. The people do not ask questions so Levi does not give them any. Levi told me once that he *'ain't fixin'* to explain to the FBI why the credentials hanging on his wall are fakes, and then he followed that with a threat about me not giving them a reason to suspect. And I do not blame him for wanting to keep up the ruse.

Levi has a good thing going here. Hiding in plain sight. And there is nothing like an impromptu alley murder to ruin everything. So hopefully I am correct in believing that the clerk is none the wiser to us.

The drive home is quiet for the most part. However as we get closer to our home, Luther speaks up and allows me to hear what has been on his mind this entire car ride, "You really think that crazy lady is crazy?"

"Who?" What?

"Mila."

No, I do not think Mila is crazy. While Mila may be a sociopath, she is also highly intelligent and extremely competent. No, I do not think Mila is insane. I believe she is brainwashed.

I let out a long sigh. I really do not want to discuss Mila again tonight. "Mila's not crazy. She's not right but she's not crazy."

"So, you think she's lying about them changing you somehow?" he asks.

I shake my head, "You mean about my being tampered with? Don't you think I would remember if somebody altered my DNA?"

I suppose Mila did not specify what type of alterations the Genesis supposedly made on me. However, in order for any stretch of her story to work, there would need to be a change on a genetic level. So it is not much of a leap for me to conclude that DNA is the type of *'tampering'* Mila had alluded to.

Luther looks over at me with no real expression, "Maybe not. You don't remember how you got home the other day. Do you?"

"I didn't tell you that," I say flatly.

I look at him waiting for an explanation but all I receive is a shrug. I suppose there are not many secrets in a house of vampires.

"Still. I've been thinking. What if they did?"

I start to tell Luther that this line of thinking is madness. I want to say that this is a waste of everyone's time and that the conversation ends here. But before I can say any of that, Luther finishes his thought, "What if they had Ulrich do it?"

That name stops my thoughts. Ulrich. I have tried to forget him so many times. I spent years erasing those memories from my dreams. The memories of my time spent captive under a tyrannical German, who claimed to be a scientist but seemed more like a sadist.

I can still see Ulrich's face hovering over me as I was forcibly held down in a tub of holy water. I can still feel the way my skin burned. Over and over, Ulrich ordered me to be held under. I remember expecting my flesh to pull off in large masses, like boiling fat from an animal.

I remember the whips. I remember the weakness. I remember feeling as though my skull would explode, my blood trickling over me, and the way my body cried with pain. I remember being given meningitis. I remember begging for it to stop. And I remember Ulrich had no mercy.

Luther continues in my silence, "You said Ulrich injected you with something, it was, um, yellow- I think," It was amber-colored, not yellow, but I do not stop him.

His words seem to rush out, "I don't remember every detail, but I do remember you weren't sure what it really was. I mean, you thought it supposed to help with your meningitis but what if it wasn't for meningitis at all. What if it changed you? What if he actually made you one of those Nexus people Mila was talking about?"

Granted Luther is using more logic and deduction than I thought him capable of, his reference to Ulrich has me on edge, and my words come across harsher than I intend them to.

I allow my British accent to coat my words heavily, adding an extra bite to them, "Let's just try to use a little bit of rationality here for a second. This is non-sense. Ulrich was a monster. He was gifted with skills in torture and destruction but that is all. He was not near proficient enough to create anything. Ever. And certainly not something the Genesis would be interested in."

Ignoring my hostility, Luther interjects, "But I'm just saying-"

"Well just don't," I snap, cutting him off abruptly. "Look Luther, there is absolutely nothing special about me."

Luther chuckles, "Well, I've been saying that for years. I'm glad you are finally ready to admit it."

His teasing catches me off guard and dismantles the anger Ulrich's name had risen in me. I let out a light sigh, no longer angry but still not willing to continue this line of conversation.

I start again but without my accent once more, "I'm sorry, Luther, I..." I let my voice trail off. What can I say? Sorry, I never really came to terms with my resentment about my capture and torture during World War Two and was unjustifiably taking it out on Luther. Well, I guess I could say that. But I refuse.

Luckily, Luther does not force me to finish my apology. "I know," he says quietly. But he does not really understand. Not truly. How could he? He was not there.

Luther had been spared capture. Of the two of us, I am sure Luther would have not survived if he had been the one who was caught. To be honest, at the time, I would have been pleased if he had been caught and killed. But things have changed, I am no longer wishing him death. Most of the time, he still annoys me with his mere presence but I do not want him to die because of it. Not anymore.

Part of me is glad that Luther was spared. That Luther will never truly understand what my time as a prisoner was like. He remembers what I told him about my experience. He remembers how I was plagued with nightmares. But he does not remember the pain the way I do.

After a brief moment of silence, Luther finally adds, "I know you don't want me to be right, Nick. But that doesn't make me wrong."

I shoot him a sideways glance full of stern reproach but offer no comment.

"I'm just saying- it might be cool if you could walk in the sun." A foolish grin spreads on Luther's face and he raises his eyebrows.

"Cool? I think you mean, hot. Like searing my flesh off until my crispy bones turn to dust." I say sarcastically.

Luther shrugs again, "I mean whether you burn up or not, either way, it'd still be exciting for me to watch."

At that, I let myself laugh. Luther has, at the very least, grown wittier with his age. I would like to think that I might have forced him to expand his intelligence with my constant berating, but I doubt he would admit to that.

As our mailbox comes into view, I look over at Luther and tell him quietly, "Hey, um... let's not mention any of this to Marcella. The Genesis, Mila, the murders in the alley. None of it. Not yet."

I have no intention of involving Marcella until I have found out more for myself. The fact the Marcella has never mentioned the Genesis does not take away from her knowledge of them. Marcella told me very little of my maker, Salem, until he tried to kill me. While I am sure that Marcella would have information to offer me, I no longer trust her answers.

"Yeah. Of course," Luther says as we pull into the driveway.

The gravel crunches under the weight of the tires but the only thing I hear is the increased beating of my own heart. There on the front steps is Krista, sitting with her arms draping over her knees.

I hit the brakes, stopping at the end of the driveway.

"Who is...? Oh, is that your wolf?" Luther babbles on.

Realizing that Krista has already seen the car and there is no possible way to avoid her, my grip on the steering wheel tightens. I should be jumping for joy at the sight of her but I am not. My nervousness tightens my stomach into a knot that is both painful and nauseating.

Without looking away from the house, I ask Luther the question I already know the answer to, "Do I smell like blood? I mean, is it that noticeable?"

Luther laughs lightly, "It's like you bathed in it."

Too many thoughts flood my mind. I need a plan and I need it now. The longer I sit at the end of the drive, the more suspicious she will become.

Recognizing my plight, Luther offers no help. He only covers his mouth in a fake attempt to hide his enjoyment of my distress. As his laughter grows, I decide on my plan of action.

I get his attention by simply calling his name, "Luther." He looks over and I plant my fist squarely in his nose. I feel the bones shift under my hand and the rush of fresh blood bursts from his face.

"What the fuck?" he yells, clasping his pouring blood.

"I had no choice," I tell him matter-of-factly. "I need a reason to smell like blood. And now you're bleeding."

I proceed up the driveway slowly as Luther continues to whine like a child, "Why didn't you break your own nose?"

I could tell him that I needed to stop his laughter so that I could think, which is not a complete lie, however, the actual reason for my punch is simply that it would be difficult to explain why my broken nose miraculously healed overnight while I am pretending to be human. But instead of giving those reasons, I only give him the one reason that will perturb him the most. I look at him incredulously, "Because that would hurt."

I stop the car near the steps but far enough away that I have time to walk around to Luther before we approach Krista. Knowing that I need Luther's blood near me to help cover my own saturated scent.

As we near the house, Krista stands up with concern on her face, "Are you alright?" she asks Luther.

Luther mumbles incoherently through his bloody hands but does not lower them to give a proper answer.

"Yeah, he's fine. He's prone to nose bleeds. It's no big deal. Really," I tell her, waving toward Luther. I stand between them with my back to Luther as though that would give us any privacy at all.

Thinking about my stance, I am sure she would mistake my nervousness for standard human jitters. Nothing about my anxiety should cause a werewolf to suspect that I am, in fact, afraid that my would-be-girlfriend might realize that I am soaked in at least six different people's blood.

"What are you doing here? I mean, if I knew you were stopping by, I wouldn't have left," I blurt out most of my words but it only makes her smile.

That is the truth. If I knew she was coming, I would not have left. I would never risk Krista being alone with Marcella. Not in a thousand years.

"It's okay. I haven't been here long."

Not long. She should not have had to wait at all. I should have been here tonight.

The heavy scent of blood begins to have an effect on me that it rarely has before. Guilt. Not regret. Regrets, I have plenty of. Guilt is different. It is not the guilt of the death I so thoroughly enjoyed tonight. No, this nauseating knot balling in my stomach is simply from being forced to look into the eyes of the one person I want to be truly honest with and lie.

Perhaps she does not smell the blood or see the guilt I am trying desperately hard to hide from her. Regardless, Krista does not ask about it either.

She simply smiles warmly and says, "I just wanted to tell you in person that my dad lifted the orders so you can take me on an official date now." She leans back against the porch post innocently but speaks with a coy tone, "You know, if you still want to."

"Yes, I definitely do."

"Good." She pushes herself off of the post, leaning close to me. She lays her hand tenderly on my chest. With her lips close to mine, she whispers, "Pick me up at eight."

I close my eyes expecting her to close the short distance and kiss my lips. However, I do not feel her lips on mine. They grace my cheek instead. Warm and soft, her gentle kiss forces my lopsided smile out.

She lets her hand slide across my chest as she descends from my porch and starts down the drive on foot.

"Do you want a ride?" I ask her.

She turns back to me with a wide smile, "Nope,"-she points to the night sky,-"Full moon. I'm going to get a run in before work."

Until she mentioned it, I had not even considered that it was a full moon tonight or that the full moon might keep her occupied while I was out with Levi and Luther. Instead, my outing only ended up keeping her away from the moon and I find myself sincerely hoping she will not think her time was wasted waiting for me tonight.

"I'll pick you up at eight, then."

"Yep. Eight." She spins back around to leave, letting the gravel crunch under her shoes, and adding, "And take a shower. Your friend's bloody nose has got you both reeking, and I will not have a smelly date."

Even though she is not facing me, I can hear the humor in her voice.

"Yes, ma'am." Just as she nears the end of the driveway, I call out, "Krista, what was the loophole?"

She does not answer my question. As she steps around the corner and out of my line of sight, she simply says with a playfulness in her tone, "Don't call me ma'am."

Now that she is gone and my secret is still safe, I smile at being able to see her tonight. I smile at the orders being lifted, and I smile at the prospect of being able to see her again the next night.

I stand there, thinking to myself, for some time. When I finally do turn around to go inside, I see Luther staring at me blankly. Unsure of how long he had stood there watching me, silently, I ask, "What?"

"That. Was. Pathetic."

Luther laughs buoyantly at me, causing me to roll my eyes. I shove him down a step but not hard enough to risk him falling off the porch completely, "Shut up."

As he steps onto the porch once more, I grab his nose and with a quick jerk, I set the broken bones.

Luther cries out with the sudden pain, "Son of a-"

Chapter 6

A *low-lying fog covers my feet* but I do not need to see the ground to know where I am. I could never forget the forest near my Montana home. Calm and peaceful, it beckons me to tempt fate by stepping inside its boundaries. Despite being in my backyard, these trees are not mine. They belong to the wolves. Werewolves who would by default hate my very presence if they knew what I really am. As luck would have it, they do not.

So why am I here waiting in the cool night air? There can only be one reason and I can still smell her on my skin. Krista. Krista Hartley. Even her name is like honey on my ears. The only werewolf I have ever wanted so completely.

Something deep inside knows she should have been here by now. Something is wrong. Yet when I hear the heavy padding of paws, my worries leave me, my heart picks up several beats, and a lopsided grin spreads across my face.

Here she comes, the one I want, the one I need and she is very close. Soon she will be in my arms. Her skin reflecting in the moonlight. The mist hanging in her hair. Her eyes locked with mine.

I will hold her close, whispering my admirations and plead the case of my merit as to why I am worthy of her heart. If all goes well, we will leave these woods together and we will spend an eternity losing ourselves in one another's body and embrace.

But just before she enters the clearing, I hear a sharp howl and realize this is not the wolf I am waiting for. I see his yellow eyes only moments before he leaps over the shrubbery that separates him from me. He glares at me as his chest vibrates with a deep growl.

"Warren? Please don't," I try but realize it is futile.

He answers me by stepping closer.

Without thinking of my response, I tell him, "Please, Warren. I love her." The words sound foreign to me. I have not loved another person in so long; I was beginning to think I was incapable of it. Yet when I said those three simple words, they feel true.

I have not known Krista for long so the fact that I could love her seems illogical. The werewolf staring back at me seems to think so too and must believe it to be a lie because he leaps at my throat. For a reason unbeknownst to me, I do not resist him. His teeth sink deep into my neck. The warmth of my blood runs along my skin and pushes up into my mouth. He shakes my body vigorously, tearing the muscles in my neck away from the bone.

He drops my limp body to the ground as he stands over me, proud of his soon-to-be kill. Unable to move, I watch as he licks my blood from his lips and know my end is near.

Stepping on my chest, my ribcage buckles under his weight. Gasping for my last breath, I watch as the wolf opens his mouth wide and lowers his teeth toward my face. His claws press into my skin and I know he intends to rip my face from my body.

I feel his cool, slick teeth slide over my cheek. With his breath beating my face, I finally find the will to fight but I cannot move. My spinal cord must have been severed because my body does not respond to my commands. Panic races over me with each painful gasp. His teeth pierce my flesh and pain shoots through my body...

*   *   *

Suddenly, I jerk awake. In my bedroom, safe from the wolves and the forest, I clutch my chest. Panting, I try to shake the image of my death from my thoughts when I hear a low knock.

"Nicolas, are you okay?" Vanessa's voice is soft.

I am not okay but still I respond, "Fine."

Staring at the ceiling, I wonder why I would tell Warren that I loved Krista and why did it seem so true. Why does it still?

"Can I come in?"

I don't honestly want Vanessa in my room right now but refusing would only make her worry about me more. "If you must."

Opening the door, she steps inside meekly, as if she is embarrassed by something. She walks to me without making a noise and sits on the edge of my bed twisting her fingers around each other.

Wondering what she is nervous about, I sit up and place my hand over hers. I do not have to say anything. Just holding her hand draws her eyes to mine where the concern written on my face allows her to relax.

"Could you tell me about your dream?" I start to answer but she interrupts timidly, "I don't have dreams anymore."

I shift a little, unsure of what to say to her. Not all vampires continue to have dreams. I, myself, have more than most but my dreams are not always a gift. They tend to be memories of forgotten lives and horrific traumas, deaths you cannot unsee. More often than not vampiric dreams are not pleasurable.

"Of course." I rub my hand over my face while I gather my thoughts. I would much rather be contemplating the events of my dream alone. Instead, I begin, "I was in a forest. It was calm and beautiful."

Her eyes light up, but there is a certain sadness to them. There is a longing for the escape that dreams provide humans. However, that is not what dreams are for us and there is no way to truly explain that. Just as Vanessa would not be able to explain to me what is it like for her to experience no dreams at all.

So, I continue, "I was waiting for someone but an angry werewolf came instead. He attacked me and I didn't fight back until it was too late. And he killed me."

"So it was a nightmare?"

I would have thought that my waking up gasping would have indicated that it was a nightmare. But actually, it was not. Not entirely. It started off nicely with the prospect of seeing Krista again and running off with her. The warmth that thought gave me was a welcome change to the usually death filled memories that flood my dreams.

I answer with a smile. "Dying certainly wasn't enjoyable."

Vanessa smiles at me briefly, "Thanks. I miss dreams."

"I know."

She lets out a long sigh, "It's going to take a long time to get used to this life."

As she stands up, I consider telling her that you never really get used to this life. You only ever learn how to live with the things you do. Instead, I give her a light smile as she leaves my room.

Once she is gone, I consider my dream for a moment longer. Consider the way it felt to say I love her out loud. Consider why it still feels true. Finally, I conclude that there is no good to come of it. Whether I love Krista or not, my actions and the results will both be the same. One way or another, I will lie until I lose her. Because that is the only thing I can do.

I call Julia into my room. Maintaining a healthy human complexion requires fresh blood, and despite my gluttonous exploits of the previous night, I am taking no chances. After all, I have a date tonight.

I should feel guilty listening to her painful, sharp breaths, but my mind is somewhere else. My inner monster is lavishing in the snap of her skin under my teeth, the warmth flooding my mouth, and the temporary relief of the burning in my throat. The monster in me rages with greed and, for a moment, I lose my control.

Once I remove my fangs, I realize I have opened more of Julia's neck than I intended to. I lie her back on my bed and sit down next to her. She holds pressure to the fresh wounds I have created. I watch the blood seep between her fingers. The sight of her blood rolling toward the pillow as she holds her neck should force my guilt but it only makes me crave to finish my meal.

Luther does not make a sound as he walks into my room but I know he is there just the same.

"I wish you would learn to knock," I say without emphasis.

"And I wish your budding personality would finally blossom into something worth wasting my time but we both know that neither of those things will ever happen."

I laugh to myself, "What do you want, Luther?"

"I was thinking about Mila again,-"

I stop him there. "No."

I do not need to add Mila to the pile of things I cannot explain away. I have too much on my mind already. I never lose control with my sheep.

"But just look at the time line, Nick-"

I cut him off again as I shove him away from my dresser, "I have considered the time line."

I take out some gauzes and a wrap for Julia's neck hoping to slow her bleeding.

"My increased tolerance of human food, my susceptibility to narcotics, my inclination toward werewolves, even my dreams have become more like actual dreams instead of my memories replaying in my head. All of it, came after Germany. After Ulrich." My English accent skirts across my words, hiding in the vowels as I continue, "I mean, hell, I never even wanted a werewolf as a friend until Tara. And now I want to shag one. So yes, I have considered it."

I help Julia sit up and move her hand away, exposing the ripped fang marks where I removed them too quickly and tore her flesh.

"You lost a lot of blood," I tell her softly. I wipe away the blood to access the wounds and begin dressing them.

Luther nods toward her as tears roll down her cheek, "Is she going to be alright?"

Fighting the urge to roll my eyes, I sit down next to her on the bed, "Of course," I tell Luther then to Julia, I add, "Do you feel light-headed?"

"Yes," she says weakly. "But I'll be fine. Tomorrow you can try again and next time I won't move so much."

Julia did not move when I bit her. Not even a little. This was my fault. I was not careful. But still she smiles at me foolishly. She should be angry like any human would be, but sheep do not feel anger or love or anything else. I look in her eyes, but they are dull and blank. She has a heartbeat, but she is not alive. Not really.

Everyone I know is damned in some way. My family, all of my friends, even the sheep are cursed. The only thing anyone from

Genesis could take from me is Krista, and possibly my sanity if I continue to follow their rabbit trail of incoherent babble.

Switching the pillows around, I lie Julia back on my bed again with the clean pillow under her.

As she closes her eyes, drifting into a weakened slumber, Luther says, "You should be more careful with her."

Without taking my eyes from Julia, I pull a blanket over her but speak to Luther, "Being careful is not my problem. Being distracted is."

Holding the bloody pillow, I walk over to Luther and add quietly, "And I cannot afford to be so distracted with Krista." Trying to maintain my secrets while attempting to discern my feelings for Krista is confusing enough without any added distractions. "So I would appreciate it if you would allow me to stop thinking about Mila, the Nexus, the Genesis, the whole lot. Because there are no answers there, only more questions."

Luther shifts as though he is about to protest my logic path, so I continue before he is able to speak, "Have you stopped to consider that if the Genesis *were* able to change me, some of those changes could make me weaker? I mean, if I were altered in a way that would give me strengths where there use to be only limitations, like a sun immunity, then common sense says that there would also be limitations where there use to be strengths."

Julia groans slightly and I pause to see if she might need me. But her moaning does not last long. Not wanting to disturb her further, I speak again to Luther but only in whispers, "I'll put it to you this way: vampires are not affected by narcotics or poisons. But I definitely can be affected, at least, by narcotics. So does that mean a poison might kill me?" I shrug.

I can see his mind mulling over my words. It honestly never occurred to him that being a Nexus would have some drawbacks. It never occurred to him why I do not have any interest in discovering if I am one of those experimental messes that the Genesis are seeking.

I place my hand on his shoulder, "You see, Luther, I don't want to think about all the new ways I might possibly die, or Mila and the Genesis, or basically any of that right now. I would rather focus on the ways my girlfriend might kill me, because honestly, if she does, none of the rest of it matters anyway."

Luther smiles at me and nods once.

I smile at him. Maybe now, he will drop the topic once and for all. I hit him in the chest with the soiled pillow playfully, "Do me a favor and put that in the wash before Marcella catches a whiff of it?"

"Sure."

Luther walks out and I am finally alone. I go to the bathroom and scrub Julia's blood from my hands. Having showered twice already, I have already successfully rid myself of the scent of the massive amounts of blood I came home in last night, so it is simply Julia's blood that needs to be removed now. Since it is still fresh, it is easier to rinse off.

Grabbing a clean shirt, I watch myself button it in the mirror but my mind is not on my reflection. It saunters through every memory I have of Krista. From the moment I saw her at the gas station I knew she would be mine. I would make her mine. I had to.

Now in a few hours, I will have my chance. My chance to impress her with more lies. I shake my head to clear the negative and decide to replay the night at the overlook instead. No use feeling guilty about lies that have not left my mouth yet.

When I close my eyes and focus, I can still feel her hand in mine. It brings a smile to my face just imaging her hand on my chest, her laugh dancing in the air around me, and her eyes sparkling when she steals a peek at me.

A shrill voice stops my proceeding thoughts, "Are you insane?"

"Shall we attempt to be civil?" I looked up at the reflection of Marcella leaning on my door. "Good evening, Marcella. How was your night?"

"Don't be contrite with me. A wolf, Nicolas? Are you mad?"

Dropping my hands to the sink, I answer, "No but you may want to watch your words carefully if you wish for me to remain so."

"It's distasteful. It's atrocious and completely repulsive. She's a dog! A mutt, hiding behind her human effigy and pretending to be more than the mongrel she really is."

I whip myself around to face Marcella quickly and step toward her. My anger keeps me from controlling the look in my eyes. Whatever is there intimidates Marcella enough to make her back into the wall.

"Hold your tongue," I snap through gritted teeth. My heart rate pushing my accent to the surface once more.

I step back and attempt to steady myself. I do not mean to be so harsh with Marcella but I suppose our rocky past is helping keep me on edge when dealing with her. A part of me longs for the relationship we once had and hopes to have again. But in this moment, I am not interested in making amends or allowing this line of conversation to continue.

She allows me a moment to collect myself before she starts again. This time she speaks much more gently, "It's unheard of. The wolves hate our kind and you cannot change that. So why even try?"

"I don't expect you to understand."

"Try me."

I look at Marcella with pity in my eyes. How do you explain love to someone who cannot and has not ever felt it? Besides, I do not dare say those words out loud. Not yet and certainly not to Marcella.

"I don't know. I barely know Krista at all but when I am with her, I know my whole life has been leading me to her." Every pleasure, every pain, every tear that has fallen was guiding me to her arms, making me the man I need to be to look at Krista and see my future, my past, my everything in her eyes. "She's not just perfect, she's perfect for me."

Marcella's hand strokes my cheek, "Perfect, save for one thing. She's a werewolf."

"You see that as a flaw but I don't."

"Perhaps not but she will see yours as a flaw. Mark my words, when she realizes what you are, she will be horrified. Her hatred for you will be your end."

I understand what Marcella is warning me of but some things are worth the risks. "We all must die at some point. I'd rather be destroyed by love than to live a thousand years without ever feeling it again."

Love. There it was. That word snuck into my conversation despite my attempt to hide it. Luckily, however, Marcella does not notice.

She holds my face gently, "I know you, Nicolas. You're not the man you show her. You're a killer, cold-blooded, murderer. You carry a monster inside, and you are *its* servant. Not the other way around."

I cannot deny what she says because deep down, I know it to be true. Grabbing her wrist, I pull her hand away from my face, "Every man, human, wolf, and vampire alike, has a monster inside them. Every person is capable of darkness. They're only waiting for the right circumstances to pull it out of them, to expose how vile they really are. I am not pretending to be better than that. I know what I am. I know who I am. But more importantly, I know that what I want and what I deserve are not the same thing. And I know that I am selfish enough to ignore that."

"Then you would condemn yourself to death for a dog!" she snaps.

I take a slow breath, trying to keep my accent from showing itself again and say, "Dying is but a small price to pay for truly living." I look over at her calmly, "Now if you'll excuse me, I need to finish dressing."

"Nic-"

I cut her off sharply, "You're dismissed."

She huffs in dismay and stomps out, slamming my bathroom door shut. I stare at myself in the mirror, arguing with myself in my mind about being too harsh to Marcella. Whether I should apologize or stand my ground and just let her be angry.

Marcella is a difficult person to deal with on a daily basis. It has taken me centuries to figure out how to keep her from manipulating me and it is times like this, times when she is hurt by my bluntness that I feel her marionette strings pulling at me again. She is my mother, for all intents and purposes, so I will always have a desire to please her but I also have a need to do what pleases me as well.

I finish dressing, letting my frustration with Marcella slowly leave. Most of the day, I lie next to Julia. The rhythmic sounds of her breathing are calming and in a strange way, there is a comfort in knowing that she will not die today.

I do not sleep for fear of another dream. As chaotic as my morning has been, I may very well dream of Krista being hurt by me or even Marcella. My dreams are too unpredictable for me to find any comfort in them. Dreaming of my own death is distressing enough but I cannot risk dreaming that I might see Krista caught in my fangs.

Instead, I lie still. Occasionally, I allow myself to venture into a day-dream but those always lead me to imagine a scenario where I might quench myself with Krista's body instead of her blood. Day-dreaming such things is awkward while lying next to a snoozing, blood deprived human. So I force myself to stare at the ceiling and attempt to think of nothing until the hour approaches that I can wander out into the night and into Krista's arms.

Finally, I feel the long-awaited night set. Leaving Julia asleep on my bed, I start up the stairs. As I enter the kitchen, I see Marcella's sheep standing near the sink washing a few dishes.

"Hey, Andrew," I begin. "Would you check on Julia in about an hour? Make sure she eats something."

Andrew smiles widely, just like any sheep who has just been given an order would. "Of course."

Grabbing my car keys, I hear Marcella's voice. It is odd how sharp her voice remains despite the low volume in which she speaks to me, "You have to tell her."

She is right. I know. I have always known it. I can feel it. Holding a secret this big will only be detrimental.

Her hands rest on my shoulders and I force my eyes not to lower to the buttons on my shirt. Keeping eye contact with her, I add, "I will. But not tonight."

"You know what will happen if she has to discover this for herself," Marcella says in her eerily smooth voice.

"Yes," I mutter quietly. "The same thing that will happen if I tell her myself."

I gently push Marcella's hand from my shoulder, "I'll lose her."

Grabbing my jacket from the back of the chair, I walk past Marcella before she could say anymore about it. I do not want to address this. Not yet. And honestly, I would rather discuss this with anybody other than Marcella. Even Luther.

*   *   *

Clearing my throat, I feel a nervous energy rip through me as I knock lightly. I can hear heavy steps as someone hurries to the door. Despite not being able to see or smell the person approaching the door, I already know that it is not Krista. Her steps are more even than these are.

Simone swings it open and smiles softly, "Nicolas. It's nice to see you again."

"Thank you. The pleasure is mine, I'm sure. Is Krista here?"

"Actually, she's not. But she should be back any minute. You can wait inside if you want."

"Okay." I step inside, hesitantly. This house smells too much like Krista. Her scent caresses my nose, causing a hunger that has nothing to do with blood.

"I'll go call and tell her you're here," Simone says as she starts down the hallway.

I nod as she leaves me, standing awkwardly. Alone in the living room, I roll my hand over the other and look around. The room is small but warm. Despite having two women living here, it does not look overly feminine.

When Simone reappears, her smile looks forced. "It's going to be a few minutes."

"Is everything okay?"

"Yeah," Simone gestures for us to sit, "her brother made her come and see him before your date and she's just not back yet. That's all."

Made her. As in, an order. I do not know that I could ever be a wolf simply for that reason. I do not take orders.

"So you can wait here or..." Simone starts with a smirk, "You could go. Rescue her from her brother."

Rescue her. I must admit, that is tempting. My smile must show my eagerness to steal her away from Mitchell because Simone only laughs lightly when I ask, "Where does he live?"

She points behind me to a tan house across the street, "Right there."

Of course, he would pick a house where he could watch his sister like a hawk. Female werewolves are rare and need extra protection, or so I have been told, but mostly the extra protection only means extra rules.

"Thank you," I tell her with mischief and a willingness to start trouble in my eyes. And why shouldn't I? I am sure that her brother already hates me despite believing that I am human. He would be in for a surprise if I overpowered him and slammed his arrogant self to the ground.

I walk over to Mitchell's house. As I get closer, I overhear voices bickering just inside. One is definitely Krista and the other I assume is her brother. I lean toward the door instinctually despite not really needing the added distance to improve my hearing.

"There's something off about him, Krista," I hear who I assume is Mitchell saying.

"Like what? You've never even met him" Krista snaps back at him.

"No, but Dad and Warren have, and I trust their judgment. And so should you," Mitchell says bluntly.

I raise my hand to knock, but it opens before I can touch the door.

"You must be Nicolas," says a petite, dark-haired lady, "Please come in."

Her werewolf scent is easy to detect as I step passed her into the home. I cannot help but to realize that her simple, kind gesture has given me permission to enter their home any time I choose. Now I could, with very little effort, sneak into this house and kill Mitchell. Eliminate one of my few real obstacles in this pack.

"I'm Renee, Mitchell's wife. Krista's told me a lot about you," the brunette tells me.

"All good I hope," I smile at her.

Smiling, she nods. "I was just practicing a dance routine with my daughter. Would you like to meet her?"

Meet the daughter of someone who hates me. Meet the leverage I could use to hurt him, to bring his world down on him if I chose to. "I'd love to."

As unusual as it might seem to introduce me to their daughter so soon into my relationship with Krista, I get the sense that Renee's real reason for the offer is simply to persuade me into going to the other side of the house and out of human hearing range of Mitchell and Krista's conversation.

She leads me to a large room full of mirrors which is most likely a converted garage. In the center of the room is who I presume to be their daughter. She is only around six years old, short, dark hair hidden partially by a top hat and dancing to an up-tempo song from a decade ago.

Huffing, she stomps and throws her arms in the air.

"Again," Renee tells her sternly even though I had not realized that she missed a step at all.

From another room, we both hear Krista's stern voice, "You're just being ridiculous! And I don't have to listen to this!"

I pretend that I cannot hear them argue because, from this distance, a human would not be able to and Renee also pretends that she did not hear anything upsetting.

"Would you excuse me for a moment? I'm going to tell Krista that you're here," she says, kindly dismissing herself to diffuse the situation in the other room.

Nodding, I try not to listen as Mitchell snaps back, "I don't like him."

Krista groans exasperatedly, "You don't have to like him! I am the only one who has to like him!"

The little girl in the dance room diverts my attention as she huffs and tosses her hat on the floor, frustrated.

"Want some help?" I ask, happy to have a distraction from eavesdropping on a conversation I would rather not overhear.

"You know about dance?" she asks incredulously.

I laugh lightly, "I know a few moves."

She waves me in, "Show me what you got."

Smiling at her challenge, I walk over to her. With my foot, I flip the hat off of the floor and bend to catch it on my head.

Astonishment floods her eyes as her mouth hangs open, "That's so cool."

With my lopsided smile spreading on my face, I tip the hat from my head and let it roll down my arm as I slide back a step and catch it with my hand.

She laughs with surprise and wonder, "How did you learn to do that?"

"Practice. Just like you." Not to mention the fact that being a vampire helps.

Her smile leaves, "I'm not good at dance. My mom is a dance teacher and we're supposed to be naturally good at this. But, guess what?" She tosses her hands irritably. "There's an exception to everything. And I am standing right here," she adds, pointing to herself.

Sighing, she lets her eyes fall to the floor. I can tell that she struggles with not being able to please her mother. And on some level, I can relate to her dilemma. However, while I do want to please Marcella, I would never distress over doing what pleases myself instead. This type of conundrum must be a werewolf thing.

I kneel down in front of her and wait until she looks up at me, "You want to know a secret? I was born in a port city which meant everyone loved boats, the water, and swimming. Everyone except me. I was the only person I knew that was afraid of the water but I worked at it and eventually lived on a ship for over a year, storms and all, and I wasn't afraid. Being born talented is not near as impressive as earning it."

She smiles slowly as the words sink in as I finish, "Being the exception simply gives you the opportunity to prove that you're exceptional."

I lay the hat on her head gently. Someone clears their throat and until then, I had not noticed them in the doorway. It is not like most people, humans or otherwise, to be able to sneak up on me so it is no surprise that it startles me and I look to the door quickly.

Krista stands in the doorway. It is not the surprise of her being there that stops my breath. Her hair is loosely pulled back as though she was in a rush to fix it but still tempts me to touch it. A few wild strands force themselves out and lightly frame her face. My eyes trail over the way her blue shirt shows off her body without seeming as though she is trying to.

Krista laughs to herself while she messes with her earring, "Sorry. Are you ready?"

For her? No. I was nowhere near ready to meet a werewolf-like her. I was not prepared to meet a wolf that I could love so quickly or at all. Ever.

"For you? Always," I tell her. Standing up, I take the girl's hand, "It was very nice to meet you..."

"Molly," she informs me.

"Molly. Such a lovely name for such a lovely lady," I smile softly as I lean down and kiss her knuckles.

She blushes lightly and the fire in my throat rages, protesting my restraint. With the heavy scent of werewolves filling the air, I had dropped my guard. The sight of her blood flushing her cheeks in a deeper pink and the aroma of her very human blood catches me off-guard.

I close my eyes to hide my blackening eyes and pinch the bridge of my nose which never really helps to stop the way my mouth waters. It is more of a response that I imitate from my distant human life for uncomfortable situations.

"Are you okay?" Krista asks as she steps closer.

"Yeah," I say, opening my green eyes, "it's just a headache. I get them a lot."

"Right. Simone said you do. She said it's why all the windows in your house are painted to keep the light out," Krista mumbles the last sentence to herself as though she is remembering.

"Just the first floor," I tell her, jokingly.

As I walk toward her, she asks, "We could do this tomorrow if you're not up for it tonight."

I stop in front of her, "I would like to do this tomorrow." Then stepper closer than I should, I smile, "And the night after that and after that but also tonight as well."

Cradling her face in my hand, I rub my thumb across her soft cheek, "It will take more than a headache to keep me from you." It will take more than her brother too.

I smile my lopsided smile, utilizing its charm in an attempt to dissuade her from anything Mitchell might have said about me a moment ago.

It must work because she smiles, "Good."

I slide my hand down her arm and take her hand, "Shall we?" She nods and I look back at Molly, "Maybe I'll see you again."

I lead Krista toward the door, trying to avoid seeing Mitchell face to face tonight. The last thing I want is for Krista to discover my secret by witnessing me rip her brother's infinitesimal mind from his insignificant body.

Grabbing the doorknob, I hear Mitchell's voice and hide the way it makes me cringe.

"You're Nick, right?" Mitchell calls to me.

I shrug, "You can call me Nicolas." I smirk despite knowing that I should not provoke him. Really though, it does fit the brash human persona her father believes I possess.

Mitchell laughs irritably as Renee takes my shoulders and nudges me toward the door, "Why don't we all get acquainted some other time. Perhaps when the moon is not so full. Yes? Good. Krista, you and Nick run along and have fun."

I open the door with Mitchell's eyes burning into me and follow Krista out to my car across the street, still parked in her driveway. Mitchell steps onto his porch and watches us closely.

Despite my eagerness to leave, Krista does not seem to pay any attention to Mitchell and says cheerfully, "I just have to grab my purse. I'll be right back."

She races inside her home. I walk around to the driver's side, careful not to move faster than a human would as Mitchell walks to my car. When I reach for my door handle, Mitchell puts his hand on my car, holding the door shut.

The convertible top is down so there is little stopping me from just slipping over the door to get in the car. However, I do not wish to be sitting when an aggressor is standing over me.

Besides, I could also simply pull the door open despite his hand. I am stronger than him but the human I am pretending to be is not.

Instead, I simply look at him irritably, "Look, this can go two ways. But keep in mind that if you, the big, bad, brother wolf, attacks me, the fragile, human, boyfriend, it will only make her cling to me that much more."

I shift my body so that I am facing him directly as I continue matter-of-factly, "She'll feel sorry for me, try to nurture and nurse me all night. And I'll probably get laid because of it."

Then with a smirk, I add, "So go ahead, take a swing."

Knowing I'm right, he exhales his frustration, "There's something different about you. Something off. You don't even smell like a normal human."

"It's called body wash, look into it."

In an instant, he grabs my shirt and pushes me back against the car, "Keep talking, boy. I don't know how you convinced my dad that you're a decent person but I won't be so easily fooled."

From the corner of my eye, I can see Renee step onto the porch. Knowing that with a little push she will be taking my side, I prod him, "You're right, I am hiding something. I'm actually a magician and I can hypnotize people."

I dangle my keys from my finger and let them swing back and forth. "You're getting angry," I say tauntingly.

His eyes tighten and I smirk, "See it works."

His hand tightens in a fist but just as he brings his hand back to punch, Renee whistles from the porch, "That's enough," she mutters, nearly in a low growl. "Reign in your testosterone and let him leave."

He turns toward her sharply, "This doesn't concern you!"

His tone would have been enough to ignite her anger but his words sealed his fate. In an instant, her face grows stern, her eyes narrow, her face reddens, and her breathing deepens to long, forced exhales.

Her voice carries a chill as she speaks her threat, "I would not suggest speaking down to the woman who lies next to you." She does not elaborate on her threat, and she does not need to. She spins on her foot and walks back into the house with her arms crossed over her chest.

Her absence is not a consent for Mitchell to continue harassing me or a submission to him in any way. Worse, her retreat is a test. I know it. Mitchell knows it. She walked away to see what he will do. Proceeding with his current line of harassing will undoubtedly be an instant failure of her test.

Mitchell can talk a good game but when it comes down to it, Renee rules that house. Some would say that she has him whipped, whatever that means, but something about the distress in his eyes tells me he simply loves her more than he loves himself. That the very thought of doing anything to disappoint her or risk losing her seems foolish and frivolous compared to her presence.

Mitchell moves his hand from my door, glaring at me, "To be continued."

"I look forward to it," I say derisively.

He walks away without another word to me but this is not over. Mitchell knows I am hiding something. He can sense that I am different. He wants me gone but that is not something we are going to agree on. I cannot just walk away. Not anymore. Mitchell will simply have to hate me as long as I am in Krista's life. He already hates the human-ruse version of me. Imagine how much more he will despise the vampire I am hiding.

Getting in the car, I start the engine. I prepare to fake a smile as Krista walks out of her house and toward the car in hopes that she does not realize what transpired a moment ago. But when my eyes meet hers, my smile is warm and gentle, and more importantly, it is real. Whether she heard all or any of my exchange with Mitchell, I no longer care.

She hops over the door, plops into the seat, and takes my hand all the while biting back a bashful smile, "What are we doing tonight?"

"I thought I might take you bowling."

She lightly chuckles, "Bowling?"

Yes, bowling. Bowling seems like a very human suggestion. Though, I am not sure what makes it funny to her. "Do you want to do something else?"

Smiling widely, she shakes her head slowly, "No, bowling is fine."

As I put the car into reverse and begin to back into the road, I hear Krista say, "I hope you enjoy losing." She looks at me with a spark in her eyes, "I'm going to decimate you."

I smile, "Oh, you think so?"

Smirking, Krista turns toward the windshield again, "Oh, yes. There will be no mercy."

Laughing to myself, I continue backing out of the driveway. "Well, then I better think up a good story about how I let you win."

Once we pull out of Lockwood Estates, I begin to feel better, a little safer, more relaxed, but looking over at her, my nerves return. The physical risks may be decreasing with each passing mile, however, when I am with her, I am at a much greater risk of danger. The risk of losing myself, not just my life.

"So," she begins, "I'm guessing you write during the day, and you're out all hours of the night with me, so... when exactly do you sleep?"

"When do you?"

"I'm a werewolf. We only need three hours a night. That makes dates like these a little easier for me. But you didn't answer my question," she smirks at me.

"Well, I have insomnia so I don't sleep either," I lie with a smile big enough that she cannot tell whether I am joking or not.

Stopping at the last traffic light before we leave the town limits, I glance over at her and attempt to change the subject, "I hope one day I will actually get to see you wear that seat belt."

She raises her eyebrow mischievously. "Well, seat belts were invented to save humans. I'll be fine but your concern is cute," she taps my nose playfully with her last word.

I laugh lightly, "I suppose keeping loopholes a secret is a werewolf thing too?" I raise my eyebrows suggestively.

Blushing lightly, and mutters to herself, "Yep."

She bites her lip and crinkles her nose for a moment. Finally, she lets out a long exhale, "Okay. But you can't let it weird you out."

Weird me out? How would anything she could ever say be stranger than me telling her I am a vampire? My eyes perk up and I shift in my seat, grinning foolishly and letting her see my eagerness. "Deal."

She plays with her fingers for a moment, postponing her words. Finally she says, "Okay. So there are a few things alphas can't order: the death of a pack member without just cause, harm to a human without just cause, and pretty much any order that would interfere with love."

Love. There is that word again. My smile fades slowly. I can guess her next words but I wait for her to say them anyway.

Pushing the loose strands of hair from her face nervously, she adds, "So in order for me to kiss you against a standing order, one of us would have to be in love with the other."

I nod slowly but say nothing. Guilt begins to creep in despite the way I try to push against it. How can I tell her that love had nothing to do with it? How can I say that my being a vampire is the only reason her alpha's order did not apply to me? So I say nothing.

Her nervousness pushes her next words out in a rush, "And it certainly isn't me, so."

No decent part of me should be capable of letting her sit there and continue to believe that. She has a right to know that despite how I think I feel now, the truth is much simpler. The rule simply did not apply to me because I am not human.

This is my moment to tell her the truth. Just do it. Say the words, 'I'm a vampire', like ripping off a Band-Aid. Quick and simple.

Here goes. I take a deep breath ready for my confession and my words freeze on my tongue. In their place, I grasp at a feeble attempt to alleviate both our nerves. "Hm, are you sure? I would have put money on it being you. After all, I am pretty irresistible. I mean," I shrug playfully, "your dad already loves me."

She laughs freely and sarcastically adds, "Oh yes, you made an impeccable first impression."

I shrug lightheartedly, "Well, a memorable one anyway."

Settling back into her seat, she smiles and shakes her head. The relief that I responded so comfortably to her mention of love scrolls across her face.

The light changes to green but I do not move. Instead, I am too busy watching her. The way her eyes drift down and to the side with some distant thought. The way her smile warms my skin. And the way the loose strands of hair sway gently with the slightest movement she makes. It is all so captivating. As though it is her own way of enthralling me.

Suddenly, she lifts her chin to the light. "It's green," she says. But I do not look at the light. I am not sure what my expression says but when she finally looks at me, she blushes.

"I know." I let my lopsided smile spread slowly.

Pulling away from the traffic light, I take her hand in mine. With our fingers tangled together, I lift her hand to my lips and kiss the back of her hand gently without saying a word. I lower our hands but I do not let go. I keep our fingers clasped in one another as I finish our drive.

We make it to the bowling alley and after a few moments, we get a lane. She sits down in front of the computer and starts typing our names in.

While I lace up a pair of ridiculous looking shoes, Krista smiles slyly, "So, you lived on a boat?"

Yes, I did. I worked on a ship in my human life a long time ago. Before I loved Ann, before I watched her die, and before I became the predator I am now. Yes, I lived on a ship but it seems so long ago that it might as well be part of a story I had read once.

"For a time," I say simply.

As she picks up her ball, a group of teenagers nearby begin snickering. We both look over as they point at Krista, whispering. Krista looks down at her ball, rubbing her fingers over its cold shell. She says that she is used to the intolerance but it is evident that she is not.

For a moment, I almost pity them. These teens have no idea what they actually hate about her or why. They have no clue of how unpredictable werewolves can be. If they did, they would whisper more quietly and hide their hate more discreetly. Werewolves do not kill humans for sport but the humans should be leery of letting themselves forget that the peace between them has always been the choice of the werewolves. Humans could do very little to dissuade an angry wolf.

I, on the other hand, know all too well that wolves can be volatile. I have felt their teeth in my skin. I understand that their phases must be voluntary in order to remain in control of their wolf. Anger, pain, and fear can overpower them enough to force them into phasing. No control of the phase, no control of the wolf.

Despite the teens' ignorance, I am pleased to have a reason to change the subject without Krista noticing. So with an upbeat tone, I ask, "So you really think you're going to decimate me?"

Her eyes light up as she smiles, "Oh, I know I will."

There is little doubt that a werewolf would be good at a game of skill and strength. However if I chose to, I also do not doubt that I could prove her wrong. Vampires also happen to be superb at games of skill and strength.

I lean back against the cool plastic seat and smirk, "You're pretty sure of yourself, Hartley. You haven't even seen me play yet."

Lining up her shot, she says, "I don't need to watch you play games to realize that you're about to be impressed." She looks over her shoulder with one eyebrow raised, "Trust me, you can't even imagine all the ways I could amaze you."

I do not know if it is the challenge in her eyes or the sultry tone of her voice but my skin warms in response.

She giggles to herself. As she turns back around, I can see the edges of her ears redden with the blushing she is attempting to hide from me. Watching her, I find that I cannot help but smile too.

She rolls the ball down the lane with precision and just as I expected, gets a strike.

"Nice follow-through."

"Thank you. You're up."

As I stand to take my turn, a plan formulates in my mind. I pick up my ball uncomfortably and look at the holes as though I am slightly confused.

"You have bowled before, right?" she asks with humor in her voice.

"Yeah, of course." I walk up to the line letting my nerves show. With a forceful exhale, I release the ball and it rolls about half-way down the lane then into the gutter.

Unsuccessfully holding back her laughter, she says, "I'm sorry." She covers her face for a moment until she gathers herself. She smiles to herself. "Are you sure you've done this before?" she reiterates teasingly.

I grab my ball from the return, "Okay, it was about fifteen years ago but, yeah, it's like riding a bike, right?"

Walking up to the line again, I close my eyes, sighing as though I am attempting to focus on my turn.

As I pull back my arm, she calls, "Wait, wait, wait." She walks to me, smiling widely. "Your technique is all wrong. It's not just about lobbing a ball down the lane. It's about the entire delivery. Approach, release, and the follow-through."

She stops near the return, "Start here."

When I reach her, she demonstrates, "Take four steps and as you do, let the ball swing back like a pendulum. Don't force it. Let the weight of the ball do the work."

Looking at me softly, she continues, "There's more to it than that but it'll get you started."

As she sits down, I mutter to myself, "Four steps, swing and release." I make my approach, roll the ball down the lane smoothly. It curves to the left but still knocks down one pin.

Turning around toward Krista, I shrug, "I'll get it."

"I'm sure you will."

Krista has no trouble bowling another strike but once her turn is over, she excuses herself to buy a snack. While she is gone, I purposely bowl another turn straight into the gutter then sit down to wait for her.

However, as I stare at the bowling balls sitting patiently in a row, I begin to feel deceitful. As much as I do not wish to admit it, every minute I lure her into falling for me is a lie. Every minute she does not realize what sits beside her is a minute stolen from her. She should know. She should be permitted to decide for herself. I should be human enough to tell her.

Yet when I see her making her return, she smiles at me from across the room and something stops me from telling her. Whether it is that I am afraid, selfish, or simply too weak, I do not know. But it matters not. Either way, I have to accept the fact that I am not going to tell her what I am. And I will justify it to myself once again.

As she gets closer, I nod towards the pins, "Go ahead. It's your turn to get another strike."

Smiling, she sets her popcorn down next to me. She rolls the ball and does not even watch as it crashes into the pins, knocking them all over.

Almost gloating, she plops down beside me and grabs her popcorn again.

"Show-off," I joke.

Her laugh is cut short as she watches the teenagers leave with disgusted looks on their faces.

In an attempt to distract her from the teens' callous sneers, I lean toward her and mutter, "It's about time they left."

She looks over at me questioningly and I continue, "Have you seen my score? It's kind of embarrassing."

Nudging me lightly, she smiles and tosses a piece of popcorn in her mouth.

"Seriously. I'd rather not have anyone else see it."

She pushes the loose strands from her face and I watch as it dances over her cheek, "You could still catch up. It's your turn."

But I do not hear her words. I only watch the way her mouth moves as she says them. The way she licks her lips just before she speaks, her tongue sliding across them, sends my heart racing. The way she opens her mouth with each syllable beckons me to caress it with my kiss. And the way she bites her lip at the end stops my breath. I stare at her mouth lost in its enchantment.

When she says my name, it takes me a moment to process and respond.

"Right. My turn. I should... yeah," I say with a half-dazed smile.

Picking up the ball, I walk over to the place she had told me to stand before. But as I look down the lane at the pins waiting, I hear her say, "You know, I'm really glad you brought me here. They have the best popcorn. Plus, it's been forever since I've been bowling."

I focus on the pins and purposely rolling the ball poorly as I respond, "Yeah, I can tell. You're pretty rusty at it."

She laughs at my words more than at my seamless attempts at rolling the ball into the gutter for a third time. And as I turn around, I see her smiling widely at me. Her knees are drawn up close to her chest with her feet resting on the edge of her chair. Several strands of her hair cascade along her face as they refuse to stay pulled back.

There is a certain comfort to the way she is sitting, smiling at me, which makes her that much more appealing. There is no anxiety about being here with me. No nervous date jitters. No worry about trying to impress me. No fear of me at all. Not even her wolf warns her against me.

She takes her turn and has to pick up the spare. The way she glances over her shoulder at me causes me to realize it is my gaze that has her distracted. I did not aim to stare at her so intently, but I am. Now that I am aware of it, I still do not pull back my eyes.

"What? Do I have some popcorn in my teeth?" she asks self-consciously.

"No," I tell her. In all honesty I would not have cared if she did, though. As I walk up to take my turn, I stop close to Krista and add softly, "You look perfect."

She scoffs, "Okay. Yeah, sure."

I continue as I make my way to the return and pick up the ball, "Well, you do."

I do not need to see the ball roll into the gutter. I aimed it there. Instead I watch her as I wait for my ball to come up the return.

Krista shakes her head and smiles, "Maybe perfectly blah."

I raise my eyebrows at her and shake my head to myself in a silent rebuttal but she just giggles at me. "Don't be that guy, Nick."

"What guy?" I ask as I roll my second attempt and manage to knock one pin down.

Nodding at the pins, she jokes, "Getting better."

Then she props her feet on the chair across from her, confident in her next words, "The guy who says sweet things just because they want a kiss."

I smile to myself. If I were human, that may have been my angle. But as a vampire, I have bigger things to lie about than whether or not I think she is pretty.

"Well, I do want to kiss you. But," I walk toward her, "I won't trick you with sweet nothings."

I gently lift her legs from the chair and set her feet down. Setting my hand on the back of her chair, I lean my face close to hers and tell her softly, "You see, when I want to kiss you, I won't waste time asking for it."

I can hear her heartbeat speed up ever so slightly. Her eyes blink quickly and she swallows hard, fighting the urge to bite her bottom lip.

Pushing off of the chair slightly, I sit back into the chair her feet had been in and smirk, "Right now, I'm busy being decimated." I nod toward the lane, "And it's your turn."

"Right." Krista walks over to the return. She picks up the ball but does not roll it right away. Instead, she slides her fingers over the cold bowling ball, lost somewhere in her thoughts.

I smile softly at her even though she cannot see my face, "I hope you realize that I don't think you are 'blah'. In fact, despite my trying, I have been hard-pressed to find anything 'blah' about you. So you should know that when I say you look perfect, I mean it."

Krista does not turn toward me or even mumble a rebuttal. She only lets out a long breath and rolls her turn. She does not watch it but we both know it will be another strike.

As she starts toward me in the settee, she smiles at me, "I know I said it before but I really wish I could do that."

Unsure of what she means, I shrug, "Do what?"

Krista spins a chair around so that the back is facing me. She sits straddling chair across from me, folding her arms across the back of the chair as she continues, "Say whatever you want. I'm too afraid of what people might say or think, to be so open."

I laugh lightly to myself. I have not needed to worry about what people might do or say in centuries. I suppose that is why I do not feel the need to hold my tongue very often. But she is wrong if she mistakes forwardness for honesty.

"Most people aren't worth fearing," I tell her simply.

Krista lays her chin on her arms, "I imagine it makes you feel very free."

"Sometimes," I say simply.

More often my unbridled compulsion to say exactly what I think tends to cause me more trouble than it is worth. But it is better not to explain that it is not just a simple lack of restraint with my words but also a simple lack of judgment that allows me to speak so freely. I blame my knowledge of death and the pain I can inflict for my impulsions and lack of empathy on how my words might affect another person. However, there is little freedom found in causing others pain.

I walk up to the return and pick up my ball as Krista asks, playfully, "So you tried to find something 'blah' about me, huh?"

My eyes dart briefly as my mind recalls my exact words. I had not realized that she caught that but still I smile at her as I respond, "Initially."

My ball rolls down the lane. It only clips one pin causing it to fall, when I speak again, "It did not take long to find that it was a futile effort."

It also did not take long to realize that persuading her father to let me date her would also be a futile effort. However, Mitchell had mentioned that I had her father fooled into believing I was a decent person so my enthrallment must have stuck. Hopefully, I can use his misplaced trust in me to my advantage when they discover what I am.

Okay, here goes. Time to finalize my plan.

"Tell you what, let's make this interesting?" I ask her.

She raises her eyebrows, intrigued.

"If I can knock down even half of those pins, I get to take you on another date. And who knows, maybe on our next date you'll be comfortable enough to say whatever you want to, with me."

She smiles widely, "And if you lose?"

I shrug. I am not concerned over the possibility of losing because it is simply not a possibility.

I grin, "I'm going to try my best not to." Shrugging, I add, "Besides, I'd very much like to know what goes on in your mind."

"Trust me, you don't want to know what's in my mind," she says quietly.

I watch her as she leans back, holding the back of the chair with her hands and sighs with fake sadness.

"There's a lot of Spice Girls' songs in there," she says with sarcastic disappointment.

I laugh to myself and nod, "That *is* shameful."

She giggles.

I can see her mull over my bet. Biting her lip for a moment, she finally answers, "Deal. You knock down half those and you'll get your second date."

That is all I needed to hear. Smiling to myself, I do not hold back. I approach, release, and follow-through smoother than any human can. With power and precision, the ball slams into the pins and I watch as the every last one falls.

I look back at her dropped jaw and wide eyes in amusement. Walking over to her, I sarcastically joke, "Wow, you're a really great teacher."

As I sit down next to her, she glances at me playfully and asks, "Did you just hustle me?"

Smiling like a kid that stole a cookie and got away with it, I answer, "Yes, I did."

She tosses a handful of popcorn at my face. "My boyfriend, the con-artist," she adds, giggling to herself but she has no idea how right she is.

My cheeks redden, warming the tips of my ears. And I smile to myself. Not because I tricked her. Not because she is right to call me a con-artist. No, I smile because of the other name she called me: *boyfriend*.

The night passes much too quickly for me. We stay until they close then I drive a little slower than usual, in a desperate attempt to prolong our night. Despite the slower speed, the car is moving fast enough for Krista to raise her arms, feeling the breeze flow through her fingers.

The way her eyes hold the moonlight makes it hard to focus on watching the road before me.

We drive further from the street lights and into the darkness of the night. The clouds hide the moon from us concealing the winding of the road in the inky black night.

I suppose if either of us were human, it would be difficult to see our surroundings and the lack of light would spark fears from our child-hoods. Some of those fears are justified even if not many humans realize it but for me, darkness is home. It is all I have known for close to six hundred years now.

She looks at me with a smile in her eyes and my heart races because I know that smile is for me *and* it is because of me. I can feel the warmth radiate from her and it is more pleasing than a thousand days in the sun.

Just as my lopsided grin begins to spread, we enter a curve much like the ones before it. This time, however, there is a fiery object ahead of us. It all happens within a brief, few seconds, but I recognize the bright red is hair. Casiana is standing in the road before us and I will not be slowing down for her. Krista misinterprets my hesitation to react as normal delayed reflexes of an average human and I feel the heat of her hand on mine.

The steer wheels jerks from my grip as the tires scream at the sudden change in direction. Krista's hands hit the dash, instinctually bracing herself.

The metal frame moans deeply as it protests the impact of my car door twisting around a nearby tree. It feels as though my upper arm explodes just beneath the skin. The momentum tosses the car which continues over the embankment.

Glass dances in the air as we roll down the hill. The fragments slice across my face as the roof of my car collapses more with each tumble. Through the unnerving sound of twisting metal, I hear Krista's scream pierce through the chaos and grow more distant as she is thrown into the trees.

My car slams into a tree, stopping our progression down the hill abruptly and I feel my neck snap.

*   *   *

Something warm streams down my arm as my eyes fight my attempt to open them. A hollow tapping sound is the only thing I hear as the pain begins rolling in. Stabbing and immense, it makes it challenging to breathe but when I do, I can smell gasoline and the heat from the metal frame being reshaped as we rolled down the hill.

The air sears my lungs as I force my eyes open but my sight is a blur of the colors and shapes of the unrecognizable cab. It takes me a moment to realize that I am upside down and it is my blood creating the tapping that I hear above the ringing in my ears.

"Kris-," I attempt to say but the haze clouding my thoughts makes it difficult to push the words in my mind out through my mouth.

Searching for my seat belt release, my hand rolls over the roughness of my shirt. Only when I feel a sharp slice in my palm do I comprehend that the grainy, rough texture of my shirt is the remnants of my windshield clinging to my clothes.

I find the buckle and press the release but my body does not fall like I anticipated, instead I continue to hang upside down. With my vision and thoughts clearing slightly, I see the dash pinning my legs to the seat. As I grab the steering wheel and begin to bend the metal away from me, I hear screaming in the distance. The type of screams I usually inflict, piercing ones that are full of pain and fear.

I shove the dash off of my legs and I drop onto the roof of my car, landing on the shattered bones in my shoulder. The pain makes me cry out but only briefly as I try to stifle my own agony and focus on the screaming in the distance.

"Krista," I call out but my voice is still weak.

Wiping the blood away from my eyes in an attempt to clear my vision, I crawl out of the busted passenger side window. I stagger a few steps before I fall against a tree.

"Krista?"

The only reply I receive is a blend of animal growls and human crying. With every bit of my body begging me to rest, I push myself off of the tree and start toward her moaning once more.

"Krista!" I yell, holding onto my side to keep my ribs from shifting with my shout. As I stumble through the indiscernible foliage, I can feel my ribs moving under my hand but I do not slow my pace.

"Stop, Nick! Don't come any closer!" Krista says between tears.

I hear her words but continue toward her voice.

"Please just get help. If I turn, I could kill y-,"

Her words are cut off abruptly which worries me much more than the idea of her becoming her wolf and attacking me.

My surroundings begin to make sense as my vision clears enough for me to see Krista lying on the ground about thirty feet from me and standing behind her is Casiana.

Krista's breathing is fast but steady. Panting, her eyes hazed over in a white fog as Casiana keeps her bare foot on Krista's cheek. I know what she is doing. Casiana has done that same enthrallment to me. A knot forms in my stomach. I long to push off of the tree supporting me and kill Casiana where she stands, smiling darkly at me, but my body does not will it.

I start toward them slowly but only manage one step before Casiana waves her finger at me, "Ah, ah, ah. We both know that I am not above crushing her skull with my foot."

I reach back toward the tree to steady myself. The ringing in my ears has all but subsided and I can tell that I am already beginning to heal. However, I am still in no condition to take on Casiana or even clear the distance between us before she could kill Krista.

"Please, don't hurt her, Cass." My voice is weaker than I want it to be. However, it would not have mattered anyway. I am sure that Casiana did not need my voice to crack to realize the advantages over me that she has in this moment.

Casiana smiles at my vulnerability. "Well then, I have good news and bad news. Good news: whether or not this mutt lives is up to you."

"And the bad?" I ask, adding pressure to keep my rib in place while it attempts to scab together.

She shrugs, "Well, I may need more from you than I originally said."

"You could have just asked."

"You would have said no. No, this,"-she taps her foot on Krista's cheek-"this is more motivating."

With my head and neck still pounding, I grow tired of her games. Krista still needs help and the labyrinth that Casiana creates when speaking is wasting precious time. "What do you want from me?"

"Just one little promise," she smiles coldly at some hidden meaning behind her words. "All I need is for you to promise that when the time comes, you will give me what I desire most."

"Which is?"

She throws her hands up, "To be determined."

Too vague. There is a trap in her elusiveness. "No."

The smile on her face faded into a look of animosity. Keeping her eyes locked on mine, Casiana leans forward, adding pressure to Krista's skull.

Krista groans with the added compression of Casiana's foot.

"Wait, wait, wait," I blurt out, stepping toward her.

She raises her eyebrow but otherwise does not move.

"Please, wait." I drop my eyes as I continue, "You can have it. Whatever you want. It's yours."

Casiana eases her pressure on Krista, "You swear it?"

Knowing it is a mistake, I meet her eyes anyway, "I swear."

She removes the pressure from Krista but keeps her foot on her cheek, keeping Krista in her enthrallment. Casiana smiles widely, "You see. I knew you could be cooperative."

She looks down Krista, "This pooch will need to turn before she loses too much blood. Be sure she doesn't kill you."

Then without any more delay, Casiana lifts her foot and with it, her enthrallment on Krista.

Krista gasps for air as the sudden rush of pain becomes a reality once more. I hurry to her as Casiana disappears into the trees. My only comfort is knowing that the enthrallment Casiana had Krista under is pleasant enough that Krista does not realize how long she has been bleeding and lying on the cold ground.

"Just go. Get help," The tears roll down her face as I drop to my knees next to her, "I don't want to hurt you."

The wolf inside her growls deep inside her chest as she fights it back. I look over her blood speckled body, analyzing her injuries. From the outside, she does not look too bad. Definitely a broken femur and dislocated shoulder but that is not what worries me. The heavy scent of blood indicates something internal.

I brush her hair from her face, pulling it from the drying blood on her busted lip and tell her calmly, "Krista, I'm going to set your leg."

"No. Nick, you can't. It's too much. I'll turn."

I know she will. And I know she needs to. And yes, I could die because of it. I know that too. Especially in my weakened state, her werewolf could kill me. But this is not just any wolf. This is Krista. Either she turns and I am at risk of dying or she does not turn and she will be at risk of bleeding to death internally.

"It has to be set now or it won't heal correctly and it will have to be re-broken later."

I slide one hand to her knee.

"Please, don't," she protests through her tears

My fingers stroke her forehead, "It's okay. I trust you." That is not entirely true. I do trust her, but only while she is in control of her wolf. Turning against her will, her wolf will act of survival instincts alone. Heal the body. Stop the bleeding. Kill the threat. I do trust her. I do not fully trust her wolf.

I place my other hand on top of her upper leg and press my lips to her forehead, smearing her blood with my kiss.

"Please," Krista says quietly.

With a one quick motion, I pull and twist her leg. Her bone fragments grind as I press down on her femur, pushing it into place.

Her sharp scream changes from a high pitch, pain-filled shrill to a deep, husky anger and I feel claws slice through my cheek. Jumping back, I watch her roll onto her hands and knees. She shakes like a dog drying itself, growling as her bones snap. Her clothes stretch and rip, trying to accommodate her changing body. White fur spreads over her while her face elongates and twists into the familiar predator she contains. Sharp teeth protrude over her lips and she closes her eyes tightly as the pain settles in.

It would not hurt if she were not fighting it. Her struggle is in vain though as her body takes her wolf shape and the growling stops. Her heavy breaths fog the air around her and the night grows much too quiet. It is as though the whole forest can feel her instinctual savagery that is reserved for vampires and is waiting like vultures for blood to spill over the leaves.

Instincts will tell her, that as a vampire, I am a threat. If I run, it will only spark her animal nature and compel her to chase me down. What little control she may have will disappear in a flash. I could outrun her but somewhere inside her, she is bleeding. Running at full speed could rip her injuries worse. She could bleed out before she even clears the trees. My freedom is not worth that risk.

No. I need her to stay calm. I need *me* to be calm, to think cautiously, and be smart.

She shakes her head wildly, whimpering, as though her head is hurting. Perhaps, she was focusing too much on preventing her phase that she had not noticed the pain sooner.

Without thinking about my actions, I step closer with my hand outreached to help her. Her eyes flash open. Bright blue, they are enchanting. So enchanting that if she did not lower her head as she gave me a low growl, I would have forgotten the dangers altogether. But her head is lowered and she is growling.

"Easy Krista," I whisper. "It's just me. Nick. Remember?"

Her eyes tighten but not from hate. She is in pain. Whining, she shakes her head once more. Her breaths grow labored and I begin to hope that she will pass out soon so I can run for help.

She looks up at me for only a second before her eyes close and she collapses. On the ground, her body shifts again. She is naked but, more importantly, she is human.

I rush to her, pulling my jacket off quickly to cover her body as best as I can. Hearing her heartbeat's steady rhythm, I scoop my arms under her. Just as I am about to stand, she moans slightly and opens her eyes. Her fingers brush over my cheek where her claws had sliced my face but the cuts have already healed.

As she smears the blood where the cuts should be, her eyebrows come together, confused. Weakly, she mutters, "What are you?" Her hand drops and her head falls against my chest as she passes out.

She was not in her wolf form long but hopefully it was enough. As long as her wolf was able to heal enough of the internal bleeding, it will be better that she is asleep. Her body will continue its healing faster if she is not distressed by pain. Besides, how would I answer her question? A vampire? Your enemy? Or, simply: a liar?

Eventually, I will have to address it. Soon she will awake and ask me again. I will have to tell her the truth but I am not sure how. The only thing I do know is that I do not want to think about that right now.

Picking her up, I hear my arm crunching inside as my busted shoulder begs me not to lift her. I disregard the pain and weigh my options. The forest would be faster because I could run at full tilt without any humans observing me. However, I could come across werewolves in the forest and the last thing I want is for them to discover my secret while I am carrying a bloody, unconscious, not to mention, naked werewolf. Still, I am not sure where Krista is bleeding from or how profuse it is so the forest it is.

I run as fast as my legs can move, attempting to ignore the way my shoulder stabs into me with every step. Instead, I focus on her heartbeat. Listening to the steady, even beats, keeps me moving through the trees despite my own pain.

As I near the edge of the tree line, I slow to a more human pace. I do not have to follow the road for long before I reach the gates to her community.

The security guard nearly spills his coffee down the front of his chest as he hops up to help me. I am not sure how bad we look but I am sure this is the first time his job has ever been remotely interesting or vital.

He grabs the radio. "I need Bryant at the gate. It's Krista."

Needing to seem as human as possible, I drop to my knees as though the pain and exhaustion from carrying her such a distance are wearing on me. I lie her on the ground gently as the guard reaches us.

"What happened?" Larry asks.

I look up at him but all I can think of is Krista. I had been so consumed with worry that I have not thought of what explanation I am going to give. All that manages to exit my mouth is mumbling, "There was a wreck."

Closing my eyes, I focus on my words but just as I am about to speak, Bryant and Warren rush through the gate.

Bryant's eyes widen and he stops at the gate when he sees us. Worry and pain flood his eyes. I look down at my shirt, smeared with blood and dirt from the accident. Most of the blood is mine but he will not see my injuries. My external wounds have long since healed. All he sees is his daughter lying naked on the cold ground, sprinkled with blood. It does not matter whose it is.

Warren senses Bryant's pain too and steps past him, kneeling down next to us. He does not open the jacket completely to assess her. Instead, Warren opens it only slightly and scans her body, then covers her once more. He reaches inside the jacket, moving his hands along her ribs.

"It was an accident." But it wasn't. Casiana meant to stop us in the forest. By any means necessary. "I think she has some internal bleeding...," my voice breaks off.

Warren does not look at me but is not looking at Krista either. His eyes are distant, focusing on what his hands feel instead of what his eyes might see.

"It's okay. You brought her here and that's the best thing you could have done," Warren says, pressing his fingers purposely along her abdomen.

"We'll take it from here," Bryant dismisses me as he kneels down next to Krista. "What do you think Warren?"

"I haven't checked her eyes but I suspect some mild hemorrhaging. Most likely from the frontal lobe. There's some bleeding around the spleen but it's stopped. Bones are already healing. Nothing too concerning." Looking at me, he adds, "She's going to be fine."

Mitchell rushes through the gate with his jaw clenched in anger.

"You," he says accusingly, pointing his finger at me as he stomps toward me. "I knew it was a mistake to leave her with you."

Grabbing my shirt, he shoves my back against the cold stone wall causing my eyes to change to black instinctually.

I turn my head and close my eyes quickly, hoping nobody noticed my natural defenses take over me.

Mitchell does not seem to have seen my eyes because he leans only inches from my face. I can feel his breath on my cheek as he adds through gritted teeth, "What exactly happened out there?"

Bryant grabs his wrist gently, "Stand down."

Mitchell only glares at me as he tells Bryant. "You can't be serious. I don't know what happened but I know it was his fault. And I know Krista wouldn't be lying there if it weren't for him."

He is right. This is my fault. If I were not a vampire, Casiana would have no interest in me and Krista would be safe at home instead of lying on the cold pavement.

"I said, stand down," Bryant says coolly. "That's an order."

Exasperatedly, Mitchell shoves me back again as he lets go of my shirt. "Not even a scratch on him and I'm supposed to believe it was a car wreck," Mitchell mutters under his breath.

Bryant looks at Mitchell firmly. "Get your wife and meet us at Krista's. We'll have Renee and Simone clean her up and dress her but nobody else needs to know about this right now. Last thing she needs is a bunch of wives cluttering up her room with casseroles and balloons. Got it?"

Mitchell is not any calmer but nods anyway. He starts toward the gate but Bryant does not wait until he is completely out of range of overhearing before he tells me, "Ignore him. He's just letting off some steam because it's his sister."

But Mitchell is not simply letting off steam. True, he does not like me and his reaction could be viewed as a gross overreaction to a mere human who was simply in a standard car accident. But Mitchell does not believe me to be a mere human. He knows something is different. What he does not know is just how right he is or how different I truly am.

Bryant carries Krista's limp body towards the gate. I know that I am not wanted inside but the further he steps away from me the more helpless I feel.

"Mitchell isn't just angry. He's afraid," I say quietly. He is afraid that his sister might be more hurt than he realizes. He is afraid that I am to blame for her injuries and that there is nothing he can do to help her. But mostly, he is afraid that he will not be able to protect her from me if he is right.

Bryant stops and looks back at me. I purposely let vulnerability show in my voice as I continue, "So am I. And if you would allow it, I would very much like to sit with her until she wakes."

I rub my hands together nervously as I add, "Please."

Bryant does not address me. He simply looks at Warren and gives a nod. Then without any other words, Bryant carries Krista through the gates.

Warren watches me curiously but does not utter a word until Bryant disappears. Finally he says, "You, uh, you don't look like you were injured in the wreck at all."

"I wasn't."

"That was very lucky. Not many humans could walk away from that. There's so much blood too... but not even a scratch on you."

"Well, I had my seat belt on," I say dryly.

He nods and mumbles to himself, "Very lucky indeed."

It was not luck that saved me. I broke my neck in that wreck, that alone would have killed any human. But not me; not a vampire.

The way Warren's lips twist and pucker makes me wonder what else he wants to ask. Mitchell's words may not have roused Bryant to question me further, but they certainly did stir Warren's mind. He would have noticed that most of the blood on me smells like my own, yet there are no visible injuries to account for it.

Perhaps he noticed my eyes turn black in that split second; maybe he is trying to make them change again with his piercing stare, or he could even be contemplating whether he saw anything at all. One thing is certain though- if he did see my eyes change, he does not know what it means. Not yet.

Before I can think of a lie, Warren adds, "Stay here. I'll call the police and you can show them where the accident was so they can file a report."

I simply nod.

There is not much else I can do. A human would wait to fill out a police report. I need to appear as human as possible, especially now. Because, whether or not Warren keeps what little he suspects to himself, it will not be long before he knows the truth. Then he will either seek blackmail or death for me.

I cannot kill him. Well, I can but I will not. I promised myself I would not hurt any of Krista's pack if at all possible. However, this might be inevitable. I would have to be very careful, be sure to leave no traces of me or signs that it was a murder at all. Krista could never find out. Consideration would need to be taken to ensure she remains oblivious.

How would I do it? Drowning? I can make that look accidental. It would be easy to stage it to look as though he drove his car off of a bridge, especially on a foggy night. Broken neck? While those do not kill vampires, they certainly stop werewolves effectively. A fall from a high enough cliff could produce a broken neck even without help from me.

Wait. What am I thinking? I cannot entertain the idea of killing Warren. I do not need to constantly worry about *another* lie between Krista and myself. Certainly not a lie more damaging than the one I am already keeping from her. That is it. It is final. I will not kill him. I will simply have let the chips fall where they may. And, hopefully, I can continue to convince myself of that.

"Warren," I call after him as he opens the gates. "I need to see her."

He lingers by the gate for a moment before he concedes, "You can come in after you make the police report and *after* she's dressed."

I smile softly, "Thank you."

He shrugs lightly, "It wasn't my call. You should thank Bryant."

Warren closes the gate behind him and leaves me alone in the cool night. Leaning back, I slide down the stone wall and drape my arms over my knees. It does not matter. Regardless of whether or not Warren knows what he suspects. Krista saw me heal. She knows I am not human and when she wakes up, she will ask me about it again. Only this time, I will have to answer.

There is no lie convincing enough to avoid this any longer. So I will tell her the truth, she will hate me, curse the day we met, and, most likely, leave me forever.

At first, memories of me will bring her anger and disgust but, eventually, the thoughts of me will become less frequent and less painful. Until, at last, my name does not phase her at all and the time we shared is merely a ghost of bad choices she made when she was young.

The hate I can handle. Most people do hate me, or at least they should. Vampires do nothing but cause pain. We slaughter families for fun. Every other word we speak is a lie. We pretend our lies are to protect our secret but that is also a lie. Most of those we lie to do not live long enough to figure out the truth. Lying is simply a convenient way to get what we want. Lying is an art and we have practiced it for centuries. We enjoy the deceit.

How am I to explain that, despite my omissions and lies, my intention was not to trick her into loving me? I was merely being too selfish to consider what keeping her in my life might cost her. How do I explain that I was fully aware of the risks to both of us but pushed them aside simply because I did not want to admit them to myself? How do I tell her these things without losing her?

By the time I hear the police cruiser stop in front of me, I have buried my face in my hands.

I look up when I hear Levi's voice, "Well hell, boy, trying to kill her ain't no way to impress a girl. I thought I taught you better than that."

Smirking, I reply, "You did. I guess just need another crash course."

He reaches over and opens the passenger door, chuckling lightly, "I see what you did there. Hop in and show me where this wreck is."

Standing up, I dust the dirt from my pants and get in the car. "It's just outside of town. You don't have to drive me to it though. Just circle around and drop me back off here if you don't mind."

I had only waited for Levi so he could drive me out of the view of the werewolves, who no doubt are watching me linger outside their walls. A human would wait for the police. A human would have the police drive them home. A human would, which means I needed to do it too; or, at least, I need to make it look that way.

As Levi drives away, he says quietly, "You know when you tell her what you are, you're gonna implicate a whole lot of others too."

I have considered that briefly. Telling Krista that I am a vampire will verify our existence and certainly increase her ability to identify other vampires in a crowd. Even if those vampires are wearing police uniforms.

Levi continues, "I cain't be having those wolves attackin' us."

I nod but say nothing.

"Just sayin', if they's britches get too big, I'm loyal to my own kind first."

I may not always understand Levi's quirky phrases but I do not need him to say anything to understand that if the werewolves attack one of *his* vampires, the entire pack will pay the price for it. Levi will make sure of it.

He clicks his tongue and adds, "Maybe if you were loyal to your own kind, we wouldn't be in this mess right now. Just sayin'."

I sit silently like a child being lectured by a parent. He is not wrong but that does not make him right. Perhaps I should have kept to vampires, stayed away from Krista. But something about her feels more like *'my own kind'* than any vampire ever has.

Exhaling forcefully, Levi changes the subject, "Tell me about this wreck. I still have to write a report tonight."

Even though the topic of conversation is the wreck that nearly killed Krista and would have killed me if I were human, I am relieved to be talking about something else other than how she will most likely dump and hunt me down this very night.

I tell Levi about the accident. I tell him about Casiana, her threat, my promise, and even about my suspicions about Warren knowing too much.

Finally, we park in front of the Lockwood gates again.

"I have to tell her, Levi. She has a right to know. I just hope you can find a way to forgive me for it one day."

I step out of the car, expecting Levi to drive away when I shut the door but instead, he stays parked along the road, staring at his steering wheel. Finally, he rolls the window down. Leaning into the passenger seat, he looks up at me. I can tell from the sorrowful tension in his eyes that what he is about to say feels like a surrender.

"I know what you have to do, Nick. I don't like it but I know. Say what you need to say. I just hope you don't make so big of a mess that I cain't clean it up."

"Thank you," I say quietly. I can tell that conceding to my disclosure of our shared secret which will inevitably put his vampires at risk bothers him more than it should. They can handle themselves, but whether he admits it or not, Levi feels a certain responsibility to them. As though allowing me to tell her, Levi is admitting that my wants are more important than their lives.

"You can thank me for a lot of things, Nicolas, but do not thank me for this," he says solemnly.

He meant for his words to show me the amount of guilt I should feel for risking impending death to another vampire. It did not really matter what he said, though. He only needed one of those words to make me feel culpable. He said 'Nicolas', not Nick, but Nicolas.

The way he uses my name carries disappointment and shame with it the same way a parent uses their child's middle name to express the gravity of a situation.

He leans over again and drives away as the window slides up. As I watch his car slip away into the night, I almost consider not telling Krista. Perhaps she will not remember what she saw. Perhaps we could continue as we have been.

As my hand touches the cold metal of the gates, I sigh but my breath does not take any of the heaviness from my chest. Whether or not she knows yet, she will know by the end of this night. I have to stop making excuses and tell her. I have to expose us as monsters. I have to make her understand that no matter how much I pretend, I will never be human.

I push the gate open and walk quietly to her house. There are not many people out on the sidewalks. With the moon being close to full, I suppose most of the wolves are outside these walls, running freely in the forest. Humans are tired at this time of night and children are all tucked into bed. The streets and houses are dark and quiet which is all the better for me. I have no desire to speak to anyone. I simply wish to sit by Krista in peace and pretend that the truth is not about to ruin everything.

Someone must have told Simone that I would be coming because she is not surprised to see me at her door. She smiles softly at me. Although she means for it to be comforting, her small, simple smile is full of pity for me. I must appear more troubled and guilt-ridden than I realize. However, the guilt I feel is not for the actions Simone assumes they are.

This guilt is not for the wreck that occurred; it is for the honesty that is coming in my confession.

Simone does not say much as she shows me to Krista's room. She does offer some attempt to comfort me by mumbling something in regards to Krista being okay. But I am not paying attention to her words. I already know that Krista will be physically fine. She is a werewolf and her body is already correcting the wrongs of the night. However, Simone cannot understand that I am not concerned with Krista's health. Only her reaction to what I will say.

Krista's room is not quite what I expected to find. The light color of the walls helps to make the small room feel larger but the pile of clothes on the floor detracts from that. Clutter lines the dresser and shoes poke out from under her bed as though the closet does not have enough space to hold them. The room is quite... Well, it's... a mess. Quite a mess.

Simone tries softly, "It's usually a lot cleaner. She's been really busy lately."

I smile at her obvious lie, "It's fine."

"Do you want me to bring you a chair?" she asks.

I do not physically need to sit down. I am much more concerned with having Simone leave us as soon as reasonably possible. So I smile softly and say politely, "No, thank you."

Simone nods and leaves me alone with Krista. I sit on the edge of her bed near her legs and focus on listening to her heavy breathing.

Part of me only wants the distraction to keep me from thinking of the disappointment that will surely be on Krista's face when she awakes and remembers the monster she saw in me tonight.

My lying eyes can hide a lot of things but it cannot hide the darkness inside me. She saw me, not the human I pretend to be, but the vampire that I am. In the morning, she will hate me. In the morning, she will want me dead like the rest of her pack will. In the morning, she will ask me to leave her sight and wish to burn my memories from her mind. Tonight, she could have died and our relationship, my happiness, surely did.

Closing my eyes, I rub my hand over my face but it does not take my angst with it. Even though it has been over an hour since we first rolled over the embankment, the smell of the accident still lingers strong enough for me to pick apart the scents. Krista's blood and my own cling to my clothes but there is something else too. I can smell the stench left by my brakes when I locked them up and burnt rubber that painted the road.

I open my eyes but that does not remove her image from my mind. Her face twisting from pain, streams of blood rolling along her hairline and framing her pale face in crimson. The helpless look in Krista's eyes as she laid on the cold ground fighting her wolf from emerging simply to protect me.

If she had not passed out when she did, there would have been nothing I could do to help her. I could not help her heal any better than I had kept her from getting hurt. If she were human, I would have lost her. There is no 'if' in that statement. She would have died.

We both would have. If we were human, my death would have been quick and painless but she would have suffered a slow torture. She would have felt every pain from every break in her body. She would have been alone and afraid, knowing that those moments were her last. She would have prayed for help but the only mercy she would have received would come hours later when she finally bled out and was released from her agony.

But we are not dead. Because neither of us is human. And it is time that she knows that. My confession will break her heart but that pain cannot be delayed any longer.

It takes a couple of hours for her to begin to stir. But just as I am beginning to wonder if the sun will rise before she does, she opens her eyes and smiles weakly at me.

"Hey," she says quietly.

"Hey," I rub my hand over hers, "How are you feeling?"

"I've been better," she smiles softly.

Sitting up in bed, her eyes dart trying to process the shuffled memories of the night. As she slides toward me, she turns my face toward hers. Her fingers are soft on my cheek as her thumb glides over my skin where her claws had been.

However, she does not seem to recall that. Her touch is gentle as she leans her forehead against mine, "I'm so glad you're not hurt."

She sighs with relief, "What about that woman? Is she okay?"

That woman. The one who threatened to kill Krista after she caused the accident and all this pain. Casiana. I wish she were dead. I wish I had hit her with the car, got out, and finished her once and for all.

"She's fine."

I take Krista's hand and shift on the bed to better face her, "Krista, I need to tell you something important. What exactly do you remember about tonight?"

Krista shrugs lightly, "Um, we went bowling. I won," she smirks before she continues.

"Um, we wrecked. There was a woman in the road. I grabbed the wheel and then I just remember tumbling over and over and over. Like being in a washing machine."

Her eyes grow large. For a moment, I believe she remembers my face healing before her eyes. But her words indicate something else entirely, "Why? What happened? Did I turn?"

She does not remember seeing me heal as a vampire does. I could continue this lie. It would be easy.

But no. I am telling her. She should know why she almost died.

I shake my head to clear my head.

"Listen, there's something you need to know about me. I'm not exactly who you think I am," I begin. "And I want you to know how sorry I am that I didn't tell you. I just... I didn't want to lose you so soon."

I shift on the bed but it does not make my confession easier. "That woman on the road. Her name is Casiana. And she was there because of me."

Krista pulls her hands from mine gently as her eyebrows come together, trying to make sense of my words.

"She is willing to go through you to get to me because of what I am." I take a breath but it does not prepare me. My mouth grows suddenly very dry. My lips begin to feel numb, making it harder to form the words, "Krista, I'm a va-," The words freeze on my tongue. Clearing my ever-drying throat, I try again, "I'm a vampire."

Once the words are out it becomes easier to say, so I do. I say it again. This time with more confirmation, "I am a vampire, Krista. An actual vampire."

Krista's face stops my confession. She purses her lips and rolls her eyes. Her eyebrow raises in disbelief as she crosses her arms over her chest, "I don't understand what this is."

What? It is the truth and she does not believe it.

Krista shrugs, "What? Is this Casiatina-chick, like your wife or something?"

Is this seriously happening? This is not where I thought this conversation would go. "Casiana and no. She's another vampire and she almost killed you tonight trying to get to me."

"Oh, well, I'm sorry I got in her way," Krista says sarcastically.

I cannot believe she is refusing to believe one of the most completely honest things I have said to her. "Krista, I am a vampire," I say matter-of-factly.

Her lips press into a thin line. "You know what I think this is? I think I got hurt and I turned and it freaked you out."

I shake my head but she continues anyway, "The least you could do is be man enough to tell me that. Not make up a bunch of bullshit just to get you off the hook."

Bullshit? My voice carries more annoyance than I intend it to but I manage to keep my British accent from appearing, "I wish I were lying. I don't know how to make you understand that this is real. I am a vampire. I murder people. I drink their blood. And I enjoy it. I'm not married and I am not afraid of your wolf," I chuckle lightly at that last line.

"I wish that were the case. I wish I was just some timid, little human that was making up lies because I was too embarrassed to say that I peed my pants when I saw a wolf rip out of my girlfriend's body. But I'm not. I'm not human. I'm not afraid of dating a werewolf. And I am *not* lying."

I turn to face the edge of the bed again and put my head in my hands. I should not have let my frustration in her disbelief show in my voice. I should not have gotten so defensive about lying, especially not when I choose to lie so often.

Forcefully exhaling, I attempt to blow away my irritation. "I'm sorry," I say quietly. "I shouldn't have..." I let my words trail off. Shouldn't have what? Gotten so defensive? Or shouldn't have told her what I am at all? In this moment, I am not sure which I regret more so I say nothing.

I look over at her expecting anger or sadness. But her face is blank and emotionless.

"Prove it," she says bluntly.

Krista reaches her arm toward me, "Bite me. Drink my blood."

I push her arm away, "No."

"Why not?" She crosses her arms once more over her chest, "Where's your fangs? Where's your Transylvanian accent? If you're a vampire, then why can't you prove it?"

I can prove it. I can show her my black eyes. My fangs and claws. But I have never wanted her to see me that way. Never intended for her to see the monster I can be.

"I can show you," I say quietly, "But please don't ask me to." I rub my hands together uncomfortably, "There are some things you cannot unsee," I tell her vulnerably.

There are some things she would never forget. Like looking into the eyes of a predator. Every time she looks at me in the future, that darkness would always be there, in the back of her mind, constantly tainting her view of me.

She looks at me expressionless, "And there are some things I refuse to believe without seeing."

I do not want to show her my true self but looking at her, I under-stand that I must. She will not believe me otherwise. Regardless of whether she is simply used to her wolf being the reason for breakups or she is subconsciously hoping this is a lie, she is refusing to accept this without proof.

"Okay," I concede, "Just... please don't scream." The last thing I want is to alert her pack that a vampire is sitting on her bed.

I close my eyes focusing on controlling exactly what she will see. My black eyes I am willing to show her now. Should she ever forgive me for being a vampire, I would not want to frighten her with my eyes when they do appear in the future.

My fangs descend from my gums and press against my lips. Fangs, I must allow her to see. But I do not let my voice grow empty or my nails to extend. She does not need to see that my fingernails become the talons of a creature you might envision crawling out from under your bed as a child. I am not the boogeyman. I am vampire. But that does not mean I need to look as frightening as possible to simply prove myself to Krista.

I can hear her breath quicken. She does not need to see my eyes or my fangs. She can already sense the difference. The change in the air urges her wolf to be on alert to the potential danger.

Despite the apprehension she already feels, she somehow is not expecting what she sees. When I open my eyes, she gasps and her eyes widen. Covering her mouth with her hand, she instinctually slides away from me.

"Please, don't be afraid. I won't hurt you," I try.

But it is not fear that causes her eyes to water and her lip to tremble. I let my fangs recede and my eyes become their usual soft green but still her eyes lock onto the bedspread, refusing to look at me directly.

"Get out," she whispers with a shaking voice.

"Please," I reach for her but she reflexively pulls it away. The simple action hurts me more than she realizes. I knew she would most likely hate me for being a vampire. Hate that I hid it from her. Hate the lying murderer before her now. But somehow despite the odds, I had still hoped she would look past it. Forgive me. Continue to love me as much as I need her to.

The dryness in my throat is suddenly unbearable, worse than the flames of hunger ever have been before. I swallow hard but it does nothing to dislodge the lump forming.

Krista pulls her knees up to her chest. Crossing her arms over her knees, she buries her mouth in her arms to hide the quiver of her bottom lip.

Her voice falters as she says, "Please, Nick. Just go."

A tear betrays her and rolls down her cheek despite her fighting it. "Please," she says feebly between shaky breaths. "I can't process this right now. I need you to go."

I should have told her sooner. I hid what I am from her simply because she would not like the truth. Not telling her was a betrayal that is scrawled on her face now. Her eyebrows pull tight, trying to hold back the pain I have caused.

I should have told her before she invested too much of her heart in mine, let her make a decision while she could instead of hoping that I could wait long enough that her only option would be to keep me anyway.

I was a fool to allow myself to continue to lie to her for my own selfish reasons. Now I may have to pay for that sin. I may have to spend every moment of every day dying inside because I put this pain, this horrible betrayal, between us. It may prove to be a hurdle too big for her to move past.

Once I walk out that door, I may never be able to touch her again. May never hear her laugh. My eyes may have to accept what my heart never will as I watch someone else, someone more deserving, hold her day after day. I will have to watch as she replaces the damages I have caused with the healing another man can bring her. Watch as she creates new memories and a whole new life without me.

My memories of her, of us, will always remain. There is no more worthy person waiting for me. Krista will always be the best part of me, even if she is with someone else. Every day there will be some small thing that stirs a memory of her. And it is the good memories that make the bad ones hurt so much more.

So without any added hesitation, I do the least selfish thing I have done since I met her. I stand up and walk to the door.

As my hand lingers on the doorknob, I look back at her even though she is staring at the bedspread. "I wish I could be something different for you. I really wish I could." Taking a deep breath, I add quietly, "There is no possible way you will ever understand just how sorry I really am."

I look at the doorknob and add weakly, "Goodnight, Krista." It would have been more honest to say, 'goodbye', but my mouth refuses to say it aloud.

I close the door behind me as I step out. No sooner than the door latches, I hear her exhale sharply. I had not realized that she had been holding her breath. Her sobbing is muffled as she cries into something. Possibly her arms, or possibly a pillow. Either way, her crying makes it nearly impossible for me to continue walking away. Everything in my body tells me to go back to her. Console her. Hold her while her heart breaks. I owe her that much.

The next steps I take feel as though my feet are cemented into the carpet. Unwilling to budge, I force my feet to move forward despite the way my body fights me.

I make my way down the hallway in more of a daze than any predator should ever allow themselves to be in. As I start to open the front door, Simone's voice pulls me back into reality, "Are you okay?" she asks.

I look in the direction of Krista's room. How do I answer such a simple question? I am anything but okay. But there is little I can tell this empathic human.

I force a slight smile at Simone, "Krista's awake. She's fine. I'm going to go so she can rest."

As I reach for the door, I feel her hand on my arm. She waits for me to look at her and see the concern in her eyes before she continues, "That's not what I asked."

Her concern is warming and it makes me smile softly at her. However, it also causes my throat to burn with hunger. Killing someone will make me feel better but it certainly will not help the situation.

However, it is the one thing I know how to do well. The rush of her adrenaline pouring to my throat would be a beautiful distraction. A temporary hiatus from facing the memories of watching Krista crumble at my confession.

Still. She is Krista's best friend, and Krista has felt enough of the pain being with me can cause. At least, this is enough for one night.

Shrugging lightly, I tell her the only honest answer I have, "It's been a long night."

She nods and I slip out before she can ask me anything else and before I can change my mind about using her blood to cool my pain.

Chapter 7

It is said that werewolves use to hunt humans too, but that was long ago, before my time. Whether that is true or not, the werewolves of today have all but forgotten that there may have been a time when they did not protect the humans. Legends say that wolves and vampires worked together to keep the human population from rising too quickly. But seemingly overnight, something changed, werewolves grew a conscience and vampires were cast aside as black sheep.

I doubt this. Legends such as that are mere constructs to help us degrade the reputation of another to justify our own crimes.

I believe we were always enemies. The smell of a werewolf to a vampire, and vice versa, has always been repugnant. I believe it is a deterrent nature put in place to ensure the separation of our worlds. Werewolves do not entertain vampires and vampires do not show werewolves mercy. Their blood does not taste as sweet as a human's but killing them is just as satisfying. I should know. I have rarely shown mercy to werewolves. Only in more recent years have I even begun to show some form of restraint in killing them.

Something is different. Something has changed; whether it is with them or in me, I do not know. Their scent does not repulse me the way it should. It is not pleasing but it does not push me away like it used to either.

Mostly, I think my hesitation of killing werewolves is simply my friendship with Tara. I am the only vampire I know of that has kept a werewolf for a friend. And while she does overlook my murderous actions, she does not excuse them.

Looking back, I should have held some bit of resistance to pursuing Krista. My mere friendship with a werewolf has always been looked down on. Dating a werewolf is a blasphemy that I should have never attempted. No matter how drawn to her I am, I should have been able to walk the other way. For both us. And I still cannot.

Regardless of our history, vampires and werewolves are definitely adversaries now. Stalked and persecuted, battered and berated, these are the constants I receive from werewolves and, now that she knows what I am, they will be the constants I receive from Krista as well.

She may hate me for the rest of her life. She may push me away but I will only go out of sight. She will not see me any time she does not want to, but I will see her. It may be wrong to stalk her, but I need to be there in case she ever finds a way to forgive me. Forgive what I am. Forgive the murder and deceit that come with being a vampire. I have to be there because her amnesty will be brief, and it is imperative that I do not miss the window of my pardon.

It took me five centuries to move past losing my first love, Ann. Death stole her from me by the hands of my maker and, like a cruel joke, left me writhing in an alley and praying to join her. The first two hundred years were merely a blur of blood and death as I tried to mask the pain temporarily. The monster inside consumed me and it changed me forever.

Yet, just as Ann's death changed me then, Krista's life has changed me once more. She made me vulnerable. Made me remember who I had once been, corrected some of the wrongs that I had allowed myself to become. To have that stripped away again will undoubtedly leave me worse than ever before. I lost my Ann becoming what I am. Now I might lose Krista *because* of what I am.

For centuries I have carried the last remaining bit of humanity in me. Used it to keep my cravings and lust in check. Loving Krista, I let her see that bit of humanity. When she leaves, she will take it with her and I will be alone with my hunger. Truly alone with it for the first time in my existence. Nothing will stand between my monster and my actions. Nothing. And that frightens me.

But there is something standing between my monster and the soothing promise of my next meal. It is silence. Mind-numbing, all-encompassing, silence. I wait patiently but there have been no cars on this desolate road. There has been plenty of time to contemplate that killing some pathetic human will not help me win Krista back but it will help alleviate my pain in some small way.

I have sat still on the edge of this gravel road long enough for the dew to settle around me. Yet I remain unmoving, like a cougar waiting for prey to emerge from a den until I hear the sound I have been longing for.

In the distance, the gravel crunches under the weight of a van. Standing up, I move to the tree whose roots have previously given way and had fallen over. My plan is simple. Murder does not need to be complicated. Sometimes the most effortless meals are the most satisfying.

As the van nears, I lift the tree upright and let my eyes glaze to black. My fangs press against my lips as my hunger anticipates the pending kill. The van rounds the corner, unsuspecting of what awaits them. As it approaches the correct position, I slam the tree down in front of their path.

The brakes lock up but it has little effect in the loose gravel. The van skids and slides for a split second before it kicks sideways and slams the passenger side into the tree. The metal bends and groans with the impact. I hear the airbags explode as I rush toward the collision.

Flinging the driver door open, I pull the dazed woman from her seat, snapping the seat belts that were meant to protect her. I slam her body against the van with enough force to leave the shape of her body indented into the metal.

My fangs pierce her neck before she can make sense of the situation. The warmth of her blood floods my mouth. Its sweetness pacifies my pain and begins filling a void that was otherwise only being consumed by self-pity.

The smell of the crash lingers strong but I can still pick apart the scents. The dust hangs in the air from sliding through the gravel. The burning scent of the grinding of brakes. The fearful adrenaline rushing through this woman as she pushes against me. The light perfume of another whimpering human still inside the van.

Looking into the passenger seat, I see the wide tearful eyes of a young girl. Her braces catch the moonlight as she lets out a shrill scream. Over the woman's shoulder, I watch her frantic teenage daughter try to open the passenger door that is pinned against the tree.

The girl watches my black eyes as her mother's blood rolls down her spine. With trembling hands, she begins rolling down the passenger window to attempt an escape. I do not take my eyes from the girl. It is not that I believe she might slip away from me. No, she would not get far. Instead, it is merely that my hollow glare drives her fear further. And her terror only adds to the gratification of a well-consumed meal.

The woman in my hands grows cold and her body begins to slump into me instead of pushing away. Despite there being a little life left in her, I toss her body over the embankment like unwanted litter.

Crying uncontrollably, her daughter attempts to evade me and begins crawling out of the window. I let most of her body exit through the window and allow her to believe for a brief moment that she might actually be able to avoid the death awaiting her.

Leaning over the seats, I grab her by the ankle and pull her toward me abruptly. Her face smacks the window seal forcefully as I jerk her back into the van. The impact busts the skin on her chin and forces her braces to rip through her bottom lip. The deep lacerations leave a trail of blood across the seats as I pull her body out of the driver's side door.

Grabbing her by the throat, I pin her against the van. The indention of her mother's body surrounds her as she tries desperately to pry my hand from her throat. Her feet scrape at the ground wildly while tears stream down her cheeks.

She mouths the word, *'please'*, but no sound escapes through my grip. As she mouths it again, I can see that the impact of her face on the van window broke her braces loose and chipped her bottom teeth as they crashed into the metal wires. The loose flesh of her lip quivers over the untamed wire.

Leaning close to her face, I inhale deeply, lavishing in the heavy scent of panic sweeping across her.

I bring my lips close to her ear as I whisper, "I'll make this quick." And without further delay, I sink my fangs into her neck.

*　　*　　*

I walk down the road, listening to the tiny rocks along the edge crunch under my shoes. The sound calms me but it cannot occupy my thoughts away from the uncertainty that hung in Krista's eyes. My mind is elsewhere, causing me to pay little attention to the mist and dew as it clings to my cheeks, making my skin clammy and slick.

As I start down my driveway, I can feel someone watching me in the shadows of the tree line. I know the person that I sense. I felt her eyes most of the way home but I had hoped she would leave without approaching me. However, that does not seem to be the case.

I stop near the bottom of my porch steps and without waiting for her to make her entrance, I smirk, "Casiana has you on babysitting duty now, how quaint."

Mila emerges from the darkness. Her smile is soft but I can tell by the hardness of her eyes that she did not appreciate my satire.

"Rough night, I take it," she says as she walks to me.

No part of me is in the mood to listen to her tripe tonight. "Goodnight, Mila. Thank you for walking me home."

I turn to go up the steps to my house when I hear the condescending tone in her Russian accent, "How is your wolf?" she asks, stopping me on the bottom step.

"You leave her out of this," I look over at her sharply, "Your boss could have killed her tonight. And if she had, we would be having an entirely different conversation."

Her eyes tighten but her smile remains, "Now Nicolas, watch your tone. I did try to warn you."

Mila lets out a long, forceful exhale, "I told you Casiana will stop at nothing to get what she wants. Resisting her wishes will only cause you more trouble," she says frankly, yet softly.

She steps onto the bottom step to be level with me before she adds, "I do happen to be the only friend you have in the Genesis, Nicolas. And I happen to have some pull with Cass, so you would be wise not to forget that. As long as you are helping us, I *might* be able to convince Cass to stop attacking your girlfriend."

My eyes drift towards the wooden planks of the porch. Krista is not my girlfriend. Not anymore. I am no longer sure if I will ever see her again. Being a vampire is not something a human can often accept, let alone a werewolf. Krista may very well choose to continue her life without me in it.

Mila's eyes roll over my face, searching. Then, with a little sigh, she says quietly, "You carry so much pain with you." She cradles my cheek in the palm of her hand, "I am truly sorry for the role you must play. But it really must be you."

Her hand feels warm against my skin. It offers minimum comfort for the turmoil of the turbulent night I have endured thus far.

I have done nothing to the Genesis, yet they follow me, they enthrall me, they poke and prod. They even tried to kill my Krista. And for what?

However before I can ask this, the door swings open and Marcella steps out with a wild look in her eyes. "Get your hands off of him," she says with venom in her voice.

Mila drops her hand but only smirks at her, "Marcella, so nice to see you again. It has been too long."

Marcella stands cold and rigid, "Not long enough from where I'm standing."

Mila scowls as she walks to Marcella with intention but Marcella does not budge. She is not intimidated and this is not a fight she would refuse.

"It does not have to be this way, Marcella. We do not hate you. We are simply taking back what you stole from us. And with a little cooperation, I'm sure we could forgive you for those transgressions. No harm, no foul."

Mila leans closer to her, "Think of it, you and me, friends once more. Think of all the havoc we could cause together."

Marcella's hard edge softens and she swallows hard. It is clear that she knows Mila extremely well and that she has hidden this from me purposely. It is also clear that a deep part of Marcella both desperately misses and dreadfully regrets whatever time they had together.

Marcella stands firm and says curtly, "Lilith is a friend to no one."

"You have not changed. Not even after all this time." A slow, dark smile spreads on Mila's face, "I truly hope I am not the one who has to kill you."

Marcella does not look away from Mila but says to me, "Nicolas, go inside."

I start up the stairs unsure of the depth of involvement Marcella has had with Mila. At this point in this particular night, there is little more that I can add to the rattling thoughts in my mind. So I decide then and there, on that step, that I will ask Marcella everything but it will not be tonight.

Stopping next to Marcella, I look at Mila and says matter-of-factly, "You tell Casiana that if anyone from Genesis hurts my Krista in any form, I will set myself on fire. No more Nexus."

Her eyes tell me that she can see truth behind my words. She can see my exhaustion from the cat and mouse games, the back and forth of lies from friends and foes alike. She can see that despite her effort to convince me that she is my best avenue when dealing with Casiana, I have decided that I am my own best bargaining chip. Without me, Casiana's plans would be foiled. At least, that is what Casiana believes.

My eyes become hard as I continue more harshly, "You tell her that if she truly believes that I am her precious Nexus, Cass would be wise to keep *me* as a friend, not the other way around. Be sure she gets that message, won't you?"

Taking Marcella's arm lightly, I tell her gently, "Come inside, Marcella. We are done here."

We both choose to ignore Mila's glaring as I lead Marcella inside. I look back only when I close the door but Mila is already gone.

From behind me, I hear Marcella begin apologetically, "Nicolas, I-"

But I cut her off abruptly, "Stop."

I turn around to face her before I continue, "I have had a long, tumultuous night. So please. Just stop, Marcella."

She stands silently which is both surprising and welcome. Depleted from the night and most everyone in it, I lean back against the wall. I rub my temples for a moment, my mind swimming in a cluster of thoughts.

When I look up at Marcella, she is watching me with questioning eyes. I am sure that she is curious and concerned about how angry I might be upon discovering that she has kept yet another secret from me. But the events of this night have made my mind weary and led to a physical exhaustion that I have not felt in some time.

"You worked for them, I presume?" I ask her flatly.

"For a time. But, I-"

I hold my hand up to stop her babbling lies. I am not interested in this conversation at this particular time. Minimum questions with short, direct answers will suffice for now.

"Do you know what they want from me?"

Marcella shakes her head slowly, unsure of how she should answer, "No. But I-"

Raising my eyebrows, I hold up my finger to silence her once more. Marcella has always chosen things for my life that she claims are in my best interest. Seemingly, most of those things tend to be in her best interest instead of mine. However, due to her constant, obstinate meddling, I am neither surprised nor saddened to discover Marcella has yet again already made my decisions for me.

Quietly, she finishes her thought, "I only really knew that she needed to be stopped."

She hesitates briefly, waiting to see if I will stop her again. When I do not, she continues, "I know that they want you for something dreadful. Something that cannot be allowed to succeed. But I'm afraid I was never privy to what exactly her plans are."

Marcella steps towards me cautiously, "I never intended for them to find you." She lays her hand on my arm gently, forcing me to look at her eyes directly, "I have failed you in that regard. And for that, I will forever be sorry."

There is an honesty in her eyes that is not typical of Marcella. And despite her usual lying and deceiving nature, I believe her. Perhaps, this night has me simply too depleted to care any more.

Marcella loves me. I have never doubted this. We have not always seen eye to eye and her constant lies have not helped that matter. But she is my mother. Forgiveness will always be hers for the taking. Even despite my trying, I will never be able to stay angry at her for lying when I am so quick with deceit myself.

There is no hostility when I take her hand from my cheek gently, "Perhaps one day, you will trust me with the secrets of my own life."

With her hand still in mine, she rubs her thumb over my skin, "Ask anything and I will answer you honestly."

Honest. That is a word I will never associate with Marcella. The most honest answer I will ever receive from her is a half-truth. Still, it is nice that she offers even that much.

"No, you won't," I shrug, indifferently, "And I am much too tired to play charades."

I let out a long exhale, "I am going to bed, Marcella. Please be so kind as to let everyone know that I am not to be disturbed."

I start to walk away when I feel her grab my upper arm, "Nicolas, wait," Concern laces her voice in a delicate way as she asks, "Are you alright?"

She walks in front of me to face me once more, "Did something happen with your wolf?"

I am unsure of my expression but something in the sadness hanging there tells Marcella all she needs to know.

"You told her," she states softly, nodding to herself.

Her face flickers with compassion briefly. But compassion is not Marcella's way and just as quickly as her sympathy appeared, her resolute expression reemerges.

Marcella's pushes her hair from her face abruptly. Clearing her throat, she adds sensibly, "Well, it's probably for the best."

It is not for the best but before I can respond, Marcella adds in a bitter tone, "It is her loss."

She crosses her arms over her body, refraining from saying aloud the obscene things racing through her mind. She has no idea what transpired tonight but that does not stop her from being insulted by the perceived notion that her son has been slighted.

Her misguided outrage makes me smile warmly at her, "Marcella," I wait for her to meet my eyes before I continue, "Do not kill her."

She smiles back at me. Neither of us believes she would be so rash as to kill Krista for such a minor affront. Not in Levi's 'no-kill' zone and especially not after she had Punzi killed all those years ago.

My smile fades, however, as I begin to feel again the despairing weight of not knowing whether Krista will ever allow me to see her again or whether she will forever despise my very name.

Before Marcella can see my pain, I reach out and pull her to me. I have not hugged Marcella in such a long time. Her arms feel foreign yet somehow still familiar in the most comforting way.

I kiss her gently on the forehead and I can hear her breath stall.

"Goodnight, mother," I tell her.

As I walk away, I hear her say quietly, trying to hide the tremble in her voice, "Goodnight, son."

*   *   *

When I awake, dark has already come again. The house is quiet and I am grateful for it. Sleeping the day away did nothing to relieve the collapsing pressure on my chest or the despondent thoughts weighing me down. I consider going back to sleep merely to escape having to fake a smile at Marcella or tease Luther with half-concocted gibes. But after a few moments of staring at the bland ceiling above me, I conclude that if I were to stay in bed all night as well, Marcella would certainly take it upon herself to remedy my situation. And I do not trust her remedies.

As I mosey upstairs, I look around but even the sheep seem to be missing. Only Julia stirs in the kitchen. Washing the dishes, she does not realize that I am even there until I speak, "Where is everyone?"

Julia spins around and smiles at me, "Out."

Despite her eyes being brighter than they were yesterday, Julia's low blood levels still cause dark circles to surround her eyes and the pallor of her skin and lips still unnaturally lacks her usual rosy glow.

"I see that. Where did they go?"

She shrugs light-heartedly, "Luther didn't say. Just that they would be gone all night and that you were to be woken if you had any visitors."

Visitors? What visitors? But before I can ask more, there is a knock at the front door. Looking toward the door, I push myself off of the kitchen door frame.

Julia starts to walk past me, but I grab her arm gently. "I'll get it," I tell her. "You should eat something and get some rest."

I walk to the door cautiously, unsure of who or what might await me. Perhaps, Casiana has come to haggle me further. Or perhaps, there is a pack of wolves waiting to pounce for my perceived transgressions. Regardless of the likelihood of either of those possibilities, I do not expect the one I see standing in my doorway.

From the look of surprise, she did not expect to see me standing here either. "Nicolas," Krista starts.

"You came," I whisper, nearly lost completely by her mere presence.

"Yeah, um, Luther called. He, um, well he explained a lot of things..." she plays with the ends of her hair nervously, "He said he wanted to talk to me in person though."

Luther? Suddenly becoming aware of the way I stand in the doorway, awestricken and staring at her, I step aside, "Sorry, um.., come in. Please."

She steps inside just enough for me to shut the door. Exhaling anxiously, she looks around briefly then says, "He said you wouldn't be here. I'm sorry. I wouldn't have-,"

Her voice cuts off but I know what her next words were going to be. She would not have come to my home had she known I would be here tonight. The knowledge of that is enough to form a lump in my throat. There are no words to express the pain behind that simple bit of truth. All I can do is simply attempt to swallow the dry, knot in my throat and nod.

"Is Luther here?" she asks.

Her eyes meet mine and we both realize the trap Luther has set for us. She does not need my answer but I say it anyway, "No, he's out for the night. They all are."

She nods and lets out a long sigh, "I guess tricking people must be a vampire thing." Pursing her lips, she taps her fingers on her forehead, "I'm just going to... I should go."

As she turns around and reaches for the doorknob, my heart races. I do not know why Luther would arrange her being here but I also do not care. I refuse to squander this opportunity.

Reaching around her, I place my hand on the door, stopping her from opening it. "Please," I tell her in a pained whisper.

Her hair brushes my arm as she drops her hand from the knob. Her scent caresses my nose. With her body so close to me, I nearly forget to continue with words instead of actions.

"You don't owe me any favors but I am asking for one anyway. Please, don't go," I say quietly. "I need to say this and I need you to hear it. Just once. After that, you can hate me all you want. Hate, I am used to. It is love that is foreign to me. And perhaps that is why I am so bad at it."

Krista turns around to face me, leaning back against the door. She looks up at me from the tops of her eyes, "I don't hate you. I only wish I could."

I drop my arm but I do not step back to create any more space between us. "Your father's orders did not apply to me because I am not human. And for me to let you believe that you were able to kiss me for any other reason was wrong. And for that I am sorry."

Something flickers in Krista's eyes but I cannot stop to ask about it now. If I do not finish what I need to say, I may never have the chance again.

"But had I told you what I was from the start, you would have never given me the time of day. I never would have heard you laugh, never would have touched your hand. And I never would have seen your smile. So for that lie, I am *not* sorry."

Krista scoffs. However, the way she looks to the side and chews her bottom lip indicates that she knows I am right to believe she would have dismissed me from the start.

"From the moment I first saw you, I have been petrified of losing you, so much that I assuredly pushed you away. But that's not what I intended. I never wanted to see that look in your eyes. That sadness, that disappointment. I never wanted you to see me as a monster." I shrug lightly, "But I am. It's every bit as much a part of me as your wolf is a part of you."

She does not meet my eyes as she swallows hard, trying not to cry.

Filling her silence, I continue, "I have spent centuries searching for the way you make me feel. And if you walk out that door now, I may never feel this again."

She places her hand over her mouth to hide the quiver of her chin. Despite her attempt to hide it, a tear deceives her and rolls down her cheek. My hand aches to wipe it from her skin but I resist. She does not need my hands as much as she needs to hear my words.

"So if you could ever find it in your heart to give me a second chance, I would very much appreciate it. I can guarantee it would not be easy. The odds are stacked against us and the risks are high. But I promise that as long as you are willing to be with me, I will never stop fighting for you."

Placing my hand on her jawline gently, I lift her chin. I wait until her eyes meet mine before I continue, "Krista, I am inexplicably, and irrevocably in love with you."

I wipe the tear escaping down her cheek as she takes a shaky breath. I continue quietly, "That monster you saw, that man who held you all night, they are the same. That's me. It's always been me. And I am telling you now that *all* of me is in love with *all* of you. The good, the bad, the hairy," I say, teasing lightly.

She chuckles despite the way her tears continue to fall. I do not attempt to stop them, instead I let the tears roll over my fingers as I finish, "You can walk out that door if you choose to. I will not stop you, nor will it change the way I feel. But I am asking you to stay. Just a little longer."

I drop my hands from her face but I keep myself close to her. "So please, Krista. Please, don't go," I whisper.

Krista does not move her hand toward the doorknob, and I am grateful for it. Because despite saying that I would not stop her, I am not certain how I might react if she does start to leave.

Instead, she looks up at me with her bloodshot eyes and says, "I am not good at telling people how I feel, so listen close, because there is a solid chance that I will not be able to say it a second time."

She sniffs to stop her tears. Drying her face with her sleeve, she exhales forcefully. She licks her lips, trying to find her words.

"Nick, my father's orders were not simply to stop dating humans."

I can see that her discomfort with saying sentiments aloud causes her words to be slower and more broken than she intends them to sound but she continues anyway, "My father ordered me not to date you. Especially you. So human, werewolf, vampire, it wouldn't have mattered. The order stood. The loophole, that kiss, everything remains the same. Right from the start, one of us was in love with the other..."

It was me. Since first seeing her in the gas station I have been captivated by her. I simply did not want to see it before. I did not want to admit that I could become lost in her without my consent so quickly or so completely.

"And both of us are now," she adds tenderly.

Her words send a sudden shiver of excitement through me with a hope that I had not dared to dream possible. However, just as quickly as that hope appears, concern takes its place. The possibility of her dashing that newfound hope by the wayside with her next words causes a knot to form in my stomach.

As much as I would like to interject and discover if my new hope is founded, I wait patiently. She simply asked me to listen. So listen is all I will do.

Krista pushes the loose strands of hair from her face as she continues nervously, "Do you know the reason I came here tonight?"

I had assumed it was because Luther told her I would not be home, but her question makes me believe I might have been mistaken.

"It wasn't because Luther tricked me." She shrugs lightly, taking another forced breath, "I came because I simply needed an excuse. And Luther gave me one."

My heart picks up a beat in anticipation.

She shakes her head with thought, "I should run. I should walk out that door and never look back. It's the sensible thing to do. Loving you will undoubtedly cause difficulties in my life that I cannot even imagine."

That is true. Being with me is indisputably a complication that her life would be better without. Yet, I still want her to choose me nonetheless.

Krista continues her thought, "But regardless of that logic, it does not matter how far or how fast I run. I will always end up on your doorstep."

She places her hand on my chest softly. Her simple touch causes me to inhale sharply.

"Because for some unexplainable reason, my wolf chose you. And the wolf always gets what the wolf wants. I am just glad that, right now, what my wolf wants and what I want are the same thing." She looks up at me, the warmth of her hand, burning into my chest, "You see, right now, all of me wants all of you, too."

Her words force a surge of heat through me and I react faster than I can stop to consider my actions. Placing my hands on either side of her face, I crush my lips into hers. The flames in my throat pale in comparison to the fire ripping through my body.

As much as I want to allow myself to succumb to the basic carnal needs that I have longed for, a thought enters my mind. Perhaps this is not what she intended for tonight. Perhaps she simply wanted to move passed my confession and continue talking. Pushing too far, we will both cross a line that neither of us can uncross. While that will not bother me, it may weigh on her in years to come. Taking advantage of her vulnerability would be wrong. I should at least offer to stop us both, for her sake.

I pull away from her but keep my face close to hers, "I'm sorry. If you want me to stop, I-"

Tugging my shirt, she puts my brief concerns at ease, pulling my lips to hers once more. She parts my mouth with hers and slides her tongue over my lip, letting me feel the desire raging inside her. She wants me. Possibly even loves me. Not my human guise. Me.

I press her back against the door, moving my lips with hers. She slides her hands to my back and pulls me closer. Her heartbeat quickens and I can feel her skin warming as I glide my thumb over her cheek.

I drag my lips along her jawline, making my way to her ear. Letting my breath warm her ear, I glide my tongue along the edge and pull on the lobe gently with my very human teeth. Her fingers press into the muscles of my shoulders.

Cradling the back of her neck with my fingers, I curve her towards me. Her breaths become jagged as she intertwines her fingers through my hair. Trailing my lips along her neck, I feel her drop her head back, exposing her neck to me. Her simple action sends a new heat pouring through me. There are no reservations about my being a vampire holding her back. No concerns that might slow this down. Her sheer trust in me causes me to crave her that much more.

My eyes glaze over to black with hunger, but this hunger is not for blood. It is for her. Grabbing her legs, I lift her up, pressing her back into the door and causing her to gasp. With her fingers still in my hair, she pulls my head back and kisses me fiercely. I could take her right here. Against this door. Or on those stairs. Or even on one of these useless tables holding useless decorative baubles. Where this happens does not matter. All that matters is that I finish what she started.

I do realize, however, that my family will be coming home at some point and having them wander in would put a damper on the mood. Well, at least, it would for her. Therefore, my bedroom is the safest option to remain uninterrupted for the night.

Stretching out my hand to keep from bumping into anything, I carry her toward the basement doorway. There is a greediness behind the way her lips course over mine. Her kiss is full of ardent desire and eagerness as I stop at the door leading to the basement. As I fumble with the knob, she kisses underneath the angle of my jaw. The heat of her breath grazing my ear, and the softness of her lips, cause my fingers to slip from the knob.

My hand cradles the small of her back as her thighs squeeze around me. I can feel her chest press into me with each heavy breath. Her hand trails over my shoulder and along my neck.

Her fingers graze over my cheek. With her lips near mine, her kissing stops briefly and her jagged breaths roll over my lips. In a whisper, I hear her say, "You may not bite but I will."

Her words send a fervent shiver over my skin and my grip on her thighs tightens. I lean towards her to close the distance between our lips but she leans back the same amount. Biting her lip, she keeps her face inches from mine.

She knows what she is doing to me. The way her directness is causing me to lose focus. The way my desire to have her is overwhelming my actions. She knows how to play on my craving for her. And regardless of what I might have thought, this is her moment. She owns me. And she is fully aware of it.

She reaches behind herself to open the door. As the door swings open, she raises one eyebrow enticingly.

Smiling, I lean towards her again and this time she does not pull away from my kiss. Her body feels natural against mine as she pulls my shoulders toward her. Her hair brushes my skin as I carry her to my room, careful not to trip down the stairs despite the distraction.

As I open the door to my room, I place Krista's feet back on the ground. She pulls off her shirt and tosses it to the side as she backs into my room.

Her fingers sear down my chest and abdomen as it descends to the top of my pants. Grabbing my belt, she jerks me into the room with her.

Her lips press into mine as she continues to unfasten my pants. She does not look around but still says jokingly, "You have a nice room."

Smiling, I lean my nose next to hers, "Thanks. I'll show you the rest of it in the morning."

She lets out a restless chuckle between labored breaths. Reaching over my head, I pull my shirt off as I kick the door shut behind us.

Upstairs I had allowed my eyes to phase into black and for the first time, Krista looks into their darkness. She was so confident just moments ago, yet as she stares into my dark eyes, it seems her nerves begin to surface and her fingers hesitate on my belt.

I assume her hesitation is due to the sudden realization of what was, and hopefully still is, about to happen. Sex with a vampire is not something that can be undone. A vampire keeping a werewolf as a lover is strange and sickening. But a werewolf having relations with a vampire is heresy. While I have only myself to obey, she will have a pack to answer to.

I lay one hand on hers gently and with my other hand, I lift her chin toward me. "Krista, I know that I want every part of you. But if *any* part of you has any doubts, now would be the time to voice them," I tell her quietly, sincerely hoping that she will say nothing at all and my selfishness may be permitted to supersede any reservation she might have.

She smiles softly at me, "You misunderstand. I am not afraid of rushing into your bed." She slides my belt off without taking her eyes from me. The newfound assurance that this is going to process further sends a surge of energy to my skin.

"It just suddenly occurred to me that, um...," she bites her lip as though the next words are somewhat embarrassing to her. "Well, every time I've pictured you naked, you've been human and well, you're not, so... It occurred to me that I might be in for a bit of a surprise."

Even though I am not entirely sure where she is going, I still smile at her mention that she has thought of me naked. As she continues, she pulls my pants slightly and pretends to peek inside them, "Just how different from a human are you?"

Letting out a small chuckle, I place my hand in the small of her back and pull her closer, "Anatomically, I am very human." And very relieved that the only concern she has is not a concern at all.

Cradling my hands on both sides of her neck, I graze my thumbs over her cheeks. I lean in and kiss her, letting her feel the desire behind my lips. Her arms tighten around me and I hear the smile in her sigh. As I pull her body against mine, a warmth spreads over me; not just from her abdomen pressing into me but from a deep need to keep her there.

Crushing her lips to mine, her hands work to finish unfastening my pants. She pulls my pants down enough to use her foot to step on them and slide them the rest of the way to the floor.

My eyes catch her reflection in the mirror. I notice that just under my fingers in the small of her back begins a path of small paw-print tattoos that trails upward along her spine.

Sliding my fingers along the path on her spine, I hear her say quietly, "Well, sir," Her hands press into my chest and shove me onto my bed. She smirks and adds, "I hope you're ready."

She wiggles her pants down in a sultry manner. As she kicks them off her toe, she continues speaking, "Cause this little wolf," she crawls onto my bed over me, tiptoeing her fingers along my chest in rhythm to her words, "is gonna huff, and puff," stopping over me, she leans her face close to mine, "and blow your mind."

She kisses me fervently and full of purpose, sending a charge of tingling heat through my body. Grabbing her waist, I roll her over so that I am on top of her. Smiling, I tell her, "Challenge accepted."

She rolls her head back to let out a laugh and I take the opportunity to place my lips on her neck. I hear her breaths grow heavy as my lips move along her jaw and beneath her ear.

Reaching down, I glide my hand along her thigh and lift her knee toward my ribs. Her hands course over my shoulders, pulling me closer and sending a river of heat through my core.

I can hear her heart racing as her fingers tangle and pull at my hair. My hand glides along her soft skin to her butt. Gripping firmly, I drive my hips into hers. Moaning, she arches her back, pressing her breasts further into my chest.

The surge of desire pushes my fangs out of hiding and I graze my teeth along her neck. Her fingers press into my back as her breaths quicken. Her soft, fragile skin would offer no resistance to my fangs yet she does not seem bothered by them. Instead, she rolls her body into mine exposing more of her most vulnerable veins.

I trail my tongue along her throat and up to her lips, tasting her flesh. There is a rapacity behind my kiss that causes her fingernails to dig into my skin. Her fingers slide along my back, scraping me enough to release a subtle hint of my own blood in the air. The monster in me rages with voracity and lust with the added scent.

Kissing her ardently, I feel her pulse pounding under my fingers as they flow over her flawless skin. The heat of her blood rushing to her flesh burns against me and her body trembles under my touch, intensifying my desire for her.

Caressing her tongue over mine, she grips my butt, pulling my hips toward hers harder. Her legs tighten around me forcing my heartbeat to quicken. Her fingers scratch into my hair once more as she drags her teeth over my bottom lip, pulling and biting lightly.

Our breaths become more ragged and uneven which only amplifies the charging heat that floods me. Her fingertips leave a trail of fire in their wake as her hands course along my spine, sending chills to my skin.

As I slam my hips into hers, she tosses her head back to allow a broken gasp escape. Her moaning grows louder with my every thrust. I slide my hand over her ribs, curving along her soft breast, then under her back to hold her shoulder as I push myself further inside her.

Using my elbow to hold myself, I lean up enough to look at her face. With her eyes closed tight and mouth open enough to accommodate the jagged gasps, pleasure twists her eyebrows tightly together. Feeling my gaze, her eyes open. I smile tenderly at her but there is no way for her to fully understand what I am feeling.

No real notion of how beautiful she looks lying underneath me. No contemplation of how I have longed for this moment since I first saw her. How I have craved to taste her lips. Or feel her skin so completely. Or how pleasingly natural she feels in my grip. I want her. This much she does know. But perhaps by the end of this night, she will understand how badly I need her.

Her hand curves around the base of my skull and she pulls my forehead to hers. As she slides her hand to my cheek, I close my eyes and feel her hot breath graze my skin in an uneven and shaky rhythm as the warmth of her hand scorches into my skin.

I press my lips to hers as she rolls her body with mine. Her skin caresses mine warmly, sending a pulse of titillating exhilaration to quiver through my body. My lips make their way along her neck once more. In the light perspiration collecting on her flushed skin, I taste a hint of the frenzy of energy escaping her body.

With a twist of her hips, she rolls us over so that she straddles on top of me. She reaches between us and guides me inside her once more as she lows her hips onto mine. Biting her lip, she leans up, displaying her body to me. Her breasts bound with each rock of her body against mine, making my grip on her hips tighten.

Her hands skim over her body, stopping to stroke her breasts briefly before continuing on. Leaning her head back, she moans loudly and places her hand on my abdomen. A fire radiates through me from the heat of her palm burning into me.

Watching her crash her body onto mine forces my heart rate to escalate. But I do not simply want to watch her. I need to taste her skin, to feel her body pressed against me, to touch every impeccable curve, and hear every inaudible gasp.

Without slowing the way her hips drive onto mine, I sit up with her on my lap. My hand pushes through her hair and pulls her face to mine. I pull her hair slightly, tilting her head back just enough for me to graze my fangs along her skin causing her body to shiver lightly in my arms.

From this position, I can watch her in the mirror. Her hair dances over the paw-prints on her spine as I take her body. My black eyes stare back at me as my fangs dangle over the thinner skin of her fine neck. Knowing the man in me wants her body more than the monster in me craves her blood sends a lascivious surge of control and power through my core and extending into my fingertips.

Her fingers dig into my back as I kiss along her neck and I feel her teeth press into my shoulder. There is no blood, however, the pain of her bite is enough to make my breath catch.

She curves into me as my hand rolls over her body, feeling the way it calls to me. My tongue dances with hers like a delicate pirouette. As she pulls me closer in attempt to close the space between us that simply is not there, I feel her heart pounding against my chest.

I have wanted this moment since my eyes first caressed her body. Then the first time I heard her laugh, I knew I would not stop until I succeeded to ensnare her. But it was the first time she touched my hand in the moonlight that I knew that I want every moment after this night as well.

*　　*　　*

Her aroma fills my room, clinging to my pillow and hanging in the air in a delicate way. As the scent of Krista fills my nostrils, I am lost. Lost in the slow smile that spreads across my face. Lost in the way her smell calms me, pulling me away from my monstrous impulses and closer to being the man I once was.

But mostly, I am lost watching the way her hair slides off of her shoulder as she closes her eyes and a warm smile spreads on her face and lost in the softness of her skin under my fingers as I stroke the path of paw prints along her spine.

Lying on her stomach with her arms folded under her head, Krista lets out a serene sigh. Untroubled and content, she lies still relishing in the tenderness of my touch. My fingers trail from the base of her neck between her shoulder blades and along her spine to the top of her butt where my sheets drape across her daintily.

Slowly, she opens her eyes and sleepily peeks over at me. Smiling widely, she says, "I'm still listening."

"Are you? It seemed like you were falling asleep," I tease.

Closing her eyes again, she shakes her, "Mm-mm." She lets out one more long sleepy sigh and pushes herself up onto her elbows. Looking over at me, her eyes are soft and I find myself longing for this moment to never end.

Wishing for no wolves, no vampires, and no impending threats. Wishing the sun would never come up, and the wolves would never come looking for her. No burning in my throat, and no need for either of us to ever go beyond these walls.

Oblivious to my desires, she pushes her loose strands behind her ear as she speaks, "So you think this Cassita lady-"

"Casiana," I correct her.

"Casiana," she continues, "You think she's crazy."

Honestly, I am not sure what to believe about Casiana so instead, I answer by saying, "I think she's crazy enough to kill you. And me."

Krista twists her mouth, "Well, I guess we better be careful not to give her any reasons to. Because I certainly do not plan on this being a Romeo and Juliet sort of thing."

I chuckle softly. Shaking my head slowly, I lean close to her. Looking up at her from the tops of my eyes, I tell her quietly, "You are most certainly not allowed to die." Then I place my lips on the warm skin of her bare shoulder.

Biting her bottom lip lightly, her cheeks flush. She crinkles her nose trying to alleviate her blushing but it has little effect on the redness of her skin. Ignoring how her cheeks glow, she leans her face close to mine and says quietly, "Well. Neither are you."

As she presses her lips to mine softly, her hair falls out from behind her ear. The weight of it causes the curls to bounce in a way that wafts the remnants of her perfume toward me.

I have never let myself be this vulnerable since Ann, but somehow, Krista found a chink in my armor. Somehow, she snuck past my carefully constructed walls. Krista means more to me in this short time than I intended for her to. But now that she is here, I cannot imagine why I would have ever tried to keep her out.

My hand cradles her neck as my thumb grazes her cheek softly. Pulling my lips back, I lean my forehead against hers and nuzzle her nose with mine. Without over analyzing my next words, I say them in a whisper, "I love you, Krista Hartley."

I do not need to open my eyes to see her smile. I can hear in the tone of her voice, "I love you too."

Smiling warmly, I lean back enough for her to see my face. "Yeah," I click my tongue, "But I did love you first, so...," I tease.

Tossing her head back to laugh, she shoves my shoulder and I let myself fall back on the bed. Shaking her head, she leans over me, "That's not fair. You knew what you were getting right from the start. I only found out yesterday."

My hand cradles the small of her back, holding her against me, while my other hand glides over her ribs and up to her neck. Cradling the back of her head, I pull her face close to mine. Keeping her lips barely hovering over mine, I let my breath warm her skin as I tell her, "You should stay."

She closes the space between us and kisses me tenderly. Then keeping her face near mine, she replies, "But I'm already late."

She pushes herself up and begins collecting her clothing from the floor.

Groaning, I exhale forcefully. "Doesn't Warren give you sick days?" I pout as she turns on the bathroom light.

She looks back at me with a smirk, "Not for this."

Smiling, I watch as she begins dressing.

"You really don't know what you promised that Cassandra chick?" Krista asks from the bathroom.

"Casiana. And no. I don't," I tell her as I roll myself out of my bed. "Do you think Marcella knows?"

I slide my pants on as I answer, "Maybe." In all honesty, I am sure that Marcella could tell me lots of things about Casiana, the Genesis, and my past. I am not sure if she would know exactly what Casiana will ask for but I am also not sure if I want to know. The more secrets that are revealed to me, the more I simply want to bury myself in Krista and pretend nothing else exists.

"You should ask her," Krista says as I step onto the cold tile of the bathroom floor.

Standing behind her, I wrap my arms around her waist and pull her to me. I lean my lips close to her ear and smile at her in our reflection in the mirror, "It does not matter what Casiana wants. The only people determining my future are in this room right now."

Without leaving my arms, Krista turns to face me, "You're not curious?"

I am curious; however, I am also certain that before my promise to Casiana can come back to bite me, Krista's family will. Her pack is more of an immediate threat than any promise I do not intend to keep. But instead of explaining to her that I am more concerned about her pack than the Genesis, I simply shake my head.

Her fingers twist at the ends of my hair playfully, "Well, I am curious about something." Smiling, she continues, "How do you have a bathroom with no toilet?"

I laugh as she pushes herself from me enough to turn back toward the mirror above the sink and resume brushing her hair. It is true that there is not a toilet in this bathroom. There is not any in this entire basement but I did not realize that she had noticed. And I have not had someone in this room who might need one in so long that I had not even considered it. "There is one upstairs if you need it."

I lean back against the tile wall next to the sink unable to stop grinning at her.

"You don't use one?" she asks incredulously.

I shake my head and shrug, "My body consumes and uses every ounce of my strictly liquid diet. There is simply no waste."

"That's weird," she jests.

I chuckle, "It's not the eyes, or the teeth, or the diet? It's my privy protocols that you find strange?"

Laying the brush on the counter, Krista smirks at me. "The only thing not strange about you is that you are going to walk me to the door like any other gentleman would. Pretty much everything else about you is going on a list called *bizarre boyfriend traits*."

She lets out a light giggle and takes my hand, "Come on."

As I walk her upstairs, I do not see Marcella and I am glad for it. Introducing Krista to Marcella would only put a damper on my memories of last night and this morning.

Luther, however, is present. Leaning against the foyer wall, he nods to Krista as we pass, noticeably proud of himself. Krista smiles back at him kindly despite his pompous stance.

When we stop by the door, Krista puts her hand on my chest and kisses my cheek.

"Are you sure you can't stay?" I ask again even though I already know the answer.

She lets out a heavy sigh. I know that we would both rather walk back downstairs and stay there wrapped in each other's bodies for the next few days but we both know that is not practical or logical at this point.

"I have cars that need me and you have a deadline," she reminds me.

True, I do have a deadline but I am nearly finished with the article I am currently writing. Besides, I do have more hours in the day to finish it than a human does. It is not as though I have to sleep. I have plenty of time to complete my article.

Knowing that explanation will not be sufficient in convincing her to stay, I slide my hand up along her arm and to her cheek, and try, "What if I need a muse?"

Luther unsuccessfully holds back a laugh and instead makes a sort of snorting sound. I roll my eyes without looking over at him.

Krista smiles, "You don't want me to be a muse. You only want me to be a distraction."

Placing her hand on my wrist, she pulls her face closer to mine, "Now say you love me, give me a kiss, and open that door. I have to go."

My fingers slide down from her shoulder and along her back, feeling the heat of her skin beneath her shirt. "You know I won't be able to stop thinking of you long enough to get anything done today," I tell her fondly.

And even though I do not want to see her leave, I kiss her dearly and open the door anyway. "I better see you tonight," I tell her with a smirk.

"You will," she assures me. She stands patiently for a moment then pushes the door closed once more, "Now, let's see." She uses her fingers to count her points, as she continues, "You kissed me. And you opened the door. But I am sure there was a third thing you were supposed to do."

Raising one eyebrow, she grins at me.

Glancing over, I see Luther grinning at me too. "You think I'm afraid to say it in front of Luther?" I ask in disbelief.

Krista crosses her arms over her chest and says with a challenge in her tone, "I know you are."

Holding back a smile, I sigh. I do not want to say this in front of Luther. I am not afraid to but I do not want to either. I do not want to encourage his wallowing in the fact that I will owe him for his meddling. I do not want to give him a reason to feel that I have to be grateful to him. But mostly, I do not want to spend the day locked in this house with a gloating, cretinous fool.

But a challenge is a challenge. So I place my hands on both sides of her face and look into her eyes as I say, "Krista Hartley, I am hopelessly and utterly in love with you. And I really do not care who hears it."

I look at Luther from the corner of my eyes, "Did you get that, Luther? Or do you need me to say it again so you can record it?"

Luther smirks and taps his temple, "Got it all up here."

Despite not wanting to encourage him, I cannot help but smile at his nonsensical amusement of the situation.

I feel Krista's warm lips on my cheek and close my eyes. The heat of her lips makes me forget about Luther's boastful posture by the wall and all of the obstacles standing in our way. For a moment, I am completely carefree.

I hear the click of the doorknob before I feel her lips leave my skin. Her breath rolls over my cheek as she whispers, "I will pick you up as soon as it's dark." She taps me on the chest as she adds, "I still owe you that second date."

I chuckle to myself as she slips out the door and closes it behind her. My lopsided grin spreads across my face as I begin to feel the tips of my ear warm with my blushing.

Pushing himself off of the wall, Luther claps quietly, "Wow. Just wow."

I look over at him with a wide smile and let him continue, "You are good. I mean, I knew she cared about you and I figured that you two would make up. But wow. You actually convinced her to spend the night. Congratulations, Nicolas, you are better than I thought."

Laughing to myself, I jokingly tell him, "That's where you went wrong, Luther. You thought. If you would practice thinking a little more often, you would have never doubted me in the first place."

He smiles wide at my sarcasm. I wait a brief moment, thinking of how to proceed. Then quietly, I continue with sincerity, "Thank you, Luther." I wait for his eyes to meet mine before I finish my thought, "I'm not sure why you called her but I do know I will never be able to repay you for it."

Sincerity and kindness are not my typical ways of communicating with Luther and I am sure that the change is what has him struggling to find his next words.

Finally, he shrugs, "Well, the only reason I called her is because you're nicer to me this way." He gestures toward me, "This Nicolas, the one who's all lovesick and confused, is too distracted dealing with his own inner turmoil to be mean to me. That's all. It was no big deal."

Then smiling again, he adds, "But I guess this means I can come to the wedding."

I laugh loudly then add, "Luther, you get to be the best man."

We both laugh at my ridiculous statement as Marcella walks in the foyer, "Congratulations. You've succeeded in having sex with every species you're legally allowed to," she half-jokes.

I shrug lightly, "Everyone needs a hobby."

She smiles a little wider but does not continue the jesting. Marcella has never been much for playful banter and I can tell that despite her attempt to keep the conversation light, she is also somewhat annoyed by my relationship with Krista.

We are both thankful, however, that Vanessa pops in and changes the subject, "Roddy is on the phone for you."

Roddy. Tara's werewolf son. I can see the disdain in Marcella's eyes as Vanessa says his name, so I simply nod to her. Today is not the day to discuss werewolves with Marcella. Today, I will simply enjoy this elated feeling Krista has left with me.

As I walk toward the kitchen to take the call, I contemplate how much I will tell Roddy about Krista. The last time we talked, he told me to avoid her at all costs and I did not exactly take his advice.

Luther's words distract me from my thoughts when he calls after me, "Another werewolf? If we entertain any more, we'll have to open our own kennel."

He laughs heartily at his own joke but I simply call back, "Luther, I am in too good of a mood to hate you today. But don't push it."

Chapter 8

Evenings with Krista passed more rapidly than I would like them to and the weeks began to add together quickly. But one thought lingers still: all good things must come to an end. However, what is always failed to be mentioned is how abrupt that end will be. Or how to prepare yourself for such a loss.

I have tried not to dwell on this thought but it is there anyway. Always in the back of my mind, lurking in the shadows. It has been haunting me for weeks now. Since that first night when Krista crept into my bed, I have wondered how long it will be before she creeps back out of my life forever. And as I speed through the dark forest with a werewolf gaining on my every step, I attempt to ignore the looming reality: vampires do not get to have happy endings.

My feet push into the soft dirt as I dodge the trees. The overgrown path through the forest offers little resistance to my accelerated speed. The dew sticks to my skin but I cannot slow my pace to wipe it from my face.

Twigs snap under the weight of the werewolf that feverishly follows my scent, making up for the head start that I stole. And I can hear its heavy panting not far behind me as I approach the small clearing.

Sliding to a stop near the creek in the clearing, I look behind me just as the werewolf bursts from the tree line. Its white fur blows in the wind as it walks toward me. Its paws sink into the muddy soil, leaving a trail of prints behind.

I step back slightly and feel the cold of the creek wick into my shoe. The icy chill of the water causes me to look down at my feet briefly but it is enough time for the wolf to close the space between us.

It looks up at me with blue eyes as I shrug, "I won."

The wolf shakes the dew from its fur then seamlessly phases back into her human form. She rises up to face me.

"You cheated," Krista tells me with a light-hearted snap in her voice.

"I do not cheat." I mean, technically, I did start before she was finished phasing but I would have won either way. A vampire is simply faster than a wolf. Besides, getting a head start was not mentioned in the rules.

She crosses her arms over her bare chest, and raises her eyebrow with a smirk, "We both know you lie." She gestures toward the backpack I am wearing as she adds, "Now give me my clothes back."

As I slide the straps from my shoulders, I stare at her milky skin. The way it shimmers in the moonlight beckons my fingers to graze across her smooth body.

I hold the backpack toward her but as she reaches for it, I pull it away, "Actually, I think I'll hang on to these for a while longer."

A wide smile spreads on my face as I dangle the backpack over the creek behind me.

Krista holds out her hand, "No, you are going to give them to me right now."

I shake my head slowly, "I think we agreed the winner gets to decide what happens to this bag."

She looks at me in playful disbelief, "Um, we absolutely did not agree to that."

She steps toward me so that her face is close to mine. She tries but fails to force her smile into hiding, "Be a gentleman and give me back my clothes."

Without bringing the bag away from the water, I tell her, "You keep using that word but I am not gentle nor a man, so...," I shrug lightly.

A mischievous smile scrolls across her face. Quickly, she grabs my side with one hand and grabs the bag with the other. Her fingers scale across me as though she were playing keys on a piano and tickling their way up my ribs.

Jumping slightly, I let out a scream and tuck my arms against myself to protect my ribs from her taunting. I shove the bag into her arms, "Stop. It's yours. Just stop."

Her fingers pluck at my sides, causing me to trip over the slick creek rocks. Somehow, I manage to land on the damp ground instead of the icy water but she continues to torture me with her tickling.

Sitting on top of me, she smiles widely at her victory and lets her fingers stop their tormenting. She leans over me and crinkles her nose. "That's what I thought you said," she gloats teasingly.

With her face still close to mine, I pull her towards me to kiss her softly. However, just as my lips inch toward hers, we hear a scream. Sharp and fearful, it pierces through the night air.

We both look in the direction the scream came from but there are no other sounds.

Krista looks at me with wide eyes and says with concern in her voice, "That came from the Lock."

Vampires do not typically meddle in human affairs. It is one of the rules that keep us a secret and that secrecy keeps us alive. However, that scream was from a human and definitely came from Krista's werewolf community.

The Lock is exactly where I do not want to go looking for a frightened human. But I rub my hand over Krista's bare arm anyway. "I'll check it out. You stay here," I tell her quietly.

She nods as she slides off of me, "Be careful."

She tosses her backpack of clothes to the ground and begins pulling out her belongings. My offer to investigate does not seem to ease her anxiety. However, she begins dressing which indicates she does not intend to phase into a werewolf. Perhaps as a human, she will stay here and stay hidden from whatever is on the other side of the tree line.

It is not a far run to the edge of the forest. I slow down as I get closer and by the time, I step out of the tree line, my speed is more of a fast walk than a run.

Looking across the dimly-lit street, I see the security booth but nothing else. No terror-stricken human, no vampires, no werewolves, not even a spider to account for the scream. But as I move closer, I can smell it. Rich, fresh blood thickens the air. The monster in me pushes to the surface, waiting to be let out. But it is not simply the blood that hangs around me that has my inner monster on edge. I can feel someone watching me as I approach the fresh carcass.

I already know what has happened. I do not need to see the massacre. No human can survive this much blood loss. Still, as I approach, I peer past the blood-smeared windows to confirm that it is Larry, the security guard, lying in a pool of his own blood.

I do not need to see the gouges in Larry's throat or taste the tapping drips of blood to know that this meal belongs to a nomad. More than one is responsible for Larry's death, yet there is only one waiting in the shadows.

As I look at the scattered pieces of tissue, I analyze who is watching me. Not someone I know but definitely a vampire. The vampire who watches me is alone but the others will be back.

The last thing I want or need is a pack of wolves sniffing around when they reappear. But there is no other way around it. The werewolves would have heard the screaming as easily as I did. They will come to check on the chaos outside their own gates. And some of them will die at the hands of these vampires.

As I contemplate my next action, Krista emerges from the trees.

"What happened?" she calls to me.

As she begins crossing the street, I rush to her and stop her in the street, knowing I cannot let her see Larry lying in pieces.

"Is he dead?" she asks urgently as she tries to peer around me.

I hear her heartbeat quicken at that realization and I take her by the shoulders firmly. Not hard enough to hurt her but strong enough for her to understand the gravity of my words. "It's not safe here," I tell her.

I can feel the weight of the air around me shift. The vampires responsible for this are nearing. Closer than they were when I first arrived and gaining ground with each passing second. Time to get Krista to safety is running thin.

"Krista, listen to me," I tell her with a palliated, panic lacing my voice, "Vampires did this and they're coming back. We have to hurry."

I take her by the hand and lead her across the darkened street toward the unmarked cemetery in the trees.

As we walk quickly, I tell her, "You'll be safe inside the cemetery. No matter what happens, promise me that you'll stay inside the cemetery."

As she crosses the property line into the cemetery, I let my hand slip from hers. She looks back at me half confused and half dismayed that I am not coming with her.

"I can't follow you in," I tell her quietly.

I can feel the vampires' presence but they are not here just yet. I still have time to say this. I can still have this moment.

Leaning my forehead against Krista's, I rub my hand along her cheek, "I'm sorry. This isn't how I wanted your pack to find out but promise me that you'll stay here until its safe. Even if you have to wait for the dawn."

The cemetery will not protect me but that does not matter. I only need it to protect her.

Heavy tears well in her eyes but she refuses to let them fall as she realizes exactly what has happened to Larry, what I am about to confront, and that her pack will see me for what I really am.

Shaking her head, Krista grabs at my shirt attempting to pull me toward her but my feet do not budge past the property line of the cemetery.

"Nicolas, you can run. Don't do this," she pleads.

If the nomads had simply moved on, running would make sense. This would not have to be my fight. I would not need to be here. Her pack would not have to see my fangs. Krista could stay safe in the cemetery until morning.

However, the nomads are too close. They will make an appearance here and her pack will know exactly what a vampire is. Warren is no fool. After tonight, he will know what I am whether I run or not. The only difference in the outcomes between running and staying is that by running, her pack will know me not just as a vampire but also as a coward.

There is no other way. These nomads are returning and I will be here when they do. I will be the one to ensure Krista's safety. I have to see that Krista lives with my own eyes. I refuse to leave her in a dangerous situation simply to save myself.

I place my hands over hers on my shirt, "It's too late for that."

Lifting her chin, I keep my face close to hers as I add, "Listen to me. This hallowed ground is the only thing that can keep me from you."

A lone tear rolls over my fingers as she says weakly, "My pack..."

I interrupt to reassure her delicately, "Only for a time. Your pack cannot keep me from you any more than the sun can."

Rubbing my thumb over her smooth skin, I cradle her cheek as I continue tenderly, "The sun burns my flesh but that is nothing compared to the way my soul burns for you. Nothing short of death will cool the way you beckon me. Nothing that can happen here tonight will matter so long as you live."

She nods solemnly but does not release my shirt until the nomads appear. Her grip loosens at the sight of them, but I do not need to turn to see them for myself. I can feel the hunger in them vibrating through the air.

"Well," a woman starts, "And here, I thought I'd seen everything," she chuckles lightly.

Ignoring her, I meet Krista's eyes and say quietly, "Remember to stay back at least three feet. Out of arms' reach."

She nods and steps back a few steps. Far enough that I can no longer touch her sweet skin. But neither can they.

I let my eyes turn black and my fangs press against my lips as they descend. "You and your people should move on."

I turn to face the woman behind me. Short, blonde hair frames her round face and she stands flanked by two other females. Supposing she is their leader, I will make a point to kill her first.

Of the females who stand behind her, a brunette stands ready to attack but waiting for any sign of approval from their leader. She waits eagerly. Her dark clothes and chestnut skin help mask her in the shadows as the brunette stands in contrast to the other female. Standing a little further back is a second blonde. Her hair is longer with blood tinting the tips of her large curls. It was her eyes I felt on me before, and it is no wonder why she waited for the rest of them. Her stance is less certain than the brunette. Of the three, she is the weakest and will be the easiest to kill.

"This is a no-kill zone and there are penalties for violating a treaty," I continue, "If you do not leave now, you will give me no choice but to impose those penalties myself."

The leader smirks at me, "Nomads do not recognize treaties."

"So be it," I say quietly.

Her smile fades and she shifts uncomfortably, "You really want to fight over a simple little snack?"

I stand still for a moment. No, I do not want to fight over Larry. Nothing about his death will cause me to lose any sleep. But I cannot leave Krista in her community knowing there are nomads nearby. I cannot risk Krista being afraid to go home simply because I would not stomp out her fears of murderers waiting at her gates. And I refuse to let Krista be trapped with the memories of being the one who finds their next victim.

Hearing the answer in my silence, she scoffs, "You're not really protecting that mutt, are you? I mean, she is a pretty little pup but still."

The leader steps closer to me as she continues, "Even if you were blind, the smell alone should be enough to repulse you. How can a shepherd expect to tend his flock with a wolf nipping at his heels?"

A *shepherd*. She says it with a sneer in her voice but it is the nomads that should be looked down on. Keeping sheep is a reliable way to maintain secrecy and mealtimes. While frolicking through towns, killing anyone you deem fit, only adds risks of exposure to the humans. Their reckless habits are the reason sensible vampires kill nomads whenever the opportunity arises.

Still, I stand very quiet, waiting for her to say her piece. After all, none of what she has to say will change the outcome. She will die. They all will.

"Perhaps you are blind. Perhaps you have not noticed there are three of us and only one of you."

"Those odds are acceptable but inaccurate," I tell her as I feel the others. I smile darkly at her as I call out her lie, "There are two of you still hiding in the woods like the cowards they are." Five to one.

I shrug, "No matter. I'll take those odds."

Her fangs shine in the dim street lights but my hands are on her before she can react. I grab her firmly, wrapping one hand around her throat and the other by her belt. She claws at me wildly, slicing my forearms. Ignoring the blood as it streams down my arms, I lift her over my head and throw her into the back of the cemetery and away from Krista.

Landing on her side, she attempts to push herself off of the ground frantically. However, sacred ground is not a trivial obstacle for vampires. We cannot simply skid across it like a water spider, ignoring the pain until we are out. Instead, hallowed ground grabs you and it claims you. There is no escape. Her desperate scrambling is in vain.

The ground burns into her, holding her body exactly where she landed as she begins to sink. She lets out sharp, piercing shrieks as she claws at the scorching dirt that pulls her in like quicksand.

Her lackeys stay frozen watching their leader's skin sear and peel from her face as the pain in her cries grows louder. Every part of her being that touches the earth melts as molten steel. Her flesh drips onto the earth until she becomes nothing more than a crater of ash.

I look at the other two females as their faces shift from shock and appall to anger. It is good for them to be angry. Their longing for her vengeance will keep them here, fighting me to their death instead of running like they should.

But simply to ensure their hate for me, I mock their leader's death by smirking as I say, "And that children is why we don't cross hallowed ground."

Both females run in my direction, narrowing in on me. But I do not want to fight so close to Krista neither do I intend on throwing any more into the cemetery. Despite the effectiveness of having a vampire melt into the ground, I cannot risk Krista getting within arms' reach of any one of them. Since I refuse to fight here, I must lead them away.

I run toward them. When they are near, the brunette swings her arms at me but I slide onto the ground on my side. As I pass between their feet, I grab the brunette by the ankle and pull her to the ground. Using my fingernail to penetrate her skin, I loop my finger around her Achilles' tendon and snap it loose from the bone.

The brunette screams in pain but I ignore her cries as the blonde doubles back toward us. Jumping to my feet, I grab the brunette's bloody ankle again and swing her body around, slamming her into the blonde. The blonde flies back and disappears into the tree line but she will not be gone for long.

Before she can return, I swing the brunette over my head and slam her into the ground, shattering several bones on the right side of her body. She screams over the snapping sound of bones shattering but I need her pain to slow her down while I deal with this blonde.

As the blonde dashes out of the trees, I run toward the security booth, putting some distance between us and Krista. The smell of the slew of parts that used to be Larry hangs around us. The decadent scent is distracting for less experienced vampires and I will use that to my advantage.

The blonde gains on me as I near the security booth. Just before I reach the little brick booth, headlights approach. The new audience will not stop this. This must be done. I only hope whoever is in the car will not become a liability to this carnage.

The car stops several feet from us but we are clearly seen in the headlights as I run up the side of the security booth. Flipping back over her, I grab her head and slam our bodies onto the cold pavement. I place my feet on both of her shoulders for leverage and ensure my grip on her head.

Pushing with my feet, I pull at her head until the flesh along her neckline begins to rip. As I continue to pull her head from her shoulders, I let out a shout to assist my strength. I fall back slightly as her body finally frees her spine and head. Her body, both what is on the ground and what is in my hands, turns to ash just before her bloody spine can stain my shirt.

A scream bursts from inside the car, and my head snaps to the sound. Finally, I see the two nomads that had been hiding in the shadows. This new female is at the passenger window of the car while the male is standing by the brunette I left writhing in pain. He helps her up from the ground. I rush toward the new female, utilizing this time that he is too distracted with the brunette to stop me from killing the other female.

As I get closer, I can smell the werewolf in the car and I recognize him. But that does not slow my pace. Krista's pack will know what I am but they will be safe. There is nothing left to consider. I must finish this.

Ignoring the frightened screaming from the human in the car, I jump on top of the car and grab the female by her hair and lift her up. She slashes at my chest, opening deep gouges. The blood warms my skin but I am too focused to let that slow me. I slam her body into the hood of the car as my blood drips down onto her. Her punch makes contact and I feel one of my teeth rattle inside my mouth.

Pointing my fingers to pierce the skin with ease, I shove my hand inside the soft tissue of her abdomen. With my hand inside her body, I reach under her ribcage and make a fist around her heart. Her eyes widen and she shakes her head desperately. But it is too late for mercy. Compressing my hand together, I crush her heart and her body turns to ash around me.

I look over at the human in the car as I wipe the remnants of her blood and ash on my pants leg. She covers her mouth with her hand in shock and horror.

The male that was near the brunette had been rushing toward us to save this female but when I squashed her heart like a bug, he stopped in the road. The realization that he is too late to save any of them sets in and he dashes. I cannot let him escape, none of them can.

I slide off of the car, snatching the license plate from the front bumper. Tossing it like a Frisbee, I thrust it deep in his back. He screams and drops to his knees as he furiously tries, unsuccessfully, to reach the metal lodged between his shoulder blades.

As I spit out my dislodged tooth, I look back at my audience in the car in time to see Simone vomit through her fingers as she had covered her mouth in shock. She looks away from me but that does not stop her retching. Despite the way she vomits on his leg, Warren does not look away from me.

I hurry to the driver's side of the car. Warren does not say anything but continues to glare as I tell him bluntly, "Stay inside the car."

Then placing my foot on his car door, I shove the car with a quick push into the stone wall surrounding the Lock. The car scrapes and groans as it slides across the street. Simone lets out a short yelp when the car slams into the wall but she is not hurt. She is simply afraid.

Seeing vampires rip each other apart can be a lot for a human to process. But I cannot slow my eradication of these nomads.

The brunette joins the male in the street and pulls the license plate from his back. As I bolt to them, the brunette slashes the license plate at me, cutting deep into my abdomen. Grabbing her wrist, I twist her arm until it snaps across both bones and as the male turns toward us, I kick him in the chest and back several steps.

Despite her injured arm, she strikes me with force. She swings a series of blows. A few are unavoidable but most I do manage to dodge, and one unintentionally strikes the male nomad. As she unleashes her onslaught, the male lands a jab to my back. A burning pain pours across my low back as I am sure his one decent blow has ruptured my kidney. It must be luck on his part since he does not seem to be altogether very skilled in fighting anything stronger than a human.

Sweeping my leg, I drop the brunette to her back. I grab the male's arm and flip him over my back. With my legs locked around his arm, a simple twist is all it takes to dislocate his shoulder and simultaneously break his humerus.

The brunette flips onto her feet and charges at me. I try to puncture her abdomen to grab her heart, in the same manner, I eliminated the other female but the brunette moves away. Unable to grab her heart, I grab the next best thing. My fingers wrap themselves around her rib. As she backs from me, I remove her rib from her body.

She grabs at her bloody, gaping side as she steps further back. Standing behind me, the male lunges. I swing the rib backward like a blade and stab him in the chest without taking my eyes from her. I do not need to see him turn to ash. I can feel his weight on my would-be blade dissipate the moment it strikes his heart.

Seeing her imminent defeat, the brunette finally does what she should have from the start. She turns to run. She does not get far. I grab her by the hair and pull her back into me. As I bring the broken rib above her, she brings her arms up defensively as though she could stop this. The brunette lets out a sharp, animalistic screech as I bring the rib toward her. I plunge her own rib into her heart and the brunette's body turns to ash against me.

I look around briefly but there are no others lurking in the shadows. The only sounds are Warren's car door as he helps Simone exit and Krista's feet drumming toward me. My eyes meet Warren's as Krista slams her body into me.

Wrapping her arms around me, she lets her tears fall. Her words spill out on top of one another but I cannot focus on her words. The intensity of Warren's eyes as he looks at the security booth says everything I need to hear.

"I didn't do that, Warren," I tell him honestly but I doubt he believes me now. "I was only protecting Krista. I had nothing to do with Larry. You have to trust me."

His mouth twists as his eyebrows come together, "But I don't trust you." He looks at Krista with his next words, "Did you know about this? Did you know what he was?"

Krista does not speak but the way she pulls me closer and her silence tells him everything he needs to know.

Nearby, the sound I knew would come echoes into the night air. Not one but many howls reverberate toward us. Warren looks at us grimly considering his next action.

Then reaching into the bloody security booth, Warren presses the door release. As the gates open, he says flatly, "I suggest you get a head start."

Without taking his eyes from me, Warren begins unbuttoning his shirt. Krista shakes her head as tears fill her eyes but nothing can dissuade him now.

Turning to face me, she takes a shaky breath and says between her tears, "You have to run, Nick. And run hard. If they catch you, you have to live. No matter what. You live."

She says, *no matter what,* but she does not realize what that entails. She would not be able to accept me slaughtering her pack in the same manner as I did these nomads.

I lean my forehead against hers and stroke her cheek with my thumb, leaving crimson painting her face and tell her honestly, "Stay here where it's safe." And where she will not see either her pack or myself be ripped apart. "Even knowing this would be the outcome, there is still no part of me that would not have pursued you. These past months have meant more to me than a thousand years ever could."

Hearing the padding of paws pounding down the Lockwood streets, I lift her chin to meet my eyes, "No matter what happens tonight, know that so long as my heart beats, I will come back for you."

I press my lips to her skin and kiss her forehead. Quietly, I add, "I will always come for you."

Then without any further delay, I rush into the trees. My feet push into the soft dirt, picking up bits of moss with each urgent step. The forest will slow me down but it is the shortest route to the ravine. As long as I am able to stay ahead of them, I can lose the wolves there. I can jump across whereas they cannot clear that distance.

Vampires are faster than werewolves but not in the forest. The trees belong to them. The wolves understand the way these trees bend, which rocks will give under their paws, and they know the paths that will help them gain on me.

The forest is not the safest route to take but it is the best option I have. Despite the deeply embedded need for self-preservation, I am attempting to avoid killing any of Krista's pack. The ravine is the only way to evade them without any more death tonight.

However as my feet push across the clearing, I can hear the heavy paws of a werewolf that is closer than the rest. It is possibly Warren, but that is pure conjuncture simply based on the fact that he was physically closer when I bolted into the forest. It could be any of them. The only one whose fur is known to me is Krista and this wolf is definitely not her.

As I cross the little creek, I try to focus on my steps and avoid falling on the slick surface of the rocks. It does not matter, however. Regardless of my careful steps, a rock shifts under my weight and slips away. I land in the icy water on my stomach. I roll onto my back in time to see the werewolf lunge at me. Sliding back, I move enough to elude its teeth. But only barely.

Growling, the werewolf snaps at me again. Placing a foot on each jaw, I block its teeth from coming closer. The force of the wolf's advancing scoots me across the slimy rocks.

Keeping my feet on either side of the wolf's mouth, I lean forward quickly and grab the fur under its jaw. My fingernails dig into the fat of its neck as I hold the fur firmly to help hold the wolf's mouth snug against my feet instead of snapping wildly at me. Keeping its mouth open, I reach between my feet and inside the wolf's mouth. I grab its tongue, digging in with my fingernails. The wolf whines loudly and struggles against me.

Pulling hard, I push my feet against its jaw for more leverage. The muscle begins to tear and blood fills its mouth. Quicker than I expect, its tongue rips and frees itself completely. I fall back onto the ground with the sudden loss of resistance.

Whining furiously, the werewolf backs away from me with blood spilling from its mouth. I toss its tongue onto the ground beside me as I see another werewolf approaching.

I look at the bleeding wolf, "Sorry."

Then, jumping to my feet, I run toward the tree line once more. I am not actually sorry. I will feel slightly bad if it does turn out to be Warren whose tongue I removed but only because Warren had been nice to the human version of me.

Removing his tongue will make it more difficult to salvage some form of friendship with Warren. I suppose if I survive the night, I can help him understand that his tongue will grow back eventually and having no tongue is better than being dead.

The new werewolf pushes across the clearly quickly. As I reach the tree line, I pull a branch back, letting the tense build without snapping the wood. I only wait a few seconds before the wolf emerges in the trees and I release my grip. The branch snaps back to its original position and smacks into the wolf's face. The force throws the wolf back several feet, breaking its mandible and causing countless facial fractures. Shaking its head wildly, the wolf whines loudly as I sprint away.

The thudding of paws grows louder than the way my heart pounds in my chest. They are closing in quicker than I had hoped for. There is little chance of making it to the ravine before them without deterring these werewolves.

The twigs grasp at my shirt as burs pile themselves on my pants. Dodging a low branch, I step into a thicker section of mud. The pull of the mud causes me to nearly losing my footing once more. The time it takes for me to recover traction allows the forerunner werewolf to join me in the heavy soil.

The werewolf jumps at me and knocks me to the ground. Grabbing fists of dew-soaked fur, I manage to keep its teeth from my throat. Warm drool drips onto my face with each snapping attempt at me. Curling my body under the wolf, I plant my foot in its chest and propel it backward, leaving the muddy print of my shoe on its light gray fur.

I leap to my feet as the werewolf regains its footing as well. Hearing the others howling as they rush to join us only reaffirms that I need to put an end to this setback and resume my escape immediately. Moving quickly, I start toward the wolf. It comes toward me as well but just before it reaches me, I leap against a tree and use it to amplify the force behind my kick as my foot slams into the side of the werewolf's head.

I take advantage of this brief moment when its teeth pointed away from me and grab it by the fur behind its head and near its hips. Lifting it over my head, I slam its body into a tree, folding its back around the trunk enough to stop this wolf from following me again. I can hear its spine crack as it separates in ways it was never meant to. The werewolf begins trembling in my hands and I drop him to the ground.

Resuming my sprint, I leave the werewolf seizing on the muddy ground. The heavy padding of paws grows closer but so does the ravine. They will not be able to make the jump. The werewolves will have no choice but to climb down the rocky slope and back up the other side. It will cost them too much time. Time enough for me to successfully evade them for tonight.

I toss my heavy mud-caked jacket to the ground. Not for speed but simply to remove any extra weight before my leap across the ravine. The drumming of paws nears and I hear a howl cut through the night air as a werewolf sees me running through the shadows ahead. However, just as it spots me, I see the edge of the ravine.

One hundred yards and I am free. They have to stop. They have to realize they will not make that jump. And they have to understand that while the fall that far would certainly kill them, it will not stop me. I would not feel much like running after hitting the ground but I would not be dead.

My feet push off of the edge as I leap toward the other side of the ravine. As expected, the werewolves slide to a stop near the edge. However, I am not expecting the jerk on my shirt as a lone wolf follows me into the air and snatches me from my escape.

With the weight of the werewolf on my shirt, my bound is cut short and the two of us fall together. Being so close to the other side of the ravine, I grasp at the rocky slope and manage to slow my descent. My shirt rips in the werewolf's mouth, freeing me from its weight as it plummets to the bottom. I, however, do not fall so directly.

Tumbling down the sheer slope of the ravine, I land on a rocky protrusion that jets out enough to allow some sparse foliage to grow there. The impact sends a ripping heat through my side as my ribs collapse against the pressure. Despite the velocity my body slams into the rock and the way my ribs protest, I attempt to grab at the overgrown as I tumble off of the projection but am unsuccessful and continue to fall.

I expect to land abruptly on the ravine floor, in pain but still able to elude the rest of the werewolves above me. However, instead of the impact of the ground, I crash into something else only feet from the floor. Sticking out wildly from the undergrowth of briers and small shrubs along the narrow creek at the bottom of the ravine, a meager tree leans away from the rocks, desperate for the sun, and into my path.

I land on the branch with enough force to push the leaves from it as it plunges into my chest. Impaled by a branch, I dangle above the shallow creek with my feet grazing the icy water beneath me. The metallic taste of my own blood pools in my mouth as the wolves begin their pursuit into the ravine.

Remaining suspended is not an option. However, neither is running. In this condition, broken and bleeding, I would not maintain the speed necessary to outrun them and certainly not through this terrain. Using my foot, I kick at the base of the branch, trying to break it from the trunk. My kick does not free me and the strike only causes vibrations to tremor up the branch and into my chest. Even with the added pain, I swing my leg again. This time the branch cracks and I fall to the ravine floor.

My body slams into the rock lining the creek, knocking the air from my lungs. However, it does not slow the way blood fills my lungs or how it tints the water red as it drifts away from me.

The icy water numbs my wounds a little as I try to catch my breath. Struggling to force my lungs open enough to be capable of defending myself, I grab the branch still lodged in my chest and pull it from my body. I let out a scream as the branch exits my chest, leaving splinters along its way.

The icy water fills the empty puncture as I look over at the werewolf lying on the ground where it fell with me. Dead and in its human form, it is not someone I recognize. Part of me had hoped it would be Mitchell that plunged to his death. Not simply because I hate him but because it is the only way to ensure that I am not the one responsible for the death of Krista's brother.

Fighting the werewolves without knowing their fur will only be a form of roulette. I do not know one from the other. I cannot discern who the werewolf is until it is dead and phases back into its human form. There will be no way to prevent Mitchell's death by my own hand. My only hope now is that he was one of the wolves I left, writhing but alive, in the forest.

I was so close to escaping, just mere feet from my freedom until one werewolf gave its life to stop me. While that is honorable in itself, it also seemingly forces my hand. I cannot outrun them like this. And I clearly cannot reason with them. Fighting is quickly becoming my only viable option.

Getting to my feet, I try to ignore the pain sweeping over me. I roll the branch over and between my hands to get a feel for the weight of it as fragments of the damp wood cling to my hands. Injured and outnumbered, I will need a weapon and right now, this branch is the best I have.

As the first wolf's paw touches the soft dirt of the ravine floor, I ready myself. The two wolves in the lead flank either side of me as they approach. Swinging the branch through the air, I slam it into the first wolf's face as though I am hitting a home run. Spinning the branch around, I swing the branch to my other side and I smash it into a second wolf's head, knocking it away from me.

The third wolf charges up the center. Stepping forward, I shove the sharp point of the branch through the soft tissue under the wolf's jaw, staking into its skull. The wolf phases instantly into its human form. With a quick thrust, I toss its dead body from the end of the branch, thankful that this too was not Mitchell.

Shoving the end of the branch into the ground, I use the branch as leverage to swing my body around and kick a werewolf in the chest as it jumps toward me. Propelling backward, the wolf crashes into another werewolf, knocking them both to the ground.

As my feet hit the ground, I pull the branch from the soft dirt and slam it into another charging werewolf. Behind it, another werewolf lunges toward me. Swinging the branch around, I lift it with both hands and use it to brace myself. As the werewolf snaps down on the branch between my hands, I hold its bite away from me.

The force behind the wolf's jump knocks us both to the ground. Rolling back, I kick the wolf off of me and leap to my feet in time to see another werewolf in the air above me. As I move toward the wolf, I spin the branch around my hand and lodge it deep into the werewolf's abdomen. The momentum of the wolf thrusts the branch through its back as I slam its body to the ground.

Removing the branch from the werewolf's abdomen, I kick down hard on its skull. The wolf's skull collapses under my foot and it phases into its human form. Chunks of tissue stick to my shoe as I lift my foot from the fragments and I look briefly to see if I recognize the wolf. However, with the lack of any real bone structure remaining, its face is indiscernible.

As another group of werewolves closes in, I hear Krista scream into the ravine, "Mitchell, stop!"

Her voice cuts through the stench of blood and death filling the ravine floor and seemingly through time itself. In the mere seconds, it takes for the werewolves to cross the damp ground, I look at her, crouching by the edge of the ravine and watching as her brother charges towards me, and I realize what I already knew.

This is the moment I choose to save my life or hers. The werewolves will not kill her but they will shred me to pieces in front of her.

Continuing to fight them off will not save me. It will only cause her to lose both me and her brother tonight.

She will not recover completely from such a loss. The guilt will consume her until it changes her. Hardens her. She will not be the same person afterward. The life she has known will be essentially over. I know this because I lived this rebirth nearly six hundred years ago.

This is the moment I have been silently pretending might not come. I do not know which wolf is Mitchell and therefore cannot spare him for her sake. But I can ensure that only one of us dies tonight. This is the moment when I discover exactly what I would do to save her. I will die for her.

Letting my eyes change back to their vibrant green color, I drop the branch so I can bring my fingers to my lips. I do not take my eyes from her as I blow her a kiss. I do not wish to watch the death that is coming so instead I let a soft smile spread across my face as I keep my eyes on only her.

Her scream echoes down the ravine walls. "No!" She cries out but it does not slow the werewolves nor do I expect it to.

Their paws pound into me, knocking me to the ground. Under their weight, I reflexively curl into a fetal position but it will only delay the inevitable. Teeth gnash at my flesh, pulling and ripping my shirt along with my skin. Their saliva burns in each new wound as the freshly exposed tissues begin constricting against the toxicity of it.

Teeth sink into my thigh. They rake through the muscles, leaving deep gouges. The blood saturates my pants and, for a moment, it is warming. However, the night is much too cool for the warmth to last and the wet blood on my clothes soon adds a chill to my tattered body.

I focus on not letting Krista hear my pain as their claws scrape flesh from my shoulder. Still, despite my trying, I am unable to stop a scream from escaping when teeth sink deep into my ribcage. The wolf's head twists violently, extracting a chunk of flesh and bone from my side.

Flesh rips from the back of my arm as more teeth tug at my body. For a moment, I think about lowering my arms away from my neck. Death would be faster that way. There is no reason to prolong the suffering when the end result will be the same. However, instead of sparing myself, I continue to endure the heavyweight of the were-wolves standing on my chest and compressing the air from my lungs painfully.

As I lie in the swarm of teeth raining my own blood down upon me, I feel the heat of breath on my ankle and the sharp, piercing burn of teeth as a werewolf bites down just above my foot. Unexpectedly and quite abruptly, I am jerked out from under the cluster of wolves and under another one.

Weakened and in pain, I cannot focus on who this werewolf is that has claimed my death for itself. I can only make out its dark fur as it steps over me, protecting me from the others. A low growl rumbles in its chest as it faces the wolves that I was stolen from. They growl back but do not move to attack the one standing over my limp body.

I lie on the cold ground as my body pours blood onto the damp grass, beginning to grow numb. I listen as the angry growls and snarls begin to lull me into a sleep I may never wake from. Through the heavy scent of the blood pooling around me, I recognize a smell I thought was gone to me.

Opening my eyes enough to confirm my suspicions, I touch the black fur lining the belly of the werewolf standing over me. "Tara," I whisper quietly. Then everything goes dark.

*   *   *

My eyes shoot open as a fire pours across my body. I let out a scream but only bubbles rise to the surface of the water. I thrash against the hands that hold me down as my skin blisters against the scorching of the holy water.

Through the blur of water splashing above me, I can make out a blond woman. Possibly Tara, or possibly Marcella, either way, she holds me beneath the searing water despite my struggling.

I know why I am being held under. There are simply too many wounds dripping with werewolf saliva to clean them individually. If they are not cleaned quickly enough, they will scar, sealing in the toxins from the saliva, and will cause constant pain for the remaining years of my life. Knowing this does not stop my struggle. The boiling of my entire body is simply too much for my reflexes to ignore.

Finally, she pulls me from the water and onto the tile floor. Finally, I distinguish that I am in my own house and lying on the cold tile of the guest bathroom. With a choking gurgle, I cough up the blessed water from my charred lungs. I lie still on the white tiles, letting them cool my scalded skin.

Tara leans close to me, offering a towel, and says matter-of-factly, "You are an idiot."

Grabbing the towel from her hands, I smile weakly at her, "You're the one who came back."

She smiles back at me as she adds, "I guess that makes me an idiot too."

She helps me lift myself from the floor into a seated position along the tub. I cover myself with the towel despite the way the fibers scratch and pull at my raw skin. Tara sits against the wall opposite of me, watching me strain to keep my eyes open.

"I hope she was worth it," she says quietly.

Without opening my eyes, I smile at her, "She is." Then once again, I drift into an unintentional sleep.

*　　*　　*

My eyes open slowly and with more effort than it should take. I can feel the dawn has set in as thoroughly as my headache already has. My pounding skull relentlessly reminds me that I have lost a significant amount of blood. Feeding would help but the drumming of my head only acts as a deterrent to moving in any way.

I can smell Julia before my eyes focus on her small figure sitting near my bed. When she notices me stirring, she smiles at me softly.

"You should eat," she tells me. She keeps her voice low as though someone has instructed her that my head would reject anything louder.

I push myself up causing the wound on my side to pull painfully. Groaning, I hold my side to help support my ribs and find that someone has wrapped gauze tightly around me.

As Julia moves to sit beside me, I squeeze the bridge of my nose but it does little to relieve the pressure behind my eyes.

"I'm glad you're awake," Julia says warmly. "I was beginning to worry."

Julia uses the phase correctly, however, she was not worried. Sheep do not feel concern in the same aspect as humans and they cannot comprehend that there is a difference.

She holds her wrist out for me as an invitation. Even though my appetite has been replaced with the thumping in my head I still take her wrist gently. The only way to move past this headache is to replenish the blood that was lost.

"Did you blow it?" she asks innocently.

I chuckle lightly to myself. It seems so long ago that I first spoke to Krista in my home. It was then that Julia had first offered her limited advice about not messing up my chances with Krista. And it was then that I realized I eventually would.

Looking over at her with a small smile, I nod, "Something like that."

Attempting to be gentle, I lift her wrist to my lips. I let my fangs extend and feel the snap of her skin beneath them. Blood rushes to fill my mouth. Richly satisfying, it cools the burning that had been overshadowed by the mass of pains and weakness washing over me. A heat pours through my body, restoring some of the strength that had been stolen from me and quieting some of the drumming in my skull.

When I pull my fangs from her wrist, I look over at Julia. She smiles at me but her eyes are empty. She sits as little more than a shell of the human she once was.

"Thank you," I tell her softly.

"No, thank you," she replies cheerfully.

There is nothing she should be thanking me for but she will never realize that. She will never remember the family she was stolen from. She will never know how they searched for her. And she will never understand that they are still longing for answers.

Still, there is nothing to be done about it. There is no reversing the effects of becoming a sheep. What is done, is done.

I pat her knee as I tell her, "You can use my bathroom to clean yourself up."

She nods and starts toward the bathroom, holding her wrist to slow the bleeding. When she flips the bathroom light on, I add, "There should be gauze in the lower cabinet."

Julia does not reply but I can hear her rummaging through the cabinet. As she searches for supplies to aid herself, I stand up and start toward the dresser. My leg aches but is minor compared to my damaged ribs.

I pull out a pair of pants. As I slide them on, I examine my legs. Most of the bites have healed and none seem to have scarred. My thigh aches where the deeper gouges had been. The gash had ripped across several muscles which will take longer to heal completely. However, superficially, there is no evidence that any injury even occurred. No uneven ridges caused by missing tissue under the skin, no lacerations, not even a bruise.

Before I pull out a shirt, I inspect my arms and torso for any lingering pains. Most of my muscles ache from the deprivation of blood but only a few cause pain from the wounds sustained last night.

Julia reemerges from the bathroom as I loosen the gauze from around my ribs to evaluate the damages. Removing the pressure of the gauze takes away the support of my sore ribs causing me to wince but I continue to unwind the material from my body.

The pain causes my breath to catch and I stop for a moment. I look over at Julia as she watches me, waiting to be of assistance.

"Julia, can you get my mother's ring for me?" I ask, offering her a task.

She nods. As she heads to my closet to search for the Bible I hide the ring inside, I resume unwrapping myself.

Once removed, I lay the gauze on the dresser and rub my hand over my sore ribs. Looking in the mirror above the dresser, I can see easily what is causing the intense pain. Even though my ribs are covered completely in smooth, healthy skin, my side is concaved, a large void left where there should be tissue.

Despite the pain, I press along the missing section of my body. There is quite a bit of muscle and bone missing, however, nothing permanent. The skin has healed completely and has not scarred. The muscle is recovering but will take some time to complete its reconstruction. The ribs will take the longest to rebuild themselves. It will take several days for this amount of missing tissue to regenerate. Until then, my remaining ribs will be unsupported, free to move in ways they should not, and free to press on the tender, healing muscles surrounding them.

It appears none of my wounds will have a lasting effect. Tara did a good job of preventing any of my injuries from becoming permanent by boiling me in holy water. I will be sore and weaker over the next few days, but I will make a full recovery.

As I begin re-wrapping the gauze around me, I can hear light arguing above me as Tara and Marcella attempt to keep their conversation quiet. I ensure the wrap is tight enough to offer the support I need before putting on my shirt. Dressing myself pulls my ribs inside my body to places they are not intended to be.

I moan as I slide my shirt down over the gauze and look at myself in the mirror. Fully dressed, I do not look injured at all. My skin is a little pale and cold to the touch from the blood loss. However, to look at me, I appear more as though I have had a flu than a fight.

Julia hands me my mother's ring and I slip it into my pocket. I focus on the argument, attempting to eavesdrop as I make my way upstairs quietly.

"I risked my life to save him," Tara says heatedly.

Marcella says in an unnaturally calm tone, "And I told you that I am grateful for that."

I can hear Tara's annoyed huff which is usually accompanied by her shaking her head and pressing her lips together tightly to keep from saying what she is thinking.

"He is a self-absorbed, arrogant asshole. He does what he wants, when he wants, and never stops to think about who might get hurt by it. You know that. And you should have stopped him," Tara snaps at her.

I walk down the hallway toward the voices coming from the kitchen. I hear the floor creak under Marcella or Tara as one of them steps toward the other, "I don't like it either but how exactly do you expect me to stop him?" Marcella replies.

"You're his mother," Tara states tartly, "Tell him no."

Marcella snorts, "We are not dogs. We don't heel simply because someone tells us to."

I see them standing in the kitchen with little more than inches between them. Listening to them continue, I lean against the wall to support myself and remain unnoticed by either of them.

"So you do nothing?" Tara snaps. "You just let him trifle with a pack too large to handle, even for him. Until it gets countless people killed. And for what? So he can put another notch in his belt?"

Marcella stands silently for a moment, her stony façade appearing callous and indifferent. I know that look. It is not Marcella's conceding that you are right, merely her way of expressing she is finished with the conversation.

Tara's eyes narrow and she adds coldly, "Then you are as big a fool as he is." Tara steps away from Marcella and grabs her coat from the back of the chair.

Just as I am about to call out to Tara to ask her to stay, Marcella sighs and mutters, "It doesn't matter what order I give, Nicolas will not comply. You know him that well. He doesn't listen."

"I'm sure I can think of at least one time I did," I say with a smirk.

They both look over at me standing in the doorway. Marcella relaxes her shoulders when she sees me. Tara huffs, crossing her arms over her chest.

Marcella smiles as she walks toward me, "You would have to think very hard, I'm sure." She rubs the back of her fingers over my cheek. "You're cold," she states more to herself than to me, already expecting me to be frigid to the touch. It will take more than one meal to replenish the amount of blood lost to me which she is already fully aware of.

Dropping her hand, she sighs and adds, "But you are standing and that is something. Still, you should rest, so make sure to not use up too much energy barking at that dog." Her voice turns condescending as she mentions Tara.

Instead of scolding Marcella, I simply call to her as she walks away, "I'll just rest here while Tara barks at me then. You'll want to write that down: *November 6th, Nicolas obeyed.*"

She shakes her head but continues walking as I chuckle to myself. I turn around to look at Tara, who only stares annoyingly at me.

"You're not funny," she says dryly.

I smile wide at her, "Am I at least irresistible?"

Tara rolls her eyes and lets out a snicker, "You most certainly are *not* that."

Grinning, she walks over to me and wraps her arms around my neck, "I am glad you're alive though."

"Me too," I say matter-of-factly.

Her hand glides over my hair smoothly, the way a mother calms her child, "You scared me, you know?"

I pull her back so I can see her face. "You thought you were scared. I'm just glad my pants were already ruined," I joke.

She chuckles lightly and pushes her hair behind her ear. Watching her, I realize how badly I have missed my best friend and a warm smile spreads across my face.

"I'm really glad you're here," I tell her honestly.

Smiling to herself, Tara walks over to the counter. As she leans back against it, she jests, "Well, I was in the neighborhood."

I watch her as she aimlessly picks at a bowl of grapes on the counter until she finds the one she wants.

"I wanted you to know how sorry I am for lying to you about Roddy," I tell her. Truthfully I am not really sorry for withholding the information I had about her son, but I am sorry for what it cost me.

Tara spins around, looking at me incredulously, and cups her ear with her hand, "What was that? Did pigs just start flapping their wings because I'm pretty sure you just said you were *sorry*?"

She knows me too well for such an obvious lie. Smiling, I correct myself, "Kind of sorry."

She chuckles lightly, "That's what I thought."

Pushing herself onto the counter, she sits facing me and says, "Well, I guess I'm kind of sorry too for sending Krista home a couple of hours ago." She tosses the grape in her mouth as she adds, "Sorry, not sorry."

"What?" I blurt out as the thoughts push through the pain lingering in my head. "Krista was here? Why would you make her leave?"

I cannot voice it to Tara but I will not leave Montana without Krista. If she were still here, it could have spared me the risk of going back to the Lock and facing her pack again to get her. Tara will not accept my blatant refusal to avoid Krista now that my secret has been exposed and the dangers of being around her are even greater. So I simply cannot tell her.

"Because you wouldn't." At least, that much is obvious to Tara. "And she would have only brought the fight to this house by sniffing around here."

Tara is right. It is not fair of me to bring the danger here to my family. Tara clearly has a more rational approach to the situation than I do and no amount of arguing will convince her that my heart should veto my head. So, instead of admitting her logic or continuing to argue, I simply redirect the conversation.

I lean back against the table to help support me without revealing my body is significantly weakened. "How come you get to make dog jokes and I can't," I tease.

She smiles wide and tosses a grape at me as she jokes, "Because I am a dog."

I do not attempt to block the grape and it hits me in the face. Tara laughs as it rolls onto the floor and I pretend to wipe the residue from my cheek.

"You know, if you're really hungry, I could make you something. You don't have to forage the fruit bowl like a caveman," I tell her.

Tara scoffs but continues to pick at the grapes, "I'm not having you cook something. I should be asking you if I could get you something."

She looks up at me, raising her eyebrows, "But that's not going to happen. I'd rather watch you starve than let you bite me again."

Giggling, she grabs at the wrist she had offered me in Germany, "That really hurt."

I smile at her and joke, "Well, aren't you selfish?"

Sliding the fruit bowl closer to her hip, she smiles as though she has missed our time together as much as I have.

"Me eat grape," she says in a deeper voice, imitating the broken linguistics of a primitive caveman. She tosses a few grapes in her mouth all at once.

With too many grapes in her mouth, Tara chomps away at them, attempting to mash them enough to successfully close her mouth. The mass of grapes muffles her laugh as she covers her mouth with her hand to keep from losing the food in her mouth.

Juice from the grapes rolls down her chin causing her laughter to advance to a snort. I cannot help but smile at her as she struggles to keep from spitting the grapes. Walking over to her, I grab a hand towel from the sink.

Last night should have been the end of my road. I should have died in that fight. I never expected to see Tara again. And I would never have had the chance to make amends with her. But here she is, dripping fruit juices onto my clean floor.

Wiping her chin with the towel, I tell her softly, "Cavemen went extinct, you know."

With a full mouth, she replies, "Probably because they choked on grapes."

Chuckling, I ask, "How is it that I was almost killed and I'm less of a mess than you today?"

Snatching the towel from me, she jokes, "Because my face might be a mess but my life isn't." She smirks, "Besides, somebody has to save you from yourself."

Tara finishes wiping her face off and tosses the towel in the sink next to her, "Actually, I've been here for about week."

A week? Have I really been so distracted that I did not realize my best friend was here? If Tara could slip by me unnoticed, it stands to reason that the Genesis has as well. They too could have been watching me these past weeks without my realizing it.

But before, I can contemplate too long on that thought, Tara shrugs as she continues, "Roddy told me about Krista. And about how far things had gotten between the two of you."

So she has been keeping tabs on me through Roddy. I will have to remember that the next time she decides to hate me.

Grinning, she shakes her head, "You had to know as well as I did that this was going to blow up in your face. I mean, she's a werewolf, Nick. Don't you remember how well fraternizing with a werewolf's sister worked in Alaska? And Jericho's sister was human. This girl is a wolf."

"This is different," I tell her, shaking my head.

She snorts as she adds, "I mean, seriously, how could you possibly think this wasn't a bad idea?"

I knew it was. Dating a werewolf is a terrible idea. For a vampire, it is dangerous. It is blasphemous. And it gets everyone killed. But dating Krista did not seem like an option. I simply could not refuse to pursue her.

"I know it is."

"Is? Not was," Tara points out. She slides the fruit bowl over, frustrated but trying not to show it.

I reach in my pocket and take out the ring before she can argue with me, "Tara, I need you to do something for me." I hold my mother's ring out between us.

She looks at it sincerely for a moment before I place it in her palm and wraps her fingers closed around it, "I need you to keep this for me. Just until things blow over."

But things might not simply blow over. The most likely scenarios all end with my death so I add, "But if something happens to me, I want you to give this to Krista."

Tara looks at me soberly as I continue, "It's the only possession that has ever meant anything to me. The wolves will come. And when they do they will try to finish what they started. You can't be here when they arrive. I won't let you get yourself killed over me."

Tara shakes her head and holds the ring out for me to take back, "They won't kill me."

I step back slightly to show that I have no intention of taking my ring back. The look on my face must show my resolution to not include Tara in this fight any further.

Tara slides off of the counter and adds, "No, seriously. They won't kill me. Part of the reason I was able to save you last night is because Bryant issued a protection order for me."

Too bad he did not decide to give an order for my protection, that could have saved us all a lot of trouble.

"You saved my life in Germany," she continues, "And he agreed that makes your life mine to protect. If I don't attack them, they will not attack me."

Orders or no orders, they will get the result they want. If they want to attack her, they will provoke her. "No, it's too risky."

"A life for a life, Nick." Tara steps toward me irritably as she continues, "Wolves are loyal. Our humans might falter but our wolves do not. You saved me, and now I must save you."

I shake my head and keep my expression firm, "No. You've already saved me once today; your debt is paid. I want you to leave before it's too late."

Tara clinches her jaw but I do not soften my expression either. With neither of us conceding to the other, I tell her, "We're leaving too. I'm going to make sure everyone gets out of here before anybody else dies."

Trying to decipher if I am lying, Tara narrows her eyes, "Promise me you're not going back for her. Nicolas, you know that would be a mistake."

It mostly is a mistake but it is a mistake that I am going to make. Even if I wanted to run the other way, I promised her I would come for her and I intend to do just that.

"I promise," I reply, too quickly to make it believable.

Seeing that she will not convince me otherwise, Tara's eyes soften and she begrudgingly nods.

Shoving the ring in her pocket, she pokes my chest lightly, "You better call me as soon as you're safe."

I give her a small, soft smile, "I already have you on my speed dial."

She lets out a reluctant sigh of surrender and wraps her arms around me again. "Be careful out there," she says, holding me tight.

As she leans away from me, I nod to her, both of us knowing this very well may be the last time we see each other. She pulls her coat from the back of the chair once more. The weight of the coat topples the chair over. I reach out to keep it from crashing to the floor but Tara does not even turn around. I stand silently in the kitchen until I hear the front door slam shut.

I may have lied about going back for Krista but at least I was being honest when I told her I intend to help my family flee. Being locked inside by the sun makes us sitting ducks for another attack. Smart werewolves will not wait for night to make an attempt on my life again. They will use the sun against us.

However, unbeknownst to them, this house is connected to other homes nearby through a series of escape tunnels. Several neighborhoods that have more than one home for vampire use has a similar network under the town. Most of the tunnels were dug by vampires who still remember being hunted by humans and werewolves alike.

The tunnels were not an easy feat to compile, however, we have an endless amount of time and strength to see us through the trials of an endeavor that large. This particular series of tunnels is not the largest network by any means. Some bigger and older cities have an enormous and elusively complex tunnel system.

The underground tunnels in Paris are wide-spread enough to be considered their own independent city. There are even sections with temporary housing, places to hide your meals, and even communal baths. Retreating into the underground worlds even helped us to deceive the humans and werewolves into believing we no longer existed at all.

The tunnels under this home are not intended to live in for extended periods of time. These tunnels are merely for escaping which also happens to be the only purpose we have for them today. At this time of year, the tunnels should not be flooded and our escape should be fairly unproblematic.

At Marcella's insistence, I find it necessary to make time to feed twice more. I indulged in another smaller meal from Julia before Marcella almost immediately urges me to consume another larger feeding from her own sheep, Andrew. I have to admit that it did improve my condition quite a bit. Although, I do not actually admit that to her.

After the second feeding, the drumming against my skull lightens enough for me to ignore it altogether. Some of my strength returns along with some of the color that was lacking in my cheeks. Even my missing ribs feel slightly better, but only slightly.

However, we cannot postpone our vacating the premises for long. The werewolves do not realize that we have the tunnels and will logically believe we are trapped inside until nightfall. If they have any sense about them, they will use the sun to their advantage. The easiest way to kill us without additional risk to themselves would be to simply burn the house with us in it. I know that if I were trying to murder a family of vampires that is the method I would use.

Coaxing the werewolves into believing that we do in fact die in the fire will take some convincing on my part as well though. Someone has to stay behind to ensure that the werewolves believe we are inside. And since this is mostly my fault, I suppose I should be the one to get the pleasure of fooling those mutts.

Marcella, however, does not agree with me. As we stand in the foyer near the stairs, Marcella keeps her voice low as she tells me, "No, there is no reason you should stay alone. Two voices are more convincing than one."

There are reasons. Good ones. These wolves will be coming for *me*. Not Marcella. This is my fight. Nobody else's.

However, before I can give my rebuttal, there is a sudden shattering of glass and an intense scream shoots through our ears. We run toward the sounds spilling out from the study.

I smell Vanessa before I see her. The stench of burning flesh pushes through the air, escaping to fill every nook of the house. Frozen by the pain, Vanessa stands in the broken, glass of the painted window as the sun pours in on her, scorching her flesh.

In the corner of the room, flames erupt from the remnants of a broken bottle, creeping up the wall. Despite its lack of originality, this amateur version of a Molotov cocktail pushes flames up the wall, quickly consuming the room. The sweet scent of gasoline and ethanol from the bottle mixes with the aroma of her burning skin in a revolting way. More glass shatters elsewhere as, I assume, other flaming bottles are tossed inside our home.

High pitch, and nearly animalistic, her screams resonate through the small room above the crackling of the wood. The intense torturing pain locks her in place, standing in front of the window that was once painted black to protect her. Her skin blisters as steam flees from her body. Vanessa claws at her sizzling skin as though removing her flesh would somehow stop the searing agony.

Attempting to avoid the streams of daylight, I hurry across the room to Vanessa. I grab her hand to pull her from the light. However, instead of freeing her, my grip only causes her wrist to crumble into ash in my hand. Her screaming does not stop as her body disintegrates, slowly inching up her arm and extending into her torso until she collapses into nothing more than a pile of ash on a dirty floor.

With her screaming suddenly extinguished, only the crackling of the wood being consumed in the flames is left echoing through her silence.

Luther rushes to us but is stopped in the doorway of the study by a wall of smoldering air. The cooking of the wooden framework of our house does not cover the unmistakable smell of Vanessa's charred body. Burning curtains drop to the floor as he stares at me, stunned by what has just transpired.

Marcella's jaw clinches and I watch as her eyes turn black. Her face grows stern but she does not utter a word as she walks out of the study.

Without stepping into the light, I look outside. Standing in my driveway are several members of Krista's pack, having just watched Vanessa's scalding demise. They stand in plain sight, protected by the sun. But it cannot protect them forever.

I do not recognize most of them. However, I cannot mistake Mitchell standing in the front with a smirk. Flanking Mitchell in their human forms, the rest wait for any signal that a more physical assault would be warranted.

Watching him, I let my eyes turn black. This fight is unnecessary. I surrendered my body to their ravenous teeth merely to keep Mitchell alive for Krista's sake and still, he persists. As long as he maintains his desire to rid his sister of me, I will not be able to prevent killing him much longer.

Eerily unmoving, I do not even breathe as I watch him gradually reach toward a knife holster on his hip. He does not look away as he slowly unlatches the button securing the knife. My unsettling glare forces him to swallow hard as he continues to move as though any sudden movement might ensue some murderous frenzy.

Having just watched exactly what the sun will do to a vampire, Mitchell should be even more confident in his affront. However, the way my disturbingly cold eyes watch him like prey still unnerves him. Me, a vampire essentially trapped inside a burning house, can still frighten a big, bad wolf while they are safe outside. The absurdity of it allows an even more sinister look to settle in my eyes.

Instantly, my attention is pulled back inside the house by the sound of a shotgun chambering. Stepping next to me and into clear view of the wolves, Marcella lifts the gun and points it at Mitchell.

"No, don't!" I shout.

Reacting without thinking, I grab the barrel of the gun and Marcella pulls the trigger as I jerk it away from its intended direction. The bullet blasts through the ceiling, raining debris and sunlight into the room near us.

Marcella rips the gun from my grip and slams the stock into my face, knocking me back to deter me from stopping her again. Perhaps in her mind, this murder is necessary and she is sparing me from that task. For Krista, it certainly would be better if I am not the murderer.

However, Marcella does not often consider others and it is far more likely that she simply wants him dead. And she is willing to stand in a house as it burns around her to ensure it.

Marcella swings the gun back into position but it is too late. I can do nothing but watch as her finger hovers over the trigger and her eyes grow wide. She sucks in a jagged breath as her arm begins to tremble under the weight of the gun.

Marcella's arm goes limp at her side and the gun drops to the floor. Looking at me, she stumbles back further into the shadows. I can feel my eyes grow heavy with the weight of tears that refuse to fall as I watch her reach to her chest. Wrapping her fingers around the knife lodged in her sternum, she collapses to the floor.

I hurry to her, kneeling next to her. Blood begins puddling around the blade in her chest as I examine the wound. If I could pull the knife out, she would heal almost instantly. She could escape with us. However, that is *if* I could.

The angle of the blade has inserted itself leaves me no options.

Moving the blade will slice her aorta and Marcella will only bleed to death that much quicker. There is no saving her from this.

A tear warms my skin as it rolls down my cheek and I look to her face. Despite the suffering she is surely in, her expression is soft as though she is aware of her impending death as clearly as I am.

Her fingers stroke over the tears rolling down my cheek as she says weakly, "There is so much I need to tell you."

The pressure in my chest crushes against my lungs, making it difficult to take an even breath as the realization sets in that I about to lose another mother.

Despite all of her flaws, she is my mother. Marcella is cold. She is selfish and vain. But she is immortal. I can hate her for an entire century if I want but she will always be there as soon as I forgive her. My world makes sense with her in it.

But now, I must face how mortal she truly is. She will not be here for me. She will not watch me make mistake after mistake. We will never laugh together. Never bicker. She will not be able to rush back to me simply because she needs me. She simply will not be *here*. But I will. I will still be here. Still needing her.

I shake my head but it does not stop the churning knot in my stomach or slow the tears from falling as I comprehend that my world is going to exist without her remaining in it.

Sniffling, I tell her, "Don't worry about that now."

The past few weeks, I have falsely believed I had time to discover and deal with all of the past lies at another time. Eventually, I would have asked Marcella for every detail about the Genesis but I took my time with Marcella for granted.

Instead, I had spent my time enjoying the blissful hiatus of losing myself in Krista and neglected to address those secrets. Now I suppose I will never know what Marcella hid from me. But somehow, in this moment, that does not seem to matter.

Marcella adopted me. She took me in, she taught me how to survive, and she loved me. She was the only constant in my world for nearly six hundred years. She has been my family for longer than any other person.

The monster in her could be darker than the ocean on a moonless night, an inky black and all-consuming frigid. But despite her cold heart, Marcella always carried a warmth for me that made it impossible for me to ever doubt her love.

Her fingers grow cold as they linger on my face. "My beautiful Noah," she says faintly.

My arms tremble as I hold her closer. Noah, the name of the child lost to her long before me. I have heard that I look like him, that it was the reason she chose me to become a vampire in the first place.

Cradling her face, I smile at her. I do not correct her on my name. It does not matter. Regardless of the name she calls me, I know that when she looks at me, she is seeing a son.

"I'm here, mother," I tell her with a broken voice. I press my lips to her forehead, knowing it will be for the last time.

As her eyes close, her fingers slide from my face. The sound of her hand thumps against the floor and unleashes a flood of pain through me, like a wave crashing into a cliff and reaching upward, touching every surface you thought was safe from the water. Its weight smashes down on me with enough force to claim my breath.

Pulling her body closer to my chest, I rest my cheek against hers. Luther watches from the doorway silently as I rock her limp body, letting my tears wet her cold skin. I let out a scream but it does nothing to release the pressure gripping at me.

Before I am ready to let go of her, my tear drops onto her cheek. The weight of it pushes through to the floor instead of rolling down her skin. Extending from my tear on her cheek, her body fades into ash in my arms. The clang of the knife falling to the floor echoes in my chest as I am left with nothing more than ash dusting the floor where my mother once was.

The house crackles around us but still Luther does not speak until I look up at him.

Tears hang in his eyes as he says quietly, "Nick, we need to leave."

He is right. Leaving would be wise. But something else sparks in me. The pain bearing down on me grows quiet and a cold hatred rises to take its place.

I tell him matter-of-factly, "You take Julia. Make sure she is safe. But leave Andrew."

Opening my hand, I let the ash pour through my fingers. Watching me, Luther asks, "What are you going to do?"

I stand up, dusting Marcella's ashes from my hand onto my pants. "Finish this," I answer coldly.

Luther does not attempt to dissuade me. Part of him knows that he cannot. And the bigger part does want not to.

He takes Julia by the hand as flaming bits of the ceiling drip around us. "Rip his head off," Luther says impassively.

As Luther leads Julia away, I take Andrew by the arm. Avoiding the sun streaming in the broken window, I step into Mitchell's view with Andrew and let an icy smile spread across my face.

Mitchell knows one on one, he cannot defeat me. He is a coward, hiding in the sun like the bitch he is. I have dealt with his type before and they are easy to play. I will simply use his anger and pride against him.

"A life for a life, Mitchell," I tell him callously.

It does not matter if I want to let Andrew live. He belongs to Marcella and now she is dead. Without her, he will die too. The removal of the bond they shared will weaken his body until he is unable to even eat. Without his master, Andrew will starve himself to death regardless of what I do.

However, Mitchell is not aware of that and I do not intend to make this easier for him to watch by informing him of it. All Mitchell needs to know is that Andrew is human and that much he can smell.

Grabbing Andrew by the head, I twist quickly, snapping his neck and let his body fall to the floor, uncaring.

I throw Mitchell's knife purposefully, embedding it into the ground near his feet as a challenge.

"If you want me, then come in here and face me like a man. Or is there simply too much *boy* and not enough *beast* in you?" I tell him with venom lacing my British tone.

A low growl rumbles from Mitchell's chest as I stare at him ominously, unconcerned by the house burning around me. I watch his chest rise higher as his anger forces his breaths to become heavy.

Knowing I have him exactly where I need him, I smile menacingly and step back further into the house and out of his view, daring him to follow. That simple action infringes on his pride enough to push him past the logic of staying safely in the sun.

A snarl rips from him as he bursts into his wolf form. The padding of his paws plummeting toward my house allows me to gauge his distance. So when he leaps through the broken window as gracefully as a tiger in the circus, I am expecting him.

Before his feet can touch my floors, I kick him in the ribs, sending him flying into the bookshelves lining the wall. The impact jolts the shelving and flaming books topple down on him. He shakes them off of his rust-colored fur as he stands up.

Watching him get to his feet, I confirm what I already believed. Mitchell is utterly unprepared to face a vampire. And I smile at how easy his murder will be.

He charges across the room at me, leaving the only saving grace he had behind him: the sun filtering in. As he leaps toward me, I grab his fur and roll onto my back, kicking his chest and sending him into the air again. The wall his body slams into has grown weak from the fire allowing him to crash through it, landing in the foyer.

Watching him mercilessly, I step through the fiery opening his body created in the wall and follow him into the foyer as he scrambles to his feet. Mitchell changes his attack and instead of jumping at me, he snaps at my leg. However, this is also ineffective.

Moving quickly, I strike his face away from my leg, feeling his jaw crack under my hand. I do not wait for him to recover from the blow. Grabbing fistfuls of fur, I hold him against me as I wrap my legs around his torso. Despite his thrashing, he is unable to free me and I squeeze my thighs together, compressing his ribs until they collapse to my will.

The flames dull his high pitch whining as I crush his ribs until his wolf can no longer stand the pain and surrenders. Mitchell's body shifts into his human form as he coughs blood onto my soot-covered floor.

I could torture him, make this last as long as the house will allow it. But his pain is much less satisfying than his death will be. He already regrets his choice to face me. He knows he will die on my dirty floor. He knows he has failed.

Leaving his naked, and broken body on the floor, I stand up and walk to the wall he had smashed through. I pull a piece of splintered framing free and walk over to Mitchell.

Pulling him by the hair, I lift his head toward me and let the darkness of my monster paint my voice as I ask, "Now who will save your sister from me?"

He groans as he tries to breathe well enough to respond but I simply drop his head, letting it slam into the floor once more.

I raise up the charred stake to finish what he started when a shot is fired. The bullet rips through the wood in my hand and I hear another round in the chamber.

My head snaps in the direction of the shot and toward the rifle pointing at me.

"Enough," Krista says matter-of-factly.

I watch her standing in my open doorway, flames dancing behind her and my eyes soften back to their green color.

"I want him alive," she says frankly.

Nodding, I toss the remnants of the charred stake to the floor. I step away from Mitchell as he moans sorely. Relieved that I withdrew my attack, Krista lets out a heavy breath. Lowering the gun, she steps toward her brother.

"He started it," I say half-jokingly.

She gives me a glance from the top of her eyes but they are soft and lacking the rebuke she intends. As she looks over her brother's body, sweat begins beading on her head from the heat of the flames.

"Do you have a car or something we can use to get you out of here?" she asks me.

Her question throws me off-guard. I was expecting this rescue to be for her brother. But she said *we*.

I could take her through the tunnels but she specifically asked about driving out of here so I find myself thinking quickly, considering what vehicles are available in the garage.

"Um, yeah. Yeah, I do."

"Good," she says to herself. She reaches for Mitchell to help him crawl to the door.

The rest of the pack could help him from there. But as she nears the door, Mitchell groans out the beginning of an order, "Kill-."

Krista drops him before he can say the words and holds the rifle to Mitchell's head. Pressing the cold of the metal barrel on his temple, she tells him bluntly, "I want him alive too."

"You would kill your own brother?" he asks between jagged inhales.

"I don't honestly know. But Tara would." Krista shoves him across the floor with her foot toward the door, "And you'd be a fool to believe I came here alone."

A smile creeps on my face. Tara is still out there, protecting me. Of course, she is. And Tara says that *I* never listen.

Heat from the flames blast against me as a crash of timber falls inside as I reach my hand toward her and tell her softly, "Krista, we have to go."

She looks over at me for a moment as though she is considering her next actions carefully before she lowers the rifle away from her brother. Stepping toward me, she slides her hand in mine forcing my lopsided smile to spill across my face.

I lead her through the kitchen toward the garage quickly. More than the dangers of the fire and the threat of the pack, waiting in my driveway, I am eager to escape with Krista by my side.

I grab the keys to the moving van that are hanging near the door leading to the garage and toss them to Krista, "You're driving."

I do not wait to see the smile I know highlights her face. Despite my desire to see her grinning at me, my house is still on fire and there are still wolves who want me dead. So, instead, I go to the back of the van and roll up the door hastily.

Jumping inside the back, I feel the van rock under the weight of Krista climbing into the driver seat and I close the door just as the engine rumbles to life.

She drives until nightfall, however, I am unaware of which direction we are going, where she intends to stop, or if she even has a destination in mind. With each passing mile, she separates us from the pack. And perhaps that is all that really matters.

The day crawls along slowly as I wait for nightfall to see her face. I would give most anything to be sitting next to her. Her hair brushing over my shoulder as she leans into me. Listening to the way her voice dances when she says my name. And smelling her perfume clutching to my clothes.

By the time she stops driving, I am eager to be somewhere other than a stale van. Standing in the cool night air is refreshing to say the least. Even the hotel room is an upgrade from the back of the van. But the place I want to be most is wrapped in her arms.

Tonight, I will not sleep. The memories of today are still too fresh to relive them in a jumbled version of a dream. So instead, I attempt to avoid thinking about the events of today by drowning myself in Krista and successfully occupy my mind for most of the night.

However, eventually, even werewolves need to sleep. So as the sun creeps up, I sit quietly on the edge of the bed, alone with my thoughts. I listen to Krista's breathes as she sleeps next to me, the sheets draping over her hips. The paw prints on her back peek out from her dark hair as it scrolls across her.

I rub my hands over one another, feeling the friction of my own skin as the events of the day replay in my mind. I lost decades with Marcella simply because I was angry with her. I will never again see her disapproving face when I do something that she would do but never admit to. Never again hear the humor in her voice when she tries to reprimand me. And never see her attempt to hide a smile from me.

Krista sighs as she stirs and moans sleepily, "You okay?"

Not really, no. I smile at her and nod, "Mm, hm."

My lie is not convincing and she shifts to stand on her knees behind my back, draping her arms over my chest to hold me against her. The warmth of her bare skin pressing into me does offer some form of escape, taking away a fraction of the pain, even if it is for just this one moment.

She lays her chin on my shoulder and says quietly, "You know you can talk to me."

But I do not want to talk about Marcella or even Vanessa. I do not even want to remember.

I brush my fingertips along her smooth arm as I tell her quietly, "I know."

Krista trails her fingers through my hair, easing my mind enough for me to close my eyes. Her lips press softly against my neck in a soothing way and I find myself lowering my walls to her.

"I grabbed her wrist, you know. Vanessa. I tried to save her. But with Marcella..." my voice trails off. I do not want to say the rest. I could do nothing. Nothing to help my own mother.

"You held her," Krista says softly, "She wasn't alone and sometimes that's enough."

Krista leans her cheek against mine, letting the heat of her body comfort me but it does not stop a creeping thought from entering my mind. Something Casiana had hinted at.

My eyes shoot open and I stand up quickly. My eyes dart, mimicking the way my thoughts shift. My eyebrows come together, trying to make sense of the way the day plays in my mind.

"I reached into the sun and I grabbed her," I say again, this time with an affirmative tone.

Krista shifts on the bed to place her feet on the carpet, "Nick, what's wrong?"

My eyes meet hers quickly but I do not answer her question as the thoughts in my mind roll over one another loudly. Instead, I walk over to the window determined to have my answer. With a curtain in each hand, I jerk them open, pouring sunshine in on me in an instant.

The sudden burst of light shoots a sharp, stabbing pain through my eyes. So many years in the dark, it is understandable why the blinding pain seems overwhelming. But the pain is limited to only my eyes.

There is no fire. No scorching flesh, not even a sizzle. I pry my eyes open, ever so slightly, to see the sunlight dance across my skin in an eerily foreign way.

"I thought vampires couldn't be in the sun," Krista states curiously.

I look over at her with concern hanging in my eyes as I answer, "They can't." But perhaps a Nexus can.

She wraps herself in the sheet and walks over to the window with me. "Then what does that make you?" she asks.

Looking at my hands, illuminated by the sun, I reply honestly, "I have no idea."